SEVEN BRIDGES

A DCI RYAN MYSTERY

LJ Ross

Other books by LJ Ross

Holy Island

Sycamore Gap

Heavenfield

Angel

High Force

Cragside

Dark Skies

The Hermitage

"That which is done out of love is beyond good and evil."

—Friedrich Nietzsche

PROLOGUE

London
Summer, 2007

Ryan knew he was not alone.

The front door clicked softly shut behind him and he stood completely still, listening intently. Nothing moved inside the immaculate Georgian townhouse; not even the air, which seemed frozen as he hovered on the threshold clutching a set of door keys tightly in one fisted hand like a lifeline.

Or a weapon.

Sun shone through a stained-glass window in a stream of rainbow light, lending the stark, white-washed walls a cheerful hue. Dimly, he heard the hustle and bustle of traffic and people outside and wondered again whether he was making the right decision.

Old doubts began to creep in.

It was not too late to change his mind.

It was not too late for *her* to change, if she really wanted to. He believed that people were essentially good; it was only their behaviour that was bad. A person could change, with the right help, the right support…

Eyes that were shadowed through lack of sleep and stress closed briefly as he thought back over the last few months. He remembered every painful encounter and every broken promise; every ounce of hurt that had almost robbed him of family, friends and, most shameful of all, his own identity.

His eyes opened again and were filled with renewed purpose.

There would be no turning back and no more second chances. His life was his own to choose, and he chose freedom.

His fingers relaxed, and he looked down at the keys before setting them on the hallway table. He wouldn't be needing them again.

"Jen?"

He called out to her and waited, head cocked to one side.

The silence was deafening.

He took a deep breath and strode purposefully towards the stairs, intending to retrieve his things quickly and quietly. Detective Inspector Jennifer Lucas was supposed to be on-shift at this hour, which was what he was banking on.

And yet, the same creeping sense of dread followed him upstairs, icy fingers crawling along his spine.

He sensed her, long before he saw her.

She stood just inside the bedroom—a room they had once shared together—eyes wild, teetering on the very edge of sanity. Her hair and clothing were unkempt and, behind her, he noticed make-up strewn around the floor, an upturned mattress and the remnants of the clothes and belongings he had come to reclaim.

She held a police-issue firearm, trained directly at his chest.

"Jen."

He stood rigid, not daring to move—hardly daring to breathe—while her hand remained steady, eyes almost black and filled with hate.

"I heard a rumour today," she rasped. "It seems that you're leaving the Met and moving north; that you've requested a transfer and it has all been very hush-hush. I told them it wasn't true, that there must be some mistake. But I see now that I was wrong."

Ryan looked at her with those devastating grey eyes, seeing past the weapon, past the threats and straight through to her very core. She could *feel* the change in him, had begun to realise it weeks ago but hadn't wanted to accept it.

She would never accept it.

"You're not going anywhere," she said.

The silence lengthened.

"I'm leaving," he said quietly.

She let out a brittle laugh.

"You're nothing without me. *Nothing*," she spat. "You'd be stacking files in the basement of Scotland Yard, if it wasn't for me."

Ryan didn't bother to argue that he'd progressed through the ranks of the Metropolitan Police on his own merit. There was nothing to be gained and his priority was to remove the immediate threat.

"Put the gun down," he said, holding out a hand to take it from her.

In response, she jabbed the weapon towards his chest and he stumbled backwards, throwing out a hand to stop himself tumbling down the stairs.

"You've found someone else, haven't you? That's it, isn't it? Did she make you feel like a man again, Ryan?" He watched spittle foam at the corner of her mouth. "Or maybe it's your sister—always whining after you, moaning about how you never see her any more. Maybe she wants a little more than brotherly love from you, eh? Is *that* it? It's always the same with people like you, Little Lord Fauntleroy, born with a silver spoon in your mouth and a poker rammed up your backside!"

Ryan felt disgust roll in his stomach.

"I'm going to turn around and leave now," he said, very softly.

"Let's not forget your bitch of a mother," Lucas continued as if he hadn't spoken, gesticulating wildly with the gun. "Does she miss breastfeeding you, Ryan? Can't she stand to know you love another woman more than *her*?"

Ryan looked her squarely in the eye.

"I don't love you, Jennifer. I never did. I realise that now," he said, enunciating each word clearly. "For a while, I was infatuated by you and I mistook it for love. That was my very grave error."

The air thrummed with tension and then her face twisted into something grotesque. To his horror, she suddenly raised the weapon to her own head.

"What do you say now, Ryan? What would you say if I pulled the trigger and splattered my brains all over that wall? Wouldn't you grieve for me, love? Wouldn't you wish you could try again and live happily ever after?"

But Ryan had walked this road many times before. For months, he had lived on egg-shells, worrying about whether he would be responsible for Lucas taking her own life if he should ever break free from the spider's web she had woven and into which he had stepped willingly.

He didn't quite know when the truth had eventually dawned but, when it had, it struck him like a thunderbolt: the last thing she would ever do was commit suicide. She loved herself, and only herself, far too much for that. All this time, she'd dangled the threat of it to keep him close, to keep him at heel and try to control him.

But not this time, he thought. *Never again.*

He heard her ragged breathing as she stood there with the sun at her back and her face in shadow. The image burnished itself onto his memory, never to be forgotten.

"Goodbye."

His chest contracted with fear as he turned his back on her, expecting at any moment to hear the hard echo of a gunshot and the searing pain of a bullet tearing into his flesh.

But there were no shots fired and, as he reached the foot of the stairs, he glanced back to find her watching him from the landing with a calculating expression. The weapon was gone from her hand and she was fully composed, her face having donned the mask that the rest of the world recognised and respected.

Her lips twisted into an ugly smile.

"Wherever you go, whatever you do, I'll be watching you," she whispered. "There won't be a corner dark enough for you to hide in because, one day, I'll come for you again. Never, ever forget that you're *mine*. I made you."

Ryan sent her a long, pitying look, then stepped outside to breathe the fresh air and forge a new life from the ashes of the old.

CHAPTER 1

Northumberland
Saturday 10th February 2018
Ten years later

"Howay, man, that's not a real word."

Detective Sergeant Frank Phillips slumped back in his chair and folded his arms mutinously across his belly, which was comfortably full after enjoying a roast dinner with all the trimmings.

"I assure you, '*qi*' is a real word."

Detective Chief Inspector Maxwell Finlay-Ryan rested his elbows on the dining table, sensing victory was near.

Phillips glanced down at the Scrabble board and then back into the innocent face of his friend, his button-brown eyes narrowing in suspicion.

"If that's a real word, what does it mean? Just tell me that."

Ryan cleared his throat, embarrassed to find that in all his years of using '*qi*' as a secret weapon against worthy adversaries, he'd neglected to look up the meaning.

"Well, ah, it's obviously of Chinese derivation—"

"Aye, and that's shady n'all," Phillips put in, jabbing an accusatory finger in Ryan's general direction. "We're playing a game in England, not bleedin' Shanghai…"

From her position at the other end of the table, Doctor Anna Taylor-Ryan turned to her friend with a look of sufferance.

"Top up?"

She waggled the bottle of vintage champagne she'd opened to celebrate their first dinner party in the new home she and Ryan had built

5

together. Its foundations stood on high ground in the picturesque village of Elsdon, on the edge of the Northumberland National Park. Every wall, window and door had been chosen with care to showcase the beauty of the landscape, which undulated in shades of green and brown as far as the eye could see. When the sun rose in the eastern skies and burned away the thick darkness that had fallen overnight, she would watch it from the comfort of their bed and wonder how in the world she had come to be so fortunate.

But now, she basked in the warmth of the log-burner crackling away in the corner of the room and enjoyed an evening with their closest friends.

"It'd be a shame to let it go flat," Detective Inspector Denise MacKenzie replied.

They clinked glasses and MacKenzie took a sip of the bubbling liquid while she studied her fiancé, who was by now arguing over the pronunciation of '*qi*' in Mandarin, in his heavily-accented Geordie dialect.

"I never knew Frank was such a board game fanatic," she mused.

"Neither did I," Anna said, eyeing Ryan with similar humour. "It'll be a shame to beat them both, one of these days."

MacKenzie sent her an appreciative smile.

The doorbell interrupted them, ringing loudly once, twice and then in one long, persistent wail that grated on the nerves.

Ryan caught his wife's glance and rose from his chair in one smooth motion.

"I'll answer it," he said, placing a comforting hand on her shoulder before moving quickly towards the front door. "It's probably nothing."

But when he checked the peephole and saw who stood outside shivering in the night air, he knew instantly that there was something very badly wrong.

* * *

"Jack?"

Ryan opened the door and came face to face with Detective Constable Jack Lowerson, whose pale face appeared like an apparition against the dark sky at his back. A couple of years ago, Ryan had taken the younger man under his wing, mentoring him through the ranks of CID and had come to think of him not merely as a colleague or a friend, but as a brother. They'd saved each other's lives in the line of duty and he'd been an usher at Ryan's wedding to Anna the previous autumn.

But they'd barely exchanged a handful of words in recent months, despite Ryan's best efforts to heal the breach. There was a distance between them now, a burning disappointment that festered in his gut and which he had tried and failed to dispel.

How could Jack fail to see the danger?

The friendship and respect they'd once shared had been built on a foundation of sand, it seemed. It had only taken the arrival of one woman to destroy it; a woman Ryan had known long ago, when he had been young and naïve himself. He knew what their new superintendent was; knew what she was capable of, and had tried to warn his friend, to explain. But his advice had fallen on deaf ears. Eventually, there had been no choice other than to let nature run its own course.

All of this flashed through Ryan's mind in the seconds it took for him to realise Lowerson was suffering from extreme shock. He was shaking badly, his whole body racked by involuntary shivers and his eyes were wide, their pupils like pinpricks in the glare of the safety light overhanging the porch. Petty disagreements and thoughts of past disappointments fled as compassion overrode all else.

"Jack? What's happened?"

Ryan reached forward to grasp Lowerson's arm and pull him into the warmth of the house, already opening his mouth to call out to the others when his eye fell on a spattering of red stains marring the other man's suit jacket. The words died on his lips and his eyes turned cool and flat as automatic training kicked in.

"What's happened, Jack? What's wrong?"

Lowerson's teeth were chattering so hard he could barely get the words out. His fingers gripped Ryan's forearms as he fought for composure.

"It's Jen—she's, she's… Oh God—"

"What's happened to Detective Chief Superintendent Lucas?"

Ryan's voice was remote, and he hated the sound of it, even to his own ears.

"Who is it?"

Anna rounded the corner and came to a halt when she spotted the newcomer, surprise flitting across her face, followed swiftly by a broad smile. Ryan watched the play of emotions and felt a sharp burst of love for her; for her natural warmth and willingness to forgive, forget and welcome an old friend into their home.

But she hadn't spotted the blood. Not yet.

"Jack! Oh, my goodness, you look frozen. Come in and see the others; Frank and Denise are here, too. Ryan," she nudged him with her hip. "You should have told me Jack was coming, I'd have made you peel some more carrots—"

Anna's friendly welcome trailed off when she caught sight of what Ryan had seen, moments before. Her eyes flew up to his and then she turned back towards the dining room to seek out the other members of the Criminal Investigation Department.

"I'll—I'll get the others."

Ryan turned to Lowerson and spoke urgently, compelling him to answer.

"What's happened to her, Jack? Tell me quickly."

"She's d-dead," came the choked reply. "I-I… You have to believe me, Ryan, I didn't do it, I—"

"Did you call it in?"

"I—"

"Did you call it in?" Ryan growled.

Lowerson shook his head numbly, scrubbing tears from his eyes.

"I—no. I just drove here, I'm sorry. I didn't know where else to go…I didn't hurt her. I couldn't—"

"Don't say anything else," Ryan said sharply, while his mind worked overtime.

Phillips and MacKenzie rounded the corner with a clatter of heels.

"Jack, lad. What's the trouble?" Phillips enquired, moving forward as if to embrace him.

But Ryan held him back with a look and reached into his pocket to retrieve his mobile phone, swiftly calling up the direct line for the Control Room. Once the number was ringing, he thrust the phone into Lowerson's hand.

"Make the call, Jack."

Phillips began to protest but then comprehension dawned. The man was covered in blood and had come to Ryan rather than going through the proper channels. He swore inwardly, already calculating what the cost might be.

"He's right, son. You need to ring it in."

"You've reached the Northumbria Police Control Room. Would you like to report an incident?"

Lowerson let out a sob, leaning heavily against Ryan who held him upright with one strong arm, staring at a point somewhere above his mousy brown head.

"This is—this is Detective Constable Jack Lowerson. B—badge number—" he stopped, shock having temporarily affected his memory. "I can't remember. I'm sorry. But I'm calling to report an incident. It's—it's DCS Lucas. She's dead. I think there was an accident… Or maybe—I don't know. I don't know."

He was almost hyperventilating now, and Ryan took the phone from him, rapping out his details for the telephone operative and ordering a couple of first responders to attend Lucas's home.

When the call ended, he found that MacKenzie held a couple of plastic bags in her gloved hands and he nodded his silent thanks.

"Jack, we need your jacket."

The man's eyes were dark pools of misery, matched only by the silent heartbreak each of them felt as MacKenzie led him towards the bathroom.

"Come on now," she murmured. "Anna's put the kettle on and we'll get you a nice cup of sugary tea."

As they disappeared into the downstairs cloakroom, Ryan and Phillips exchanged an eloquent look.

"Sweet Jesus," Phillips muttered. "D'you think he's—"

"I don't think anything until I've seen a crime scene," Ryan said. "I'll put a call through to the Chief Constable. They need somebody senior to oversee the first response, if there's anything to find."

Phillips nodded.

"She can't keep either of us on the investigation," he warned.

"I know. But she'll still need somebody making sure the scene doesn't turn into a circus."

"What about Jack?"

"MacKenzie will have to take him in," Ryan replied. "There's nothing else for it. You know that, as well as I do."

Phillips nodded sadly.

"Aye, I know. I s'pose I was hoping…" He shrugged heavily and then shook his head. "I'll have a word with Denise."

Ryan stood for a long moment watching his sergeant's burly figure retreating down the corridor, his balding head bent in defeat. He thought of the dinner they had shared and wondered how long it would be before they laughed like that again.

CHAPTER 2

It was almost nine-thirty by the time Ryan drove south along the A1 motorway towards the city of Newcastle upon Tyne. At his side, Phillips occupied the passenger seat and stared sightlessly out into the night, watching the flicker of headlights flare up against the glass.

"How'd Morrison take it?" he asked, eventually.

Ryan thought back to the difficult conversation he'd had with their Chief Constable. Sandra Morrison had been enjoying a quiet Saturday night in with a rom-com and a Chinese takeaway, no doubt congratulating herself on having finally restored calm productivity to the Criminal Investigation Department after two years of turbulence.

He'd been sorry to burst her bubble.

"She's a professional," he said, blithely ignoring the stream of expletives she'd emitted when he'd first relayed the news. "Morrison was shocked, but she took it in her stride. We're to oversee the first response while she gets in touch with Durham CID, then hand over to whoever they send, no arguments."

"Durham?"

"Yeah. We can't have anyone from our end handling this. There'll be enough talk, as it is, without fanning the flames with any suggestion of bias."

"Aye, that's two superintendents in as many years," Phillips agreed. "The papers will have a field day."

"And then, there's Jack."

Silence fell once again while scenarios and possibilities ran through their heads.

"Did he say anything else?" Phillips asked, turning away from the window. "Did he tell you what happened?"

11

Ryan flicked the indicator to overtake a slow-moving caravan, his profile silhouetted briefly in the passing light.

"Jack said she was dead and he was adamant he didn't hurt her," Ryan replied. "But he was covered in blood and I cautioned him not to tell me anything further."

He felt Phillips eyes boring into the side of his head.

"What else could I do? He came to me before he rang it in. He turned up, covered in blood. I didn't want him to incriminate himself."

Phillips sighed.

"Aye, I know. It was the right thing to do. But…look, it could have been an accident— Jack wouldn't hurt a fly."

"I know that. But even the most non-violent of people can be tested to their limits," Ryan said, softly.

He thought of the man he had been, all those years ago. He remembered the whispered threats from the very same woman who now lay dead, the daily insults that had chipped away at the very fabric of himself until there had been hardly anything left to call his own. He remembered the terrible urge to make it stop, the animal need to defend himself in any way he could.

Though that half-broken man was a distant memory now, he still recognised it in others.

"We don't know what happened, yet. But, if Jack says he didn't hurt her, then I believe him."

To his embarrassment, Phillips felt a lump rise to his throat.

"I didn't know they were—I didn't know they were, ah…" He came to an awkward halt.

Ryan's jaw tightened.

"You didn't know they were together, out of hours. Are you surprised?"

"She's fifteen years older than him," Phillips argued.

Unbelievably, that brought a reluctant smile to Ryan's face.

"Love is blind. Just ask MacKenzie."

Phillips let out a bark of laughter.

"Aye, I'm hoping she doesn't gan' to Specsavers any time soon, or I'll be for the boot."

* * *

Twenty minutes later, Ryan manoeuvred his car through a network of residential streets in an upmarket part of the city known as Jesmond. It was conveniently located near the centre, which made it popular with singles, couples and well-heeled families alike. A few streets further afield, Saturday night revellers enjoyed a liquid dinner after the working week in the bars and clubs of Osborne Road but, as Ryan pulled into a parking bay near Lucas's smart Edwardian terrace, there was nobody to be seen except the shadowed figures of the first responders who had been dispatched to protect the scene.

"Pinter lives around here," Phillips remarked. "Might be worth giving him a call."

He thought of the chief pathologist attached to Northumbria CID, who was usually their first choice in cases such as these.

"Not ours to make," Ryan reminded him, though it stuck in his throat.

They slammed out of the car and hurried across the empty street, huddling into their coats to protect themselves against the cold wind that whipped along the row of houses and left a thin layer of frost on the tiny patches of lawn separating them from the pavement.

When they reached Lucas's front door, they were greeted by two police constables from Tyne and Wear area command, who came to attention as they approached.

"Been here long?" Ryan asked, making a mental note of their badge numbers.

The shorter of the two decided to act as spokesperson from behind a thick, magenta pink woollen scarf that was not police issue. He could hardly blame her; the wind was so cold it cut through to the bone.

"About thirty minutes, sir. We've been taking it in turns to do shifts on the door, to keep warm."

Ryan nodded.

"What've we got in there?"

The woman's eyes clouded as she tried to focus on her report and not on the nausea that still rocked her system.

"We, ah, we arrived at DCS Lucas's home at approximately nine-fifteen, responding to an order from Control. The door was closed but the lights were on inside the house, as they are now, sir. We touched as little as possible."

Ryan looked over her shoulder to the front bay window, which was illuminated behind a set of voile curtains.

"We rang the doorbell and knocked repeatedly, calling out a warning before we tried the door. It was unlocked, so we entered using the appropriate warning."

Ryan nodded, watching her bear down against the memory of what she had seen, admiring her for the attempt. It was a hard line they walked, particularly when they didn't deal with the most serious crimes every day, as he did. You got used to it, after a while.

"Go on."

"We entered the property and began a search, in case DCS Lucas needed medical attention. We found her almost immediately, in the living room."

Ryan's eyes strayed back to the window.

"Alright," he murmured. "Reinforcements are on the way. Set up a cordon, keep an eye on the door and log anybody who so much as looks at the house."

With that, Ryan covered his hands and feet, took a deep breath and prepared to face his past, one last time.

* * *

Ryan felt an acute sense of déjà vu as he stepped inside Lucas's home.

He stood just inside the entrance hall and looked around, thinking that it might have been a replica of the house she'd owned in London, all those years ago. Her tastes had changed very little and every wall had been painted white or palest grey; there were no photographs on display nor any mementoes that might give the casual observer any clue of her personality or preferences. Lucas had chosen to live inside an expensive blank canvas, leaving her free to paint the day however she chose and to reinvent herself depending upon her mood.

"You ready?" Phillips rumbled, from somewhere over his shoulder.

Ryan gave himself a mental shake and headed towards the living room, following the ripening scent of death that carried on the air. Beneath it, he could detect the heavy floral perfume Lucas had favoured and the sensory memory made his stomach turn. He steeled himself, preparing his body for worse to come. The sight of death in all its untarnished glory did not grow any easier with time or experience but at least he'd learned how to manage his reaction to it.

Mostly.

They came to a standstill outside the living room door and Phillips looked across at the huddled, shrunken figure of his former boss lying on the far side of the room. He experienced the same wave of compassion he always felt for the dead, a basic sadness at the loss of a life but no more than that. He was no hypocrite and would not pretend he had thought a great deal of the woman in life or that he would greatly mourn her death. But then, he had not had the dubious pleasure of truly knowing her, unlike the tall, silent man standing beside him.

He looked up at Ryan's face, which was so hard it might have been cast in granite.

"Y' alreet, lad?"

Ryan surveyed the room with calm, watchful grey eyes. He noted the deep gash on Lucas's head, saw the drying blood matting her dark hair and pooling out in a fan on the polished wooden floor where she had fallen, and waited to feel pity. He waited to feel outrage at the premature loss of a life half-lived but, instead, his overriding emotion was relief. The feeling soared like a phoenix, as though an enormous weight had been lifted from his shoulders.

And what did that say of his character? he wondered.

It was his vocation to seek justice for the dead and to avenge them for the sake of those who lived on. He made a point never to discriminate between those who had lived 'good' or 'bad' lives. Who was he to judge? He was not their Maker, even if he believed in such a thing.

For all that, Ryan found himself unmoved by the sight of the woman's body lying crumpled on the floor and he knew then that the Chief Constable had been right to appoint somebody else to run the investigation. It was chastening to admit that he could not promise Jennifer Lucas the impartiality she deserved because he could not look upon her body and muster the pity to try. It was a watershed moment for him, one he would need to think about at some other time.

"I'm fine," was all he said.

Phillips searched Ryan's face and opened his mouth as if to say something, then thought better of it.

"Looks like there was a tussle," he remarked instead, pointing to a spilt cup of coffee and a small crystal vase that had fallen from the mantelpiece, scattering shards of glass and artificial flowers across the floor.

Ryan had seen it too.

"I'd say she was holding the cup when she fell," he said. "It shattered across the room, nowhere near the coffee table. She must have had it in her hand when it was dislodged."

Phillips tried to imagine it, wishing he had Ryan's unique ability to reconstruct a crime scene.

"Maybe she tried to steady herself and caught the edge of the vase as she went down."

Ryan looked at an empty spot on the mantel.

"Faulkner's the expert," he said of their senior crime scene investigator. "But I'd say you're right on that score, Frank."

Phillips sucked in a breath and asked the burning question.

"Well? How would you call it? Suspicious or accidental?"

"Once again, that's not my call to make," Ryan murmured, but his eyes continued to trace the details of the room. "And we haven't heard Jack's story, yet. But I know one thing: a woman doesn't usually fall to her death in her own living room without some outside force to ease the journey. Look at the edge of that radiator, Frank."

Phillips peered across the room and noted the remnants of blood and brain matter on the sharp, heavy edge of a cast iron radiator not far from Lucas's body.

"Aye, that'd do it," he agreed.

Ryan turned away and faced his friend.

"I can see two wounds on her head and there might be more once Pinter examines her properly. I might have passed off the first as an accident but how in the hell did she come by the second?"

Jack Lowerson's name hung on the air between them, unspoken. Neither man could even dare to think it.

CHAPTER 3

DCI Joan Tebbutt was an attractive woman in her late fifties with a quiet manner, a penchant for reading and over twenty-five years' experience on the force. She might have been away from her usual turf—and that made things harder—but she considered herself both ready and able to take up the challenge of investigating the death of a high-profile colleague from a neighbouring constabulary.

She hadn't needed a brusque conversation with her superintendent to know what the media reaction would be in response to the latest misfortune to befall Northumbria CID. It had been a while since the papers had seen their last juicy murder and it was a gift to have one involving local detectives the public trusted to solve rather than to perpetrate crimes. Understandably, the bigwigs wanted it all tied up in a neat little bow as quickly as possible.

Well, they'd just have to see about that.

The late DCS Jennifer Lucas had been a forty-seven-year-old woman at the top of her game. She'd been glossy and polished with a cloud of shiny brown hair and open blue eyes that looked great on camera. If the in-house gazette was to be believed, she'd done wonders for public relations; revamping operations and making sure plenty of 'lessons had been learned' from past mistakes and corruption that had been rife during her predecessor's tenure. She'd succeeded in a Man's World and, in other circumstances, Joan might have admired her.

But a woman like that didn't just turn up dead for no good reason and Tebbutt hadn't been born yesterday. It would take more than a few good news stories in the Police Gazette for her to overlook more basic methods of communication, such as the gossip chain in the staff canteen. In her experience, it was amazing what could be learned by

18

sitting there and listening while she munched on a ham and cheese panini.

As she pulled up on the street outside Lucas's home, her keen eye took in the police cordon and the constables diverting passers-by away from the crime scene, both measures meeting with her approval. A dark van she recognised as belonging to the team of CSIs was parked nearby and she spotted one of them talking to a tall, good-looking man she presumed to be DCI Ryan and an older man she knew to be DS Phillips.

Ryan peeled away from the small group to meet her. She watched his face closely for the usual signs of displeasure at having been passed over for an investigation but was pleasantly surprised to find it lacking. He flashed a brief, professional smile and she couldn't help but think that the younger female officers in the staff canteen hadn't over-exaggerated his charms on that score either.

But that was neither here nor there.

"DCI Tebbutt?"

"DCI Ryan," she shook the hand he extended. "I understand you've been overseeing the first response. Thanks for holding the fort."

Ryan nodded, and she had the fleeting impression that he was assessing her. That was fair enough; she was doing the very same thing.

"DS Phillips and I entered the property just before ten-thirty. We're both in agreement that the circumstances of the case point to a suspicious death but, of course, that will be your call to make."

She inclined her head in the direction of the CSIs, who were zipping themselves into polypropylene suits.

"Did you call them in?"

Ryan gave a slight smile.

"No, the Chief Constable had them on standby. Faulkner's waiting for your go-ahead before they make a start. We're not looking to tread on any toes."

Tebbutt stuck her hands in the pockets of her waxed green jacket.

"You're good at this," she told him, forthrightly. "I'd heard you were good but, frankly, I was expecting to find a bit more testosterone flying around."

Ryan huffed out a laugh.

"It would accomplish nothing. You're very welcome to this one, believe me."

Tebbutt sensed a thread of discord.

"We'll need to have a chat soon, Ryan. You'll need to make a statement—both of you," she added, as Phillips left his discussion with Faulkner and moved across to join them. "I understand you were both present when DC Lowerson turned up at your house, unannounced."

Phillips shuffled his feet, but Ryan simply nodded.

"Lowerson was in a state of shock when he arrived but we've followed procedures to the letter. We bagged up his clothing and DI MacKenzie took him and the evidence down to the station, so he could make a full statement."

Tebbutt nodded.

"I know. I've just come from there," she said, surprising them both. "I thought it would be prudent to strike while the iron was hot, as it were."

"How's he doing?" Phillips burst out. "He had a bad shock—"

"*If* it was a shock," she put in, smooth as you like. "Whatever happened here tonight, Jack Lowerson is a grown man. You should remember that." She raised a hand to greet her sergeant, who trotted along the pavement towards them, then gave Ryan one last searching look. "I'll be in touch."

With that, she tucked her chin inside the collar of her coat and headed off.

"She's good," Ryan remarked, once she was safely out of earshot.

"Aye. Maybe too good," Phillips muttered. "She doesn't know Jack like we do. What if she walks in there and assumes they had some sort of lover's fight that went wrong? God only knows what he told her."

Ryan had a brief flashback to the times he'd fended off similar quarrels with Lucas and of how close each one might have been to the grim scene they'd just left.

He pasted a reassuring smile on his face.

"Tebbutt knows her business, just like we do. We have to trust her to do the job."

* * *

The foyer of the Northumbria Police Headquarters bustled with activity when Ryan and Phillips stepped through its reinforced glass doors, just before midnight. There were few industries that truly came to life in the Witching Hour but theirs happened to be one of them. People in varying degrees of inebriety and undress were sprawled in the waiting area and they represented a cross-section of society; there were as many in smartly-tailored business suits as there were in muddied rags, men and women of all ages and races who congregated together under one uninspiring, boxy roof.

"Home, sweet home," Phillips declared, breathing deeply of the comforting smell of pine-scented bleach mingled with a variety of bodily odours.

"You're becoming institutionalised—"

Just then, Ryan caught a movement in his peripheral vision. Across the foyer, one of the newer police constables was thrust against the wall as a woman elbowed him squarely in the stomach and made a valiant bid for freedom, racing towards the automatic doors with single-minded panic.

Ryan covered the ground between them with lightning speed, stopping the woman in her tracks. The timing was perfect, and he braced for impact as she hurtled into his torso, nearly winding them both in the process. His arms banded around her skinny body like steel rods and she began wriggling against him like an angry wasp in her desperation to break free.

"Calm down," he muttered. "*Calm down!*"

She began to kick out and he narrowly avoided a sensitive encounter.

"*Hey*! Do you want to make things worse for yourself? Calm down, or find yourself booked for evading arrest and assault on a police officer."

His words must have penetrated her brain because she stopped struggling suddenly, her thin arms falling limply to her sides as she sagged against him.

By now, the arresting officer had recovered himself sufficiently to hurry across and lend a hand, while the crowded foyer watched the brief drama play out with avid interest.

"Sorry, sir, I don't know how she managed to—"

"It happens," Ryan said, holding the woman's arm in a gentle grip. He looked down at her crestfallen face and realised she couldn't have been more than nineteen or twenty.

"What's your name?"

Her lips trembled, and she swiped the back of her hand beneath her nose. Absent-mindedly, Ryan rummaged around his jacket pockets for a packet of tissues and offered one to her.

She hesitated, then snatched it up and blew her nose loudly.

"Charlie," she muttered.

Ryan sighed.

"Why are you here, Charlie?"

She craned her neck to look up at him, surprised to find there were no aches or pains where he had restrained her.

"Soliciting," she whispered, and a tear escaped.

"First offence?" he enquired of the constable, who watched the exchange with goggle-eyed fascination.

"Yes, sir. A pop for shoplifting but nothing else on record."

Ryan watched as she blew her nose again. He didn't consider himself a bleeding heart and he'd certainly heard his share of sob stories over the years. But, every now and then, he met one who had barely begun their path into the cycle of drugs and crime and it gave him pause.

He warred with himself, then reached inside the pocket of his jeans for some change.

"There's a vending machine over there," he said, quietly. "Go and get something to eat and drink."

She searched his face but there were no conditions attached.

"Th-thanks," she mumbled and walked directly to the vending machine to do as he suggested.

"Sir? What should I do now?"

Ryan waited to see whether the girl would run, but she scooped up a can of coke and a variety of sugary goods and then took them to one of the plastic seats nearby, where she settled down to eat.

Good.

He turned back.

"What do you think, Webster? You could book her for assaulting you and for soliciting and nobody would question it," he said, with a meaningful pause. "On the other hand, you could give one of the women's charities a call to see if they can give her a bed for the night. They're usually full but it's worth a shot. If not, book her in here. If she's got a pimp, he'll be waiting for her to come out or he'll have one of the other girls waiting to snatch her up and they'll have her straight back on the streets before sunrise. Let's at least give her a fighting chance," he murmured.

"But it's not our job—"

"Our job is to protect," Ryan said.

The younger man's eyes strayed across to the pitiful sight of a girl savouring her first chocolate bar in a very long time.

"I'll call them now," he decided.

Ryan gave the constable a manly clap on the shoulder and then moved quickly to re-join Phillips, who was standing on the far side of the foyer with a small, knowing smile on his face.

"What?" Ryan demanded, a bit defensively.

Phillips lifted a shoulder.

"There was a time when I thought it was all black and white for you, all 'right' and 'wrong' with no shades of grey."

"There's black, white, grey and everything else in between," Ryan told him. "Come on, let's go and find out where Lowerson lies on the colour chart."

* * *

They had barely made it down to the interview suite when they were met by MacKenzie, who headed them off at the door.

"They're not letting any of us see him," MacKenzie said, without preamble.

"What d'you mean? The lad's not under arrest," Phillips fumed.

She laid a gentle, restraining hand on his chest.

"They've booked him on suspicion of murder."

"*What?*" Phillips growled.

"They have to," Ryan said. "You saw the scene back there, Frank. There's no way Lucas fell and hit herself repeatedly. It looks suspicious and Jack was the one who found her. Tebbutt needs more time to gather evidence and she has to treat him in the same way she'd treat any civilian suspect, or there'd be hell to pay."

"His solicitor'll get him straight in front of the Mags and he'll be out on bail, if the charge isn't dropped by then, anyway," MacKenzie put in, to reassure herself as much as anybody else. Phillips ran a frustrated hand over his thinning hair.

"Oh, aye, and in the meantime, he'll be suffering all kinds of torture down there," he said.

"It's not so bad," Ryan mused, and two pairs of eyes swivelled towards him. "I spent a night in the cells after Bowers died up at Heavenfield Church, remember? And I seem to recall it was *you*, Frank, who did your duty back then and booted my sorry arse behind bars."

Phillips turned an embarrassed shade of red.

"Oh, aye. I forgot about that," he admitted, sheepishly. "It was nothing personal, y'nah. I was just—"

"Doing your job," Ryan nodded. "Just like Tebbutt."

Phillips glowered.

"That's as maybe. But the lad's traumatised, he needs to see a doctor."

"He's seen one." MacKenzie took the wind out of his sails. "Tebbutt saw to it. Jack's been fed and watered, and the medics have pronounced him fit as a fiddle, just a bit shaken up. A solicitor was in with him when he made his statement and he had a change of clothes and a shower after his prints and swabs were taken. Even before he was formally arrested, he volunteered the swabs," she added.

Their ears pricked up at that. Lowerson was unlikely to volunteer anything if he felt there was something to hide.

"That's encouraging. Did he tell you anything else on the journey over?" Ryan lowered his voice.

MacKenzie scrubbed a tired hand over her face and let it fall away again.

"Not much more than you already know," she said. "Jack says he went around to Lucas's house after his shift, at around seven-thirty. He used the door key she'd given him and let himself inside, where he found her dead on the floor. He went across to see if she was still alive and that's how he ended up covered in blood. He says he panicked and drove to the safest place he could think of."

She looked across at Ryan, who gave a brief nod of understanding.

"And we know the rest. Where are his parents?" he asked. "Are they here?"

MacKenzie nodded.

"They're in conference with his solicitor now," she said. "His mother was almost hysterical when she came in."

"It's not every day your baby boy is arrested for murder," Phillips said, heavily.

25

All three turned at the sound of running footsteps echoing down the corridor and spotted their colleague, Trainee Detective Constable Melanie Yates, hurrying towards them with a sheet of paper flapping in her hand.

"Uh oh," Ryan murmured, and put a hand on her arm as she came to a skidding halt. "What's the matter, Mel?"

Yates didn't waste any time on pleasantries but came straight to the point.

"Sir. This e-mail has just been forwarded to us from *The Enquirer* news desk."

She thrust the paper into his hand and Ryan skim-read its contents in the surrounding silence, his face darkening into a worried frown.

> *At midnight tonight, the Tyne Bridge will burn.*
> *This is the first.*
> *You have been warned.*

A second ticked by, then Ryan looked up and checked the time on his watch.

Eleven-fifteen.

"Yates, I want you to get straight on to Morrison and tell her we've got a major bomb threat. Then, I want you to call the news desk back and ask them why the hell it took them so long to report this to the police. When they give you some bogus answer about how they didn't pick it up, I want you to threaten them with the full force of the law if they so much as breathe a word of its contents before we've made the area safe. There's probably a battalion of reporters already down there, waiting for bad news."

Yates seemed rooted to the spot while the reality of the situation set in.

"*Now,* Yates. There's no time to lose."

Galvanised, she rushed off and Ryan turned to the others with blazing eyes.

"We need to get on to the bomb squad," he said shortly, not stopping to wait for them as he began to move swiftly towards the Criminal Investigation Department.

"*Wha—?*" Phillips demanded, of Ryan's retreating back.

"It's a bomb threat," he threw over his shoulder. "Somebody calling themselves *The Alchemist* wants to see the Tyne Bridge burn at midnight, tonight."

They pushed through a set of security doors separating the interview suite from the main office building, all thoughts of Jack Lowerson temporarily forgotten.

"It's probably a hoax," Phillips said, huffing a bit to keep up with Ryan's longer strides. "It might be some whacko looking for attention. It happens all the time."

"Yes, but there's usually a ransom of some kind," Ryan said, as he shouldered through a set of double doors and into the long corridor that led to the bullpen.

"And they're not asking for anything?" MacKenzie was incredulous.

Ryan shook his head and lengthened his stride, never more conscious that the clock was ticking.

"It's like firing a warning shot, to show us they're serious." His eyes strayed to an enormous, white plastic clock fixed on the wall and felt his stomach jitter.

"It'll be some daft kid," Phillips was adamant. "Or maybe some crackpot fanatic looking to make a name for themselves. We've dealt with their type before."

"Yes, but there was always a motive or ideology behind those," Ryan muttered, tightening his fist around the paper he still held in his hand. "And if it was a terror attack, they wouldn't go to the trouble of sending us a warning first."

"It has to be a hoax," MacKenzie reasoned. "Otherwise, they'd ask for something. They always do."

Ryan gave a slight shake of his head.

"But they are. They're asking for it to be splashed all over the news, or why else send that message to *The Enquirer*? They want everybody to admire their handiwork."

"If that's the case, they'd have a better audience on a Saturday afternoon," MacKenzie said.

"Not necessarily," Ryan argued. "Flames look so much better at night, don't they? It'd be like a beacon, visible for miles around."

"There'll be crowds of people on the streets tonight," Phillips said. "It's a Saturday and there's clubs and bars scattered on both ends of the bridge, not counting the night buses and pedestrians crossing the bridge."

As they reached the door to the open-plan office space that housed the Criminal Investigation Department, Ryan pulled out his phone and punched in the number for the Explosives Ordnance Disposal Unit, who were part of a military regiment based out of Otterburn Training Camp and Barracks. It was a cool, thirty-minute drive west of the city and he knew it would be a miracle if the EOD Unit made it into the city before midnight. As the phone began to ring at his ear, he thought of the quickest way to evacuate the area around the bridge.

"Mac, I need you to speak to Control. Tell them we need all available units down at the Quayside. We have no way of knowing if there's a real threat or where it might be on the bridge, but we need to start evacuating everybody within two hundred metres of either entrance. We need police covering north and south sides of the river. We can't take any chances, I want the whole area locked down."

"Consider it done," she said simply.

"Frank? I need you to speak to the fire and ambulance services and have them on standby."

"Aye, I'll get on to it," he said. "What're you going to do?"

Ryan finally heard the *click* of a telephone being answered at the other end of the line.

"I'm going to hope I'm wrong."

CHAPTER 4

The river undulated between the cities of Newcastle and Gateshead in waves of inky-blue, all the way to the North Sea. The bridges spanning the river were illuminated by a series of enormous floodlights, reflected in the rippling water below. In the centre of it all, the Tyne Bridge rose in towering arches of bottle-green steel, a matriarch to six smaller bridges fanning out on either side in the space of a mile. Swathes of people hopped between the twinkling lights of numerous bars and clubs lining the water's edge, while lovers braved the cold weather and shuffled along the Quayside as they made their way home, hand in hand. There was a steady chorus of happy noise, a thrum of merriment that followed the crowd from one drinking hole to the next and, from his position on higher ground, Ryan watched them with a sinking heart.

There was no time.

It was ten minutes until midnight and police squad cars had formed a barrier on the main access roads above and below the bridge. Officers in high-vis gear spilled onto the streets to push back the crowd and set up a cordon but were inevitably outnumbered as they struggled to deal with all the usual scuffles and misdemeanours that were the by-products of an alcohol-fuelled Saturday night in town.

"Any sign of the bomb squad, yet?"

It wasn't their official name, but Phillips was a creature of habit.

"They're on their way," Ryan said, and turned his collar up against the biting wind. It rolled in from the water and curled its way through the cobbled streets, up to the exposed rooftop of the multi-storey car park where they'd made their temporary base.

"Fingers crossed, it'll be a wasted journey for them."

Ryan nodded.

On the southern side, MacKenzie was helping to coordinate the evacuation effort and her disembodied voice crackled down his police radio, informing them that a roadblock was now complete at either entrance to the Tyne Bridge and traffic was being diverted. Apartment buildings and hotels within striking distance of a blast had been informed and residents were being removed, although there was little chance of completing that mammoth task in the time they had left.

"Five minutes to go," Phillips said, with a nervous glance at his watch. "Still no sign."

"It's like having a talking clock," Ryan muttered and raised his field glasses to look down at the roads below, which were deserted in every direction.

His police radio fizzed again and, this time, the distant voice of one of the officers stationed on the Quayside came down the line.

"Sir, we've got a police line in place but quite a large crowd has gathered and is refusing to budge. Over."

Ryan sighed.

"How large?"

"A couple of hundred," came the reply.

There would be no way to move that kind of crowd in the space of three or four minutes, Ryan knew that much.

"Just keep them back," he ordered.

"Yes, sir. There are some television crews, they're stirring it all up—"

Ryan sighed inwardly. He understood the need for a free press and believed it was important, but there was a time and a place for everything. The last thing any of them needed was vultures circling around an already loaded situation, just so they could secure a headline for the morning papers. There may be lives at stake.

"If they cause any kind of obstruction, book them," he said.

"They're getting two for the price of one, tonight," Phillips observed. "Big night for the news desk."

Ryan said nothing but slipped the radio into his back pocket and raised his binoculars again to scan the empty streets below, watching for any sign of suspicious activity. He had officers situated at various check-points with orders to be vigilant and several members of the Firearms Unit were stationed in office buildings with a clear view of the bridge, should they need to disable a suicide-bomber on a mission.

As the clock crept ever closer to midnight, they heard the roar of a vehicle's engine as it made its way up to the roof of the car park. The sound reverberated around the concrete walls and an army jeep emerged, coming to an abrupt halt in one of the parking spaces nearby. Two men and a woman dressed in military gear jumped out and ran across to where Ryan and Phillips stood beside the far perimeter wall.

"Which one of you is DCI Ryan?"

A fit-looking man of around forty addressed them in the kind of no-nonsense tone that might have set their teeth on edge, had the threat of an imminent explosion not been uppermost in their minds. He wore head gear but, from what they could see, he had a year-round tan on his chiselled face, a pair of arresting blue eyes and what might have been sandy blond hair beneath his cap, all of which reminded Phillips of a plastic Ken doll.

"Captain Nobel? Thanks for getting down here so quickly."

"I'm sorry we couldn't get here sooner. There's no time to send a robot to look for any explosives, so I'm afraid we'll have to hope for the best." He gestured towards the two other military personnel standing beside him. "This is Sergeant Sue Bannerman and Corporal Kevin Wilson. We've got the rest of the team heading to the south side to liaise with your DI MacKenzie. What measures have been taken so far?"

But there was no time for discussion as they suddenly heard the distant sound of chanting voices carrying on the night air.

"What's that?" Phillips tried to judge the direction.

"It's the crowd on the Quayside," Ryan said, without rancour. "They're counting down the seconds until midnight."

Ten, nine, eight…

"For God's sake, it's not New Year's Eve!" Phillips cried. "Do they think this is a bloody joke?"

31

"Let's hope it is," Nobel remarked. "Nine times out of ten, these things are a false alarm and it gives them all something to talk about in the morning."

Ryan still didn't like those odds.

"How far back is the cordon?" Bannerman asked quietly, coming to stand on Ryan's other side.

…seven, six, five…

"At least two hundred metres in any direction," Ryan murmured, his eyes still scanning the road for any sign of life but finding none.

The tension in the air was palpable and the people on the roof fell silent as the remaining time slipped away, five pairs of eyes coming to rest on the shadowy arches of the bridge which dominated the skyline.

Ryan felt his heart hammering against the wall of his chest, powerless to stop what was about to happen before their very eyes.

…four, three, two…

Time hung there, suspended for a terrifying moment. And then—
One!

A cheer erupted from somewhere far below and they held their breath, hardly daring to move, never tearing their eyes away from the bridge which remained blessedly intact. Elsewhere in the city, people tuned into the news or streamed it on their smartphones, caught somewhere between excitement and dread as they watched live footage from the cameras that were dotted around the city, their long-range lenses trained on the bridge from every possible angle.

When nothing happened, Phillips let out a long, quivering sigh.

"There, y' see! I told you, it was nothing but kids—"

The explosion rocketed through the night air, sending smoke and rubble up in a billowing cloud of dust. Shards of tarmac and burnt metal flew through the darkness and cheers turned to cries of panic as shrapnel fell like glittering raindrops, wounding those who refused to be moved. Ryan felt the air contract, buffeting against his body in a hard burst of energy that rocked him back on his heels. He threw up a hand to shield his eyes against the bright ball of white light that flared up and then simmered into a steady yellow glow, staring in horror as the fire raged on.

They stood in silent vigil as one of the city's most iconic landmarks was altered irrevocably. Its lines could be re-drawn, and its arches repaired but it would never again be the same steel that had been forged and moulded, hammered and bolted into place by the hands of men nearly a hundred years ago.

When Ryan was sure he could trust his own voice, he raised the police radio to his lips.

"MacKenzie? Do you copy?"

The sound of the radio's crackle broke through the unnatural hush, serving to remind them that there was urgent work to be done.

"All fine here," MacKenzie replied. *"No casualties reported. From what I could see, the blast seemed to come from the north end of the bridge."*

Ryan agreed with her.

"We'll have to wait until the dust has settled before we can assess the true damage." Below, they heard the wail of ambulance sirens making their way down to the Quayside. "Keep me posted with any developments."

Ryan ended the exchange and then turned to the three army officers.

"How soon until you can get down there and find the source?"

"Not for a while. That might have been a partial blast," Nobel said, with a note of warning. "We need to wait to see if there's a second explosion. You should warn your officers of that possibility."

Ryan nodded towards Phillips, who began making a series of radioed warnings to that effect.

"If we don't see a second blast, we'll send a robot down there to look around. It'll be easier in the morning, when we have a bit more light to guide us," Nobel continued.

Ryan looked back at the dust cloud spreading further downstream.

"What do you make of the level of explosion?" he asked. "It was in a different league to the usual pipe bomb in a carrier bag."

All three EOD officers made a kind of synchronised, non-committal sound.

"It looked bad but, sometimes, once the air has cleared, you find it's only made a small dent," Wilson explained. "That bridge is pure steel and it was built to last. It'd take a truckload of explosives to bring it down."

"Unless the bomber had access to military grade materials," Bannerman pointed out. "That would make more of an impact but they're harder to come by."

"What were they looking for this time?" Nobel asked. "Money?"

The distant glow of the fire was reflected in Ryan's eyes as he thought of the planning it must have taken to pull off the attack they'd just witnessed.

"We won't know what they're looking for until the second blast," he said. "This was just a practice run, to get our attention."

"Aye, well they've succeeded in that," Phillips said, with a catch to his voice. His grandfather had been a scaffolder, one of the many who had built the bridge piece by piece until it had become a permanent part of the skyline. The explosion was more than an attack on concrete and steel; it was an attack on their shared history and on the community that had built up around it.

"You reckon there'll be a second?" Wilson asked, curiously. "How can you be so sure?"

Ryan spared him a brief glance.

"It's your department, but I don't need to be an expert to know that a device was planted in advance. Whoever did this probably held a remote detonator of some kind in the palm of their hand. They triggered it and watched the bridge go up, maybe even from the crowd down there on the Quayside. They'll have heard all the cheers, seen the audience in awe of it all."

He paused, struggling to find the right words.

"I know there'll be more because whoever did this has had a taste of real power. It's like a drug to some people and the need doesn't diminish, it only grows stronger."

He lifted a mute hand towards the bridge.

"This is only the beginning."

CHAPTER 5

There was a picture of a heart on the wall.

At some time or other, a previous inmate had scratched its outline onto the wall of the cell and written one word beneath it that read, 'SAM.'

Lowerson stared fixedly at the small mural from his position atop the uncomfortable single bed which, despite being fairly new, had already attracted the lingering smell of urine. He wore the freshly laundered jeans and shirt his mother had sent down for him, and when he lifted the material to his face, he recognised the scent of her laundry detergent and could almost imagine she was there beside him.

His eyes were red-rimmed but bone dry, all his tears having been spent.

How had it come to this?

He stared down at the clothes he wore and remembered he had bought the jeans a year ago, although it felt like much longer. Wearing them again, it was like donning a different skin, an old skin that felt smooth and worn-in, yet uncomfortable at the same time. He'd stopped wearing many of his old clothes because Jennifer had told him, ever so gently, that he needed to dress like a man, not a boy.

"It's no wonder you were practically a virgin when I met you, Jack. I'm surprised any woman ever touched you, before me."

He pulled his knees up to his chest and rested his elbows on top, spearing his fingers through his hair. The tiny heart on the wall opposite seemed to mock him, reminding him of what a fool he had been.

But even now, even *knowing* how she had felt about him before she died, a small, treacherous part of himself wanted to deny it. His heart, now battered and torn, wanted to cling on to even the smallest hope that the last four months of his life had not been completely, utterly wasted.

He wanted to mourn the woman he had loved, to believe she had been a good person. For, if she had been anything else, how could he forgive himself for being so taken in?

"Blah, blah, blah, Jack. That's all you ever say. Always whining at me to tell you 'I love you', to rub your belly like a puppy. Is that what you are, Jack? Are you a dog, that I can kick?"

"No. I'm not, I'm—"

Then, she'd walk to him and place a hand on his face. She'd look into his eyes with every sign of sincerity and whisper the words he longed to hear.

"Of course I love you, Jack. I just want what's best for you, that's all. I just wish you'd change, only a little. Just for me, okay?"

Lowerson thought of how he'd lapped up her words, and anger washed over him in a wave so strong it was almost painful. He felt the rush of adrenaline burst through his veins and he leapt off the bed to walk it off, pacing around the room as his mind went around and around in circles, thinking of everything and nothing.

And every time he closed his eyes, he saw her lifeless face staring up at him.

He leaned back against the wall of his cell and sank to the floor, holding his head in his hands.

* * *

"Ryan, come in."

Chief Constable Sandra Morrison pushed her office door shut and gestured vaguely towards one of the over-stuffed visitor's chairs arranged on the other side of her desk.

For once, Ryan took up the offer and settled himself as comfortably as he could, stretching out the tired muscles in his neck. Somewhere over his shoulder, he heard the sweet sound of a coffee machine percolating and wondered if there might be a god, after all.

"Here," she said, thrusting a cup into his hands. "You look like you need one."

"Thank you, ma'am," he murmured, and chugged back a grateful swig while Morrison hesitated, then decided to break with her own tradition and take the seat beside him rather than facing him across the expanse of her desk.

Ryan noted the action and polished off the last of his coffee in three large gulps. If they were about to have a serious discussion, he needed his wits about him.

"Tell me some good news," she said, in the residual silence.

He almost smiled.

"Ma'am—"

"Oh, for heaven's sake, let's cut out the formalities, too. We both know the Department's up shit creek without a paddle. That qualifies for a frank discussion on first name terms."

"Alright then," he gave a slight shrug. "I wish I could tell you some good news, Sandra, but I can't. Not yet, at least. We need time to figure this all out."

"We don't have much time," she shot back. "This has hit every major international news outlet. I presume you've spoken with the counter-terrorism unit?"

And there was the difference between them, Ryan thought. Of the two major events that had occurred in the space of a few hours, Morrison's priority was to pacify her colleagues in centralised departments, whereas his first duty was to the young man holed up in one of the basement cells, three floors below.

"Yes, I've spoken with them. An investigation is already underway, and we'll know much more in the morning, once the EOD team have had an opportunity to assess the site. Meanwhile, the tech team are working together with *The Enquirer* to find out where that e-mail came from and I've authorised the resources for them to work through the night on this. If we can find the source, we can find the person responsible. I've sent the rest of the team home to catch some shut-eye, with orders to report back for a briefing at eight o'clock tomorrow morning or, rather, this morning."

Morrison checked the time on her smartphone. It was already past two o'clock, so she could hardly ask for a quicker response than that. The windows were dark except for the dim, yellowish glow of the streetlamps in the staff car park below and she'd turned on every light in her room, just to stay alert.

She set her cup on the desk and turned to the next troubling matter on her agenda.

"Tell me what happened to Jack," she asked him, as gently as she could.

"I've already told you all I know."

Morrison raised a hand to push back the untidy fall of ash-blonde hair flopping into her eyes. There had been no time to run a brush through it after she'd first heard the news and hurried out of the house, back down to the office where she belonged. Although it was the worst kind of news to receive on a Saturday night, she had not been cuddled up on the sofa with anybody special, or enjoying an Aperol Spritz with a group of giggling friends down at her local drinking hole. There was a reason she lived alone; she had made her choice years ago, after her marriage collapsed. There had been a choice to make then between devotion to her work, or to her ex-husband. She'd chosen the work. But, every now and then, she wondered what life might have been like if she'd made a different decision, as Ryan had done.

Irritated with herself, she shoved the thought aside and focused on the present.

"No," she said. "You've told me what you plan to tell Tebbutt, when you give a statement. I want to know what happened to Jack *before*—I want to know how it came to this. Why was he the one to find Lucas at home?"

How did I miss this? she nearly added.

Ryan looked at her for a long moment with calm, all-seeing eyes, until she had the grace to look away. Months earlier, he had come to her to warn her of the kind of woman she had chosen to appoint as their new superintendent. He'd tried to tell her about the danger, to warn her of Lucas's insidious nature. Morrison hadn't listened, hadn't wanted to hear it. She'd needed a poster girl for CID, somebody with an impeccable track record who could sweep in and white-wash the blemishes left over from the old days, and she'd believed the person to do that was Jennifer Lucas. He'd been forced to watch as the culture of their team had become one of fear and mistrust, where officers learned never to speak out or find themselves reprimanded. He'd watched his friend, his colleague, lose himself a little more each day and he'd been powerless to stop it. Ryan had almost taken the decision to leave or take a long sabbatical, when Lowerson had arrived on his doorstep.

"You know why," he said, quietly. "I tried to tell you."

The seconds dragged on and then Morrison lifted her chin to look him in the eye. She hadn't made it this far in life without having to take difficult decisions, ones which sometimes cost her sleep, but she was always willing to take responsibility for them. If an apology was due, it deserved to be said face to face.

"I know you did," she acknowledged. "I don't know what happened to you in London, Ryan, and when you tried to tell me I silenced you, told you to stop being unprofessional. I needed to believe it was professional differences or old scores between you and Lucas, so that I could get the department back on track. I didn't want to know."

He said nothing, and she dug a little deeper.

"I'm sorry," she said, baldly. "If it had been MacKenzie or Yates who came to me with a concern about a male colleague in a position of power, I'd have treated them differently. I understand that, and I hope you'll accept my apology. It should never have happened, and it pains me to know that, because of my inaction, Lowerson may have found himself compromised."

Ryan opened his mouth to speak but she surprised him by continuing.

"I want us to be friends again," she said, and her voice wobbled slightly. "I trust your judgment as a police officer and the staff love you. You're an outspoken so-and-so," she added, for good measure, "and God knows you don't always follow protocol. But you've got an unswerving moral compass which is bloody hard to find in our business. I don't want to lose that, none of us do. Tell me what I can do to make things right again."

Ryan listened, then gave himself a second to collect his thoughts. When he'd walked into her office, he'd expected to give a report and then be on his way. He hadn't expected her to delve into all that and he found himself momentarily at a loss.

"The first thing you can do is fire up that coffee machine again," he said, bringing a smile to her face. "We've got a lot of work ahead of us and it's going to take more caffeine."

Morrison's eyes crinkled at the corners.

"What's the second?"

He held out his hand, and Morrison took it gladly.

* * *

Half an hour later, Ryan crossed the foyer on his way to the staff car park. The place was empty except for the duty sergeant at the desk and the reclined figure of a local homeless person whose rumbling snores were oddly comforting.

As he passed the stairwell that led down to the basement, Ryan's footsteps slowed.

"Bugger it," he muttered, and changed direction.

He took the stairs two at a time and emerged into the corridor leading towards lock-up. There was a constable on duty, as always, and Ryan hesitated. As much as he wanted to see his friend and offer his support, it would not serve Lowerson's best interests if his case were scuppered because of police meddling.

He borrowed a piece of paper and a pen, instead.

"If Tebbutt gives her permission, can you pass Lowerson this note?"

The constable looked down at the note and nodded. It read, '*Keep your chin up. Nobody expects the Spanish Inquisition*', on account of their shared appreciation of Monty Python.

"I'll ask."

Ryan raised his voice a notch, on the off-chance it might carry down to whichever room Lowerson was occupying.

"Thanks. Just tell him we're thinking of him, alright?"

As his footsteps retreated down the corridor, Lowerson put his head back on the pillow and was finally able to sleep.

* * *

Elsewhere in the city, another person lay wide awake.

Memories of the moment kept replaying in slow motion, showing every perfect detail. It had been so exquisite, so powerful.

There had been a momentary doubt, a slight hesitation when the clock struck midnight. But with all the people cheering and counting down the seconds, it seemed right not to disappoint them.

The colours, the sound of metal splintering, the cries from those too stupid or too stubborn to heed the warning—it had exceeded even the wildest fantasy.

There was no guilt or shame, nothing but a potent sense of release, as if a caged animal had been set free into the wild. It was remarkable to think that, all this time, the feeling had lain hidden beneath the surface, trampled upon and repressed for so long. The animal had lain dormant, waiting to strike forth and become its true self. There was no better time than the present.

What could be built, could be destroyed.

And what was once born must also die.

Nothing was meant to last forever.

CHAPTER 6

Sunday, 11ᵗʰ February

Ryan didn't return home until the early hours of the morning, when the sky was already beginning to lighten to a deep shade of mauve, heralding the start of a new day. There would be little chance of sleep, but he needed the comfort of home and to be with the woman he loved. He was bone-weary after spending hours on his feet speaking to colleagues across three command divisions, overseeing the aftermath of the explosion and totting up the human cost. Luckily, nobody had lost their life, but the injury list ran to at least thirty reported cases of minor burns and cuts caused by falling debris. He supposed he should be grateful the damage was no worse.

As he suspected, the media had started a feeding frenzy, reporting every detail through the night and replaying the moment the bridge had gone up in a constant loop. Each time another news outlet picked up the story it served as a fresh reminder, rubbing salt into a wound that was already bleeding and raw.

The EOD team had deployed one of their robots to enter the blast zone and complete a thorough check of the site, but the smog and lack of natural light were both barriers to finding out anything meaningful about what had caused the explosion. The decision had been taken to complete a full inspection of the site in the morning and, until then, roadblocks remained in place throughout the night, causing further havoc with the city's infrastructure.

Still, it was better than the alternative.

The passing landscape changed dramatically as Ryan left the city lights behind and drove north along the A1 motorway towards the outer reaches of Northumberland, where houses and offices gave way to fields

Ⅎ

and trees coated in a light frosting of snow that had fallen sometime amid all the chaos. Soon, he followed the turning for Elsdon and wound his way into the heart of the countryside, passing through smaller hamlets and the elegant town of Rothbury until he reached the scenic little village where he and Anna had chosen to put down roots.

Anna.

He smiled, just at the thought of her. Who could have thought a murder detective and a historian would build a life—a good life—together? He never imagined the happiness that awaited him, ten years after he had sworn never again to place too much of himself into the hands of another person. His eye caught the shiny gold band on the ring finger of his left hand. It was starting to scuff a bit with wear and tear, and he liked that just fine.

Presently, he drove up a small incline, following a narrow country road that would lead him to the spot where they'd built their home. The tightness in his chest began to ease as its stonework came into view, just visible against the purplish-blue sky. He spotted the porch light and the glow of a lamp inside the hallway which had been left burning for him. Her love was there in that small gesture, and in her every act of kindness each day. Anna asked nothing of him that he was not prepared to give, nor did he ask it of her. Theirs was a partnership of equals; of two souls that had found one another in the wide expanse of the world. She understood his mind just as he understood hers and they were bonded by their shared experience.

They were both survivors of a different kind.

Yes, he thought. He could say that now. Anna had given him the strength to say the word aloud and feel no shame.

He was a survivor.

Ryan's thoughts strayed back to Jack Lowerson and he leaned back against the leather headrest. They, too, were bonded by a shared experience with the same woman who lay on a metal trolley down at the mortuary. Had Lowerson been pushed once too often, once too hard?

Or had he been the one to do the pushing?

Time would tell.

* * *

"Ryan?"

Anna's sleepy voice sounded across the shadows of the bedroom.

"Shh, go back to sleep," he murmured, shrugging out of his jacket. "I'm sorry, I didn't mean to wake you."

"I was only dozing," she said. It was always hard to fall into a deep sleep when she knew he was out there somewhere, facing untold dangers.

In the twilight, she watched him strip off his shirt and jeans, and then the bed dipped beside her. It was as natural as breathing for his arm to curve around her, for her head to rest on his chest.

"I saw the news," she said. "It all happened so fast, I can hardly believe it."

Ryan brushed his lips against her hair and tugged her a little closer.

"There was no time to prevent it," he said, softly. "We barely had enough time to clear the streets. The blast could have been a lot worse; there was no way of knowing."

"Do you think it was a terror attack?"

Ryan rubbed his cheek against the top of her head, breathing in the scent of her.

"Whoever did this is a terrorist, but not in the way you mean. I don't think they're fighting for any holy cause, any ideology except one that promotes their own ends."

"You'll find them," she said, with conviction. "You always do."

Ryan thought back to a recent case at Kielder Water and his jaw clenched.

"They don't always get the justice they deserve," he said. "Or, at least, not straight away."

She looked up at his profile in the darkness.

"Do you still want to take a leave of absence?"

Ryan thought of his plans to hunt Nathan Armstrong, the man he knew to be a killer. He was out there, somewhere, probably hurting somebody else's child, somebody else's mother or brother, and it was a constant ache to know it.

"I've been in touch with my counterparts in Paris and Vienna," he said. "They tell me there's no evidence to support an investigation and, besides, he's a celebrity. Apparently, that means he can't be a killer. I'd be going out there without the approval of those police departments, without the full force of the law backing me."

All the same, he was ready to do it. He'd been ready to hand in his notice, if that's what it took to get the job done.

"You can't leave now that this has happened," Anna said. He would never leave his team in a moment of need.

"No, I can't. We're no closer to finding out what happened to Lucas and, until we do, Lowerson will have a question mark over his head. Tebbutt seems like a decent woman but I'm not going anywhere until I see his name cleared."

"You're certain, then, that he couldn't have done it?"

Ryan had thought of little else. As the Tyne Bridge had gone up in flames and he'd gone through all the necessary motions, he'd still been thinking of Jack's character and of how far he might have gone.

"It isn't in his nature," he said, simply.

Anna nodded her agreement.

"Tebbutt rang me, earlier," she told him. "I need to go in and give a statement later today."

Ryan stared up at the skylight overhead, watching the passing clouds.

"We all need to," he said. "I was granted a reprieve owing to extenuating circumstances, but I can't put it off much longer."

"Do you think she'll want to talk about how you knew Lucas from before?"

"Probably."

Anna thought of how to ask the question that was uppermost in her mind.

"Ryan, how did you feel when you saw her? I mean, when you knew she was dead?"

He closed his eyes, unwilling to relive the shameful memory of how relieved he had felt; as if somehow the cosmos had decided there were enough bad people in the world and had removed one of them, to even the score. Whatever her past, Lucas had not deserved to die prematurely, and it was unlike him to feel such little compassion.

"I felt…" He took a shaky breath and decided honesty was always the best policy. "I felt happy, Anna. I'm ashamed to say it."

There was a small pause and he wondered if she was disappointed.

"Then we can be ashamed together, because I felt happy too."

He looked down into her eyes, then bent his head to bestow a lingering kiss.

"There's nothing to worry about any more. She's gone, Anna. She can't hurt anyone, ever again."

CHAPTER 7

The new day dawned crisp and clear. Long, watery rays of amber sunshine trailed across the hills and valleys, brushing warm fingers of light against the houses scattered in between. The wintry air was cold, nipping at their cheeks when Ryan and Anna left shortly after seven and made their way back into the city, she to give her statement to DCI Tebbutt and he to hold the first briefing of what had been aptly named, 'OPERATION ALCHEMY.'

There seemed to be an unnatural hush as they drew closer to the city, as if its people were in mourning. With road closures still in place, people had taken to the streets to make their way into town and see for themselves what had happened to one of the most famous monuments to their industrial heritage. The morning news had been unrelenting in its coverage of the disaster and had, by now, amassed numerous quasi-intellectuals who were on hand to give an 'expert' view of the situation, ranging from former Metropolitan police officers to retired army personnel. Opinion was divided, with most believing ISIS would come forward and claim responsibility before the morning was over, and a few outliers believing it would be the IRA who would claim that dubious honour instead.

Yet there had been no statement from either party.

Northumbria Police Headquarters rested on the eastern fringes of the city, in an area known as Wallsend. It took its name from the Roman wall which began within striking distance of their new offices and ended eighty-four miles away on the western coast of Cumbria.

"Strange to think of how different the landscape must have looked when the wall was built," Anna remarked, as they stopped at a set of traffic lights just outside the gates to the archaeological site. "I must go back and visit the heritage centre sometime."

Ryan smiled at her, then put the car into gear as the lights changed.

"I've never known anybody love history as much as you," he said. "I worry, sometimes, that my work gets in the way of your career. I know you're writing a book and there's your teaching at the university, but is there anything you really want to do? My work can be…" He tried to find a delicate word for 'all-consuming' and settled on, "Cumbersome."

Anna thought of the regular offers she received to lecture at universities around the world. Sometimes, she took them up; other times, she didn't.

"Your work doesn't get in the way," she replied. "And I don't feel held back. My specialism is in North-Eastern early-religious history and practices. I'm in the very best place to keep learning about that. If I want to gallivant abroad, nobody's stopping me."

"Quite the opposite," he said. "I only hope you need a groupie to carry your bags."

He wriggled his eyebrows at her, and she laughed.

"You'll tell me, if the situation ever changes?"

Anna nodded.

"Shy bairns get nowt, as my granny always used to say."

Now, it was Ryan's turn to laugh.

* * *

Ryan stepped into one of the larger conference rooms in CID just before eight o'clock and was pleased to see it already had a handwritten sign declaring it to be the Major Incident Room. He found it half-full of staff ranging from data analysts to specialist technical support personnel, as well as some of the usual suspects. In the corner, a television had been tuned to the news channel with its sound muted and the subtitles enabled.

"Mornin' lad," Phillips was the first to greet him.

Ryan presented his sergeant with a takeaway cup.

"Ah, you're a goodun'," the other man declared, taking a delicate sip to check its contents had been sweetened to his taste.

"How'd you sleep?" Ryan asked.

Phillips made a rocking motion with his hand.

"So-so," he replied. "What with Jack…and then the bridge?" He shook his head, sagely. "No chance of me getting any shut-eye."

"You could've fooled me, Frank."

Phillips turned to find his fiancée sauntering towards them with a disbelieving look on her face.

"Morning," she said, and waggled her thumb in Phillips' general direction. "*This* one's snoring probably kept the whole neighbourhood awake last night. That, or a rhino broke loose from the zoo and went on a rampage through the streets."

Ryan snorted a laugh while Phillips butted out his chin.

"I'll have you know, I never snore," he said, with some dignity.

"In that case, somebody better call the zoo," MacKenzie replied, deadpan. "Where's Yates?"

"She's down at *The Enquirer,* taking a statement from the bloke manning the news desk, or whoever picked up the incoming messages last night," Ryan said.

Further conversation was forestalled by the arrival of Captain Gary Nobel from the EOD Unit, who framed himself inside the doorway with the kind of practised air that drew all eyes in the room. Although it wasn't strictly necessary, he had chosen to wear slim-fitting khaki trousers and a skin-tight, long-sleeved jersey that clung in a manner that made Phillips regret the bacon butty he'd wolfed down earlier that morning.

"Thanks for joining us." Ryan gestured him forward. "You've already met my sergeant, but I don't think you've met DI MacKenzie?"

Without his safety gear, they could see that Nobel was a little under six feet tall, with lightly tanned skin, bright blue eyes, blond hair going grey at the temples, and an athletic build. In other words, Phillips thought, he looked like Brad Pitt's less famous brother.

Damn him.

"No, I don't think I have. It's a pleasure," Nobel reached a muscular arm across Phillips' face to extend his hand, which MacKenzie shook as a matter of politeness. "I'm only sorry I stayed on the north side of the bridge, last night. Clearly, I should have opted for the south."

He flashed a winning smile.

MacKenzie raised a single, unimpressed eyebrow, while Phillips bristled. Sensing an altercation might not be far off, Ryan stepped in.

"Are the rest of your team still down at the bridge?"

Nobel dragged his eyes away from the attractive redhead and folded his arms across his chest, which had the added benefit of drawing attention to his pectorals. Women loved that, didn't they?

"Yes, Bannerman and Wilson are down there with the other two lads. They'll head up and join us as soon as they can, but I thought you'd want to have an update in the meantime."

Ryan nodded.

"Thanks. We'll make a start."

When Nobel headed towards the front of the room to take a seat, Phillips turned to MacKenzie.

"I don't trust him," he growled.

MacKenzie stuck her tongue in her cheek and tried to stifle a laugh. "Now, Frank…"

"I mean it. I don't care if he's GI Joe, I don't like the cut of that bloke's jib."

* * *

Ryan walked to the front of the room to stand in front of a long whiteboard he'd set up with a series of significant times and events from the previous day. There were no names or faces tacked to the board other than the pseudonym of their unknown quarry, *The Alchemist.*

He waited for the room to settle, which didn't take long. Chairs scraped, chatter died, and they awaited his instructions.

Ryan swept his gaze around the room.

"For those of you who've been living under a rock for the past twelve hours, let me remind you that we are tasked with uncovering the identity and whereabouts of the person or persons unknown, calling themselves *The Alchemist*. This person or organisation sent a warning e-mail to *The Enquirer* at approximately eleven o'clock last night, which they did not report to us until twenty-past eleven. The contents of the e-mail were straightforward; we were told that the Tyne Bridge would burn at midnight and that it would be the first."

Out of the corner of his eye, he noticed Chief Constable Morrison slipping into the room to stand at the back, out of sight. He nodded an acknowledgment and then continued.

"We were left with forty minutes in which to assess and evacuate a radius around the bridge, on a busy Saturday night. There was no time to prevent the blast itself."

"Sir? What about Superintendent Lucas?"

The interruption came from one of the crime analysts, an eager-faced young man with no sense of tact, or timing.

But Ryan decided to address the elephant in the room.

"I'm only going to say this once, so listen up. As you will have heard, Superintendent Lucas passed away last night. Her death is being fully investigated by DCI Tebbutt, of Durham CID. I am sure that if there is anything untoward, she will uncover it." He paused, allowing that to sink in. "Now, there will come a time when we can pay tribute to DCS Lucas's long service in the Metropolitan and Northumbria police forces, as is right and proper. However, as recent events have proven, life very much goes on and the longer we stand around, the less chance there is of finding out which fruitcake was responsible for last night's destruction. First rule of CID, constable: know your priorities."

Ryan's reference to cake did not go unnoticed by Phillips, who turned to MacKenzie with a fatherly smile.

"I taught him that phrase," he said, proudly.

"Aye, and many more useless things, besides," she replied.

"I'm pleased to welcome Captain Gary Nobel, who heads up the bomb disposal unit, otherwise known as EOD," Ryan said. "He's going to give us a brief update on what his team have been able to find out following the blast last night."

Nobel stood up and faced the room.

"Members of Explosives Ordnance Disposal are elite and highly trained military personnel who assist civilian authorities by providing counter terrorist support," he said, as if he were addressing a roomful of army cadets. "The regiment is based at several locations around the UK and our squadron has a small out-posting at Otterburn. It's thanks to those arrangements that we were able to get down to the Quayside so quickly last night but, as Ryan's already told you, not quickly enough to find and dispose of the device before it was detonated."

Phillips wondered if Nobel could possibly stand with his feet any wider without falling face-first on the carpet-tiled floor.

Wishful thinking.

"Once we had a bit more natural light, we sent a robotic device into the blast zone and found what we believe to have been the epicentre, just underneath the northern end of the bridge on the westernmost edge," Nobel continued. "We were able to go in afterwards on foot, where we found remnants of an improvised explosive device that packed enough power to blow a hole with an approximate radius of two and a half metres through the tarmac and under-layers of the road. Thankfully, it was only able to shave off a small amount of steel rodding and suspension that must have been vulnerable."

"Why d'you say it was vulnerable?" Phillips piped up, his natural curiosity overriding his subtler feelings towards their guest speaker.

Nobel tucked his thumbs into the belt loops of his trousers, dragging them down a half-inch.

"Ah, just things like corrosion or wear and tear. The bridge is ninety years old and, even with plenty of upkeep, it's natural to suffer a degree of weakening in the nuts and bolts. To be honest, we should be pleased it wasn't a hell of a lot worse."

"How many people were injured by shrapnel?" MacKenzie enquired, of nobody in particular. "Thirty-two?"

"Thirty-four," Ryan corrected, and appreciated her subtle point. The outcome was bad enough, even without fatalities.

He turned back to Nobel.

"You said it was an improvised device? Do you know anything about its components?"

"We've taken samples and we'll work with your lab boys—"

"And girls," MacKenzie muttered.

"Yeah, them too," Nobel said, dismissively. "We'll work with them to confirm the ingredients. My money's on military grade, given the size of the explosion. If it had been placed beneath the bridge, maybe in one of the towers at either end, we might have seen a very different outcome."

"How do you think somebody transported it up there, in the first place?"

Nobel shrugged.

"A sports bag or even a large rucksack would have been enough to transport a homemade bomb," he said. "We've scooped up a few bits and bobs that might turn out to be what you're looking for. Your perp would've needed to plant the bag well ahead of time or risk exposure and, given the direction of the blast, I'd say they hid it between the pavement railing and the outer edge of the bridge. It's the only way they could be confident it wouldn't be picked up by some observant passer-by."

Ryan had to agree with the logic.

"Phillips? How are we coming along with the CCTV footage?"

The previous evening, he'd instructed a requisition of all available footage from both sides of the bridge. It was in the centre of town with several cameras trained on either end, so there was a good chance they'd pick something up.

But his sergeant pulled an apologetic face.

"Nobody's answering from the Council office," he said. "I've left messages, but the offices don't open until eight-thirty—"

He paused to check the time, which was just after the half hour.

"There should be no trouble getting hold of whatever they've got. Fingers crossed the cameras were working."

"Don't forget the buses," MacKenzie thought aloud. "Buses go back and forth over the Tyne Bridge and the onboard camera at the driver's side usually has good visibility of the road ahead. You never know, we might get lucky and see a pedestrian carrying a large bag."

Ryan nodded.

"Good thinking. Request footage for the last couple of days, to start with. We can review older footage if we need to, down the line."

He turned back to Nobel.

"As far as you're concerned, it's more a question of looking at what was used to make up the device, isn't it? We can start tracing the source of the materials, as soon as we know."

"Yeah, I'd say so. GCHQ will be able to give you a steer on any internet searches for certain components, unless you've got a smart bastard who's using the Dark Web, which will slow things down."

Ryan thought of the planning and execution of last night's explosion and had a sinking feeling their perpetrator would have covered every angle.

As Nobel took his seat again, Ryan turned to the tech team.

"Patel? Any update on the e-mail trace?"

The head of their specialist information technology division came to attention. Jasmine Patel was a shy, introverted woman most of the time, but she happened to be possessed of a first-class brain and a knowledge of computers that was second to none. In cases such as these, Ryan knew there was nobody better.

"Um, yes and no, sir," she said, softly.

"Speak up, love!" Nobel called out, then nudged Phillips as if they'd just shared a joke.

"Sorry," she muttered, feeling her palms begin to sweat.

"I think you were going to tell us about the source of the e-mail," Ryan said, kindly.

"Yes. We spent most of the night trying to trace the IP address of the server used to send the e-mail," she said. "We hopped from Hungary to Brazil and then to Russia and finally Ukraine, where we've stalled. Whoever sent that e-mail has a sophisticated level of knowledge but I'm afraid I can't tell you much more at this stage. I've got the team working on it and, if we make any further progress, I'll let you know straight away."

She ducked down again, feeling like a failure.

"That tells us something important," Ryan said, to the room at large. "If we were in any doubt, we now know that our perp is no fool. It sounds obvious, but they often are."

"Like that one who called himself *rubberducky2001* and thought he'd bought himself a few deadly bombs off the internet?" Phillips chimed in. "He ended up strapping two hundred quid's worth of bath bombs onto himself and walked into City Hall smelling of lavender and roses. Priceless."

There were a few chuckles around the room.

"Unfortunately, there was no sign of any bathing produce last night," Ryan said, hitching a hip onto the corner of the nearest desk. "Right now, our priority is to keep trying to chase that e-mail server, to identify the ingredients—"

He broke off at the sound of a mobile phone ringing, and was embarrassed to find it was his own.

"Sorry," he muttered.

He slapped a hand against the pockets of his jeans until he found his phone and then yanked it out, intending to bin the call. Instead, he glanced at the screen and saw that the caller was his trainee, Melanie Yates, who was on site at *The Enquirer* taking statements from the staff manning the news desk.

His stomach gave a funny little lurch he recognised as a premonition of things to come, then he raised the phone to his ear.

"Ryan."

The rest of the room watched the quick tightening of his jaw and looked amongst themselves, gearing up for the news they'd been waiting for.

"Understood. Get back down here as quickly as you can."

He ended the call and held the inoffensive piece of plastic in his hands for a moment longer as he thought of what the hell to do.

He looked up at the clock on the wall, noted the time was exactly nine o'clock, then drew himself up to face his team.

"*The Enquirer* have received another e-mail. We have until noon before one of the other bridges goes up."

He watched heads turn to check the time, as he had.

"Which bridge?" MacKenzie asked, and Ryan raised a hand to rub at his temple then let it fall away again.

"It doesn't say. All I know is, we have three hours to find out."

CHAPTER 8

"**D**octor Taylor-Ryan?"
In another part of the building, Anna looked up from an idle inspection of last month's dog-eared magazines in one of the Constabulary's informal meeting rooms.

"Yes?"

Tebbutt flicked the sign to 'OCCUPIED' and stepped inside, pulling the door shut behind her.

"I'm DCI Joan Tebbutt," she said, and offered what she hoped was a friendly smile. "Thank you very much for coming down."

"No problem," Anna murmured, not quite knowing what to do with herself. It made little difference that she was married to a high-profile murder detective, or that she counted several police officers as her friends. They operated in a different world and, at times like these, she felt it keenly.

Hers was the world of quiet, academic study; of losing herself in textbooks and old parchment to uncover the stories of the past and of what made up their shared history. Theirs was a world rooted in the present, where the action happened quickly and decisions were taken almost immediately. They could not afford to do otherwise.

Anna watched as Tebbutt settled herself in one of the slouchy visitor's chairs beside her, leaving a comfortable distance between them yet close enough to create a sense of confidence. Unfortunately for her, Anna happened to live with a man who was adept at reading human behaviour and some of his experience had rubbed off over the years. Consequently, she was familiar with the ploy, which greatly diminished its effect.

"Once again, thank you for coming in to give a statement," Tebbutt began. "I'm going to make a note of what you tell me, then you can read it back and sign it. But first, I'm going to set out the standard caution, okay?"

Anna nodded after Tebbutt went through the proper motions.

"I understand."

"Great, let's get started," she said, and shuffled more comfortably in her seat as she flipped open a fresh notepad. Anna took the opportunity to study her face, noting it was smooth and clear with very few lines. There was a tiny scar just visible beneath her chin and she wondered how Tebbutt had come by it.

"You're wondering how I got my scar, aren't you?"

Anna almost jumped, but found herself laughing instead.

"How on earth did you know that?"

Tebbutt looked up from behind a pair of slim gold spectacles and smiled.

"Experience," she said. "And the answer is very boring. I cut myself a long time ago when I took my nephew ice-skating one Christmas on Princes Street, in Edinburgh. No tales of gun-slinging or knife-fighting for me, I'm afraid."

"That's no bad thing," Anna was bound to say.

"True," Tebbutt said, briskly, and did a little survey of her own.

Ryan's wife was a very pleasant surprise. Often, she'd found men in positions of power preferred a little woman at home, one with mammary glands bigger than their brains. It was a simple formula, but it repeated itself with worrying regularity. Instead, she found herself looking into a pair of intelligent brown eyes and listening to a woman with a gentle Northumbrian accent and an air of calm authority.

The doctor and her husband made an attractive couple, Tebbutt thought.

The kind of couple some might like to break.

"So, perhaps you could start by telling me what you do for a living? I like to build up as full a picture as possible."

Anna let out the breath she'd unconsciously been holding and tried to relax.

"Ah, sure. I'm a senior lecturer in the history faculty at Durham University. I spend the holidays working on new research, or writing, and term times are eaten up with teaching duties too."

"I see. And were you working at the university yesterday?"

Anna shook her head.

"No, I reduced my teaching hours this term, so I could work more from home and press on with the book I'm writing—"

"Which is?"

Anna blinked.

"Oh, it's a pocket history of Holy Island, where I was born and grew up."

"Lovely place," Tebbutt murmured, then dived into the heart of the matter.

"So, you were working from home all day, yesterday?"

"Yes, although I popped into town for an hour or so, around five o'clock, to catch the shops before they closed. I wanted to pick up some things from the food hall, in *Fenwick.*"

Tebbutt smiled and made a quick note.

"For dinner?"

"Yes, we were expecting Frank and Denise—that is to say, DI MacKenzie and DS Phillips—around seven-thirty."

"So, you were in town for five o'clock, which means you left at, say, four-fifteen?"

"Yes, around then. I got home about six-thirty," Anna said, helpfully.

Tebbutt's face remained impassive but, privately, she thought it was unfortunate that the good doctor happened to be in the vicinity of the late DCS Lucas's home at that hour. She'd spoken to the police pathologist first thing that morning and he'd given his best estimate of a post-mortem interval, telling her Lucas had died somewhere between three and six o'clock the previous day.

"And at what time did Phillips and MacKenzie arrive at your home in Elsdon?"

"Right on time, around seven-thirty give or take a few minutes either way."

"And what time would you say DC Lowerson arrived?"

Anna thought back.

"It must have been around nine o'clock when we heard him ringing the doorbell," she murmured, and thought of his shocked face standing there beneath the greyish-white light of the security lamp. "We'd finished dinner and were just chatting, playing Scrabble, that sort of thing."

"Scrabble?" Tebbutt queried, and Anna's lips curved.

"Yes. We live a rock and roll lifestyle."

"I see," Tebbutt smiled briefly, then it was gone. "Who answered the door?"

"Oh, Ryan answered. I joined him after a minute," Anna said.

"So, DCI Ryan spoke to DC Lowerson for around a minute before you joined them?" Tebbutt repeated, just to be sure.

Anna frowned and sat up a bit straighter in her chair.

"Well, yes, but—"

"That's fine," Tebbutt murmured, and gave another mild smile. "Can you tell me what happened next?"

Anna swallowed.

"Well, I thought perhaps Ryan had invited him to dinner and forgotten to tell me, or that Jack had decided to pay us a visit, after all," she said.

"After all? Doesn't he usually come to visit?"

Anna wondered how to phrase her answer but, ultimately, fell back on the unvarnished truth.

"Not recently, no. We hadn't seen Jack in quite a while."

"Why?"

Anna sighed.

"He had been very busy, I think, and…" She paused, thinking of how best to put it.

"And?"

"He had become quite insular. He used to come around every couple of weeks for dinner or to have a Sunday roast with us," she said.

"What changed, do you think?"

Tebbutt continued to look at her with a patient, unyielding expression on her face.

"Jack had different priorities, I think, and…people grow apart," she finished, lamely. She would not be the one to incriminate her friend, certainly not on the basis of hearsay and gossip.

"Back to last night, then. You came into the hallway and saw DC Lowerson in the doorway? What happened next?"

"I noticed the bloodstains on his shirt and went back to get Frank and Denise."

"What did you think, when you saw the bloodstains?"

"I thought he might have hurt himself," Anna lied. It was half-true, at least. "Either way, I thought the others could help. He seemed very upset."

"In what way? Do you recall what was said?"

Anna cast her mind back.

"He was very agitated and looked unwell. As though a gust of wind could have blown him over," she said. "I was worried about him."

"Mm," Tebbutt made a note. "Did he tell you what had caused him to be upset?"

"I heard him say, 'Jen's dead.' I presumed he meant DCS Lucas."

Tebbutt cocked her head.

"What led you to make that automatic assumption?"

Anna swore, inwardly.

"Common sense," she said quickly. "I don't know anybody else called 'Jennifer', and Jack had been working with her for months."

Tebbutt set her pen on top of her notebook and sat back, folding her hands.

"Could it be, you thought of DCS Lucas because her name is very recognisable to you? She was, after all, your husband's former girlfriend."

Anna's face paled.

"That has absolutely nothing to do with what happened yesterday," she muttered. "Now, if there's nothing else, I'd like to go home."

Later, when the door clicked softly shut behind her, Tebbutt sat there in the quiet room and thought back over the cases she'd dealt with over the years. The circumstances varied but the motives rarely differed.

What might a woman do, to protect the man she loved?

In her experience, an awful lot.

She put a call through to her sergeant and instructed him to check the Automatic Number Plate Recognition cameras on the main roads leading into the city, to see whether Anna Taylor-Ryan was telling the complete truth.

* * *

Anna sat behind the wheel of her car, staring off into the distance. Across the car park, the infamous Pie Van was doing a decent morning trade in breakfast butties and all manner of baked goods, but she hardly noticed.

When she'd first met Ryan, her past had been a matter of public record. The sad, sorry story of the Taylor family had been an open secret on the tiny island where she'd grown up, with tales of domestic abuse and suspicious deaths accounting for part of the shame she'd carried for years. Ryan had stood by her side as she'd mourned her sister's murder at the hands of a madman and held her hand as she'd battled the grief that followed.

But then, Ryan was uniquely qualified. His past was a matter of public record, too, having also lost his sister in the worst possible circumstances. It had helped to forge an understanding between them, a connection that could not be broken. They were both independent, free-thinking people who loved their friends and their work. Add in a generous portion of good, old-fashioned lust and they had it made.

But there had been many years of living *before* they met; a whole lifetime of events that moulded and shaped a person.

Jennifer Lucas represented one such event for Ryan.

When they'd first learned of her transfer to the Northumbria Police Constabulary, Anna had lived in a state of constant dread. What possible reason could she have to move north, except to torment him?

And when Lucas swept through Ryan's team, breaking things apart bit by bit, removing the stability he'd worked for ten years to build, Anna knew she had been right to be suspicious. For a long time, she'd worried that the woman would try to attack their marriage; to stretch them to breaking point as a kind of private revenge.

But Lucas had inflicted her punishment in a different way.

She'd targeted another man instead; a younger man who was lonely and eager to please. Jack was also kind and honourable, the kind of person they were grateful to have in their lives. Systematically, the woman had broken him apart, until Jack Lowerson was nothing but a shell of his former self.

Worst of all, he had been complicit in his own downfall.

Minutes passed while she watched dust motes dance on the quiet air, then she reached for her sunglasses to offset the glare of the morning sun.

Yes, Anna thought. It was a good thing Lucas was gone, and gone for good.

She caught herself in the rear-view mirror and saw a young woman with tired eyes, a product of restless nights. There were shadows beneath that would fade, just as Lucas would.

She turned the key in the ignition and looked forward to sleeping like a baby, when all was said and done.

CHAPTER 9

"There are seven bridges connecting Newcastle and Gateshead."

Ryan addressed his task force, which had by now set up permanent operations in the Incident Room and would remain there for the duration of the investigation. Against one wall, a bank of telephones was manned by support staff who fielded reports of supposedly suspicious behaviour and sifted through eyewitness accounts ranging from sightings of the late Michael Jackson to the Yorkshire Ripper.

Time wasters, every one of them.

"Aye, but who's to say it's just that stretch of the river?" Phillips said. "The Tyne is seventy-odd miles long and splits into the North Tyne and South Tyne. It could be any one of the bridges from Tynemouth to Deadwater Fell."

Ryan had considered the possibility.

"You're right, Frank. There are over forty bridges, if you consider the entire length of the river. In theory, the next attack could target any one of them."

"But he won't," MacKenzie said, and moved across to study a large map of the city tacked to the wall. "The likelihood is, he'll go for one that has more impact."

"*The Alchemist* wants two million pounds' worth of bitcoins to be transferred via a purpose-built website before noon," Ryan said. "To extort that kind of money from the city, I agree with MacKenzie. We have to assume he's bargaining with one of the major bridges."

"That narrows it down a bit," Sergeant Bannerman remarked, then looked to her colleagues Captain Nobel and Corporal Wilson. "Three hours isn't long, but it could be long enough for us to find and disable a bomb, if we have the whole EOD Unit working on it."

Nobel opened his mouth to agree, but Ryan shook his head.

"This time, our bomber was more specific with his conditions," he told them, and reached for a printed copy of the e-mail received by the news desk at *The Enquirer*.

"The message reads: '*Unless bitcoins to the value of two million pounds are paid via www.savethebridges.org by* NOON *today, another bridge across the Tyne will burn. Do not attempt to find or disable the explosives, or I will detonate. Do not attempt to evacuate the bridges, or I will detonate. Do not attempt to remove the website, or I will detonate. This is the second. You have been warned.'"*

Ryan slapped a hand against the paper.

"He wants money and he's prepared to send another bridge up if there's any suggestion of police interference," he said. "D'you know what that tells me—aside from the obvious fact that he couldn't give a fig about the safety of others? It tells me he's just another commonplace criminal with an eye on the bottom line."

"A criminal with some special skills, surely?" Wilson argued.

In answer, Ryan crumpled the sheet in his hand and lobbed it across the room, where it fell neatly into the wastepaper basket.

"That's how special I think this lowlife is, Kevin."

Phillips barked out a laugh.

"So, what're we gonna do, guv?"

Ryan considered the timescales and the threat to public safety.

"There's a strong suggestion that the bridges are being watched. We know this isn't an idle threat; last night was enough warning to show us he's not afraid to press the big red button," Ryan replied. "We can't be seen to evacuate the bridges, which means he's expecting to see people walking around as usual—or, at least, in vastly reduced numbers, after last night's scare."

The light dawned on all of them.

"We could go in plain clothes," Nobel said, jabbing a meaty finger in the general direction of his teammates. "Sue and Kev can take the High Level and the King Edward VII Bridge, and I'll take the Millennium and the Swing Bridge. I'll get Paul and Stevie to do the

Metro and the Redheugh," he said. "We can wander across and keep our eyes open."

"And what if he sees us?" Bannerman asked, a bit worriedly.

"Howay man, grow a pair of balls, will yer?" He smirked. "If you're scared, one of us can take your place."

Bannerman bristled.

"I wasn't suggesting that," she muttered. "I was thinking of risk assessment."

"Just leave that to me, sweetheart," he replied.

Ryan watched the exchange with distaste and made a note to have a word with Nobel at the first opportunity. Bannerman might not be a part of CID but, for as long as she was attached to his task force, he was responsible for her working conditions.

And that included dealing with her misogynist boss.

"Do your risk assessment," he told Nobel. "If it's safe to do a visual assessment, then try. In the meantime, we have less than three hours in which to create a city-wide panic."

"*Eh?*" Phillips said, with his usual eloquence. "What d'you want to do that for?"

The light of battle shone in Ryan's eyes.

"Because, Frank, if we can't evacuate the bridges by fair means, we need to do it by foul. As soon as EOD have had a chance to scope out the bridges in their civvies, we'll lift the media ban. The press will push the word out much faster than we can. It's the best way I can think of to shut down pedestrian and vehicular traffic in both directions without setting up a police blockade."

Phillips grinned.

"Aye, you'd have to be bonkers to use the bridges, especially after last night."

"Let's just hope we can get the word out in time," Ryan replied.

* * *

David and Wendy Lowerson were blissfully ignorant of the new threat laying siege to their city. They waited anxiously in the foyer of CID Headquarters for any sign of their youngest son who, they had been told, was being released that morning without charge. Beside them was seated a tired-looking woman sporting a purplish-black bruise on her left eye and a vacant expression. On their other side, an elderly man was seated beside a boy who might have been his grandson, silently sharing a bag of cheese and onion crisps.

David glanced across at his wife and laid a hand over hers.

"It'll be over soon, just wait and see," he whispered, giving her fingers a quick squeeze. "You know that our Jack would never hurt anybody."

Wendy's hand shook as she thought of her son.

"I know, Dave. I've known he was a gentle soul ever since he was born," she said, and her other hand touched her belly, ever so briefly, in remembrance.

"Makes you wonder what happened to the woman," Dave continued, in weary tones. "Maybe she fell, after all."

Wendy nodded blankly, not wanting to think of it.

"I just—Jack's always been on the other side of the fence, on the side of what's right. I never imagined he'd end up—"

"Ah, now," he said, rubbing her cold fingers. "Jack's a tough nut. Remember when he was in that coma? Six months, six long months we visited him in hospital. Didn't you worry that he wouldn't be strong enough to pull through? We both worried," he corrected himself. "But, in the end, Jack was stronger than we thought."

Wendy's breathing hitched as she battled against tears.

"I thought we'd lost him," she managed, then turned to look at her husband. "But, in some ways, this is worse. I can't stand knowing what this might have cost his reputation."

"Nay, lass," he reassured her, although he'd thought of it too. "The solicitor told us Jack's of good standing, he's no flight risk and he's volunteered to hand over his passport which is why they're letting him go. They would be keeping him longer if they had any doubts about that, now, wouldn't they?"

Privately, Wendy wasn't so sure, but she didn't have the heart to argue.

"If you say so."

"He'll come and stay with us for a while—just until he's feeling stronger—while it all blows over," David continued, then a thought struck him. "We'll need to go and pick up his cat. Marbles will need feeding."

"She's gone," his wife replied, dully.

He looked at her in surprise.

"He didn't mention—"

"I found out the last time I managed to see him," she said, and her fingers twisted as she thought of the measly scraps of time she had enjoyed with her son over the past few months.

Ever since…

Ever since he'd met *that woman*.

"Jack told me Marbles had run away but, I'm telling you, that cat would never run away. She loved him, and he adored her."

"D'you think something happened to it?"

Wendy just shook her head.

"He was very vague. All I know is, Jack was heartbroken."

They both fell silent for a few seconds, then his father said, "I'd give anything to see him smile again."

Wendy closed her eyes and a single tear escaped.

"So would I, love. So would I."

CHAPTER 10

To say that Ryan was angry would be an understatement. He was livid.

The city was under threat of another major incident, one which carried the potential of widespread harm to people and property, and it was his duty to remain on the ground overseeing operations to prevent it. Instead, he had been waylaid by DCI Tebbutt, who demanded that he provide a statement. The timing could not have been worse.

"Can't this wait?" he demanded. "I don't know if you've heard, but we've had another bomb threat. I'm sure you understand that comes with a certain time pressure."

Tebbutt continued shuffling her paperwork.

"I'm sorry, but I have a similar duty to ensure that the investigation into DCS Lucas's death is not delayed in any way. I'm sure I don't need to tell you that the first few hours of a murder investigation are crucial."

Ryan drummed a finger against his thigh and admitted that was nothing more than the truth.

"Let's get it over with, then."

"I'll make it as painless as possible," she assured him, with a small smile. "Despite what you may think, I do appreciate that you have a job to do."

They settled themselves at a table in one of the smaller meeting rooms in CID.

"Now, let's get the formalities out of the way," she said, reading off the standard caution.

"You're making this an interview under caution? Does that mean you consider me to be a suspect?" Ryan was incredulous.

"I just thought it would save time later if we do things by the book from the start. Of course, you're welcome to consult with a solicitor, if you feel you need to."

Ryan raised an eyebrow but shook his head.

"Do you understand the caution I've just given you?" Tebbutt continued.

Now Ryan did smile, and Tebbutt watched it transform his face.

"Yes, I think I understand the general gist," he said, gravely.

"Good," she murmured, and felt a momentary pang of regret that she would be responsible for dimming the humour she saw fleetingly in his blue-grey eyes. "How long have you known DC Lowerson?"

Ryan found himself irritated again.

"Look, Joan, that's the kind of information you can see from his employment record. I'm already pressed for time and I hardly need any warm-up questions."

Tebbutt scratched her earlobe and held up a pen, patiently.

Ryan almost swore.

"Fine. To the best of my knowledge, Jack has been employed by the Constabulary for eight years and I've known him throughout that time in a general capacity. Three years ago, I saw his potential and suggested he try for the detective pathway, which he did. He worked for my team in CID for just over three years, following which he accepted a transfer to work directly for the late DCS Lucas, as part of the training pathway to becoming a detective sergeant."

Tebbutt frowned at that.

"That's an unusual job spec," she observed, then shrugged when Ryan said nothing. It was one of the main reasons he and Jack had argued; it had been clear to everybody except Jack that his so-called promotion had been a sham arrangement.

"How did you feel when DC Lowerson took up the new job?"

"It's completely irrelevant how I felt," Ryan snapped. "Ask me something that relates to the events of last night, or I'm walking out of that door."

Tebbutt realised that he meant every word.

"Alright, Ryan. We'll turn to last night, for now. Can you tell me, in your own words, what your movements were from around 3pm yesterday afternoon?"

Ryan raised a single eyebrow.

"So, she died earlier in the day, I take it?"

Tebbutt gave him a warning look and he held both hands up.

"Alright—alright. I was on-shift until around two o'clock, when I headed home. I stopped off to run some errands—"

"Such as?"

Ryan pushed an irritable hand through his dark hair and sent her a frustrated glare.

"*Such as* stopping off at the petrol station and collecting a couple of suits from the dry cleaners," he said. "The ordinary, prosaic things that make up the fabric of life."

"Which petrol station? Which dry cleaners?" Tebbutt asked, and Ryan stared at her in shock.

"You're checking on my *alibi*?" he threw at her.

"Wouldn't you?" she threw back, and honesty compelled him to agree.

"It was the Esso garage off the West Road and a little dry cleaners called Filigree's."

Her pen stilled.

"Which is where?"

He swallowed.

"It's on Sandyford Road."

"Near Jesmond?"

His eyes flashed molten silver.

"You know it's near Jesmond," he muttered.

"I see. A little out of your way, isn't it?"

He said nothing.

"Okay, Ryan. So, what time did you get home?"

"Ah, I don't know. Maybe around four, four-thirty?"

"And was Anna at home?"

"No, she wasn't."

Tebbutt nodded, thinking back to her conversation with Anna earlier that morning.

"What did you do?"

"I did a bit of cleaning and tidying ahead of guests arriving."

She spared him a disbelieving glance and his anger reached boiling point.

"Look, Joan. If you're so jaded that you don't believe me capable of picking up a vacuum cleaner and a mop, that says more about you than it does about me. Like it or not, that's what I was doing."

Tebbutt pursed her lips.

"What time did Anna arrive home?"

"Oh, I don't know. About six, six-thirty, maybe? She came home, we prepared dinner and then Phillips and MacKenzie arrived around seven-thirty," he rapped out, staccato style. "At nine o'clock or thereabouts, the doorbell rang. We weren't expecting anybody else and I answered it to find Jack Lowerson looking shaken—"

"Is it usual for a murder detective to be so shaken up at having discovered a body? In our line of work, that's par for the course, wouldn't you say?"

"I'd say that's a matter for the individual."

"Very diplomatic," she purred. "But, you were saying you opened the door to find him shaken. Then what?"

"I noticed he had blood on his clothing and I thought he might have hurt himself, but then he told me he had found DCS Lucas."

"Did you question why he would be the one to find DCS Lucas?"

"I did not."

Tebbutt almost sighed.

"You didn't find it strange that Lowerson was at DCS Lucas's house, after hours?"

"I have no opinion on the matter."

There was an awkward pause but, unlike other witnesses, Ryan was impervious to Tebbutt's usual questioning techniques.

"Lowerson was obviously shocked," Ryan did say. "I advised him to telephone the Control Room to report the incident and you know the rest."

"Yes," she murmured, setting her pen aside for a moment. "But, tell me, Ryan. Why do you think Lowerson came to you, rather than calling it in first?"

"I imagine he had a bad shock and decided to seek out his friends," Ryan said quietly. "That's what many of us would do."

"But not a trained detective, who should know better," she remarked.

Ryan folded his arms across his chest and, when no comment was forthcoming, Tebbutt pressed on.

"When was the last time you saw DCS Lucas alive, Ryan?"

His lips firmed.

"I submitted a report on the progress of several active cases on Saturday morning, before each of us was due to go off-shift. We had a brief conversation in her office and, presumably, her assistant can attest to the fact."

"Was DC Lowerson there, too?"

"No, I believe it was his day off."

"Was it awkward to work with DCS Lucas, given your previous relationship?"

If Ryan was disappointed to find the office rumour mill had been at work, nothing of it showed on his face, which remained entirely impassive.

"That is none of your business whatsoever."

"I disagree," she said. "I understand that relations between you and the late DCS Lucas were extremely strained, owing in part to an acrimonious relationship you had many years ago."

"Ancient history," he snapped.

Tebbutt seemed to consider something, then reached for a cardboard folder she'd placed on the empty chair beside her. Ryan frowned as she pulled out a sealed evidence bag, drew on a pair of gloves, then retrieved a series of photographs.

His face drained of colour as she laid them out on the table in front of him.

"Do you recognise these photographs, Ryan?"

His gaze swept over the small collection of images, taken of himself and Lucas over a decade ago. He hardly recognised the tall, black-haired young man together with the petite brunette, smiling together in St. James' Park on a sunny afternoon. He remembered that day vividly; it was the day she'd first threatened to ruin his career, should he so much as look at any other woman, even in passing. Lucas must have kept the pictures, for posterity.

"We found these in DCS Lucas's home," Tebbutt was saying. "Were you aware that she had these images in her possession?"

His eyes swirled with emotions when they swept up again to look at her and Tebbutt had the uncomfortable sensation of having gone too far, though she was only doing her job.

"Ryan—"

"The interview is over," Ryan told her.

A moment later, he was gone.

CHAPTER 11

A lesser person might have been intimidated by the sight of Ryan storming down the main corridor of CID with a murderous expression on his face, but Chief Constable Morrison was not one of them.

"Ryan? A moment, please."

"I'm sorry, I can't. I need to get down to the Quayside."

"Phillips and MacKenzie are more than capable of managing for now. I need a word," she said, with an edge to her voice that told him the 'word' would not be a pleasant one.

And it wasn't.

"What the hell do you think you're playing at?" she stormed, as soon as the door shut smartly behind him.

Ryan planted his feet.

"I'm afraid you'll need to elaborate," he said.

"Oh, I'll be happy to."

Morrison moved around to the other side of her desk and flung her bag on top of it. To her chagrin, a half-used tissue and a tube of lipstick rolled out, which did not escape Ryan's notice and spurred her to even greater heights of irritation.

"I've just had the Editor-in-Chief of *The Enquirer* on the phone, asking me to explain why the media ban hasn't been lifted despite an obvious threat to public safety. You can imagine my embarrassment at having to find this out from him, rather than from my own DCI."

Ryan stuck his hands in his pockets.

"I was going to update you, but I was accosted by Tebbutt on my way out of the door."

Morrison almost chuckled at the thought of Joan Tebbutt hoodwinking one of her best men, but managed to keep herself in check since there were more pressing matters at hand.

Ryan was impatient.

"Look, Sandra. I've given the EOD Unit half an hour to do a quick risk assessment and a recon of the bridges, in case there's anything obvious. I don't expect there to be," he added, "but we have to look."

Morrison lowered herself into her desk chair and Ryan took a couple of steps further into the room.

"Okay," she said. "What then? Have you spoken with the local police? What's being done?"

Morrison tapped an anxious finger against the edge of her desk.

"As soon as I hear from EOD that their recon is complete, I'll lift the media ban," Ryan told her. "We still have two hours for the press to work their magic and traffic should reduce across all the bridges as soon as word gets out. We can't risk uniformed officers going anywhere near the river, but I've got plain-clothed police officers and specialist firearms officers stationed on foot on both sides of the riverbank with orders to intercept with extreme caution. I'm waiting to hear from my contact at GCHQ to see if they can trace the website or the e-mail server IP and I've asked our own tech team to keep working on that angle, too."

Morrison rubbed the heel of her hand against her chest while she listened. It all sounded reasonable and, if she were in his position, she might have taken the same action.

But the desk she occupied required a different approach, one where she needed to consider the politics of a situation, which was something she knew Ryan struggled to understand. In his world, actions and consequence were what mattered most, not spreadsheets and approval ratings.

She drew in a deep breath.

"The terms are two million pounds in bitcoins," she said. "Who knows whether GCHQ will come up with any useful intel before noon? It's almost ten o'clock, already, Ryan. There's no time to waste and, as soon as the motorways, the rail network and the bridges are effectively shut down, that's going to cost the city millions with every passing hour. We can't afford it."

Ryan frowned.

"I hope you're not suggesting that we pay the ransom, because it's cheaper than the alternative?"

Morrison shuffled in her seat.

"Look, if we pay this lunatic off, everybody wins and nobody gets hurt."

"You don't know that," he ground out. "We're dealing with an unknown quantity and there's every chance they'll detonate another bridge even if we meet those terms. There's a bloody good reason why we don't negotiate with terrorists. If you pay the ransom, it sends out a clear message to every other maniac that it's open season. You might as well send personal invitations to each and every one of them, telling them that bomb threats will be paid off under our jurisdiction."

"You'd rather see another bridge go up than pay the money to stop it?"

Ryan didn't so much as flinch.

"Sandra, so long as nobody is hurt, I'd rather see *every* bridge go up, because bridges can be rebuilt. The liberal values we fight every day to uphold, the ones that allow us all to live together side by side with as little animosity as possible, aren't so easily rebuilt."

Morrison looked away as his words hit home.

"Alright, Ryan, you've made your point. You've got until eleven o'clock to make the area safe. After then, I can't make any promises we won't be overruled from the powers above."

Ryan took that as dismissal and turned to leave.

"Ryan?"

He paused with his hand on the door.

"Yes?"

Morrison opened her mouth and then closed it again, waving him away.

"Nothing. Good luck."

"Thank you, ma'am."

* * *

Phillips and MacKenzie stood on the rooftop of the mediaeval 'new' castle, a stone fortress from which the city of Newcastle took its name. Situated on high ground between the railway station and the cathedral of St. Nicholas, it boasted panoramic views of the river which made it the perfect choice for a temporary base. From their position, they were afforded a birds-eye view of all seven bridges crossing the busiest section of the Tyne, including the Tyne Bridge itself which, although battered and bruised, was still standing tall and proud in the steel-grey of a winter's morning.

"You doin' alright, love?" Phillips enquired of his fiancée.

There were very few things that frightened Denise MacKenzie, but heights happened to be one of them.

"Mm-hmm," she said, injecting a bright tone into her voice. "I'm fine. Really."

But her stomach shuddered dangerously as she glanced over the edge of the crenellated parapet and caught sight of the ground, eighty-one feet below.

"Well, just say if you need to take a break. There doesn't really need to be two of us up here," he said.

MacKenzie looked across at Phillips with an affectionate smile. She already knew him to be a kind, thoughtful man, but she'd forgotten about his chivalry. Smiling to herself, she trained her binoculars on the High Level Bridge, which stood directly in front of them. It served as a one-way road for buses crossing from Newcastle to Gateshead as well as a functioning railway bridge. Aside from its larger neighbour, it was arguably the most noteworthy of the seven bridges, having been designed by Robert Stephenson to form a rail link towards Scotland in the early days of railway infrastructure.

"It hasn't kept people away, Frank," she muttered, from behind the binoculars. "I've seen plenty of buses and taxis crossing over the High Level, and that doesn't count the number of pedestrians and rail traffic." She lowered the glasses and turned to Phillips with worried eyes. "Ryan's right. As soon as EOD have finished here, we need to lift the press ban and put the fear of God into the people of this city, so they'll stay away and be safe."

Phillips had been thinking the same thing as he watched a mainline train chug slowly across the King Edward bridge, which served as another main railway bridge in and out of the city.

"The rail companies have reduced their services for today after what happened last night, but they haven't stopped altogether. Morrison doesn't want to cause a panic and she doesn't want the city grinding to a halt," he said. "But, if I were batty as a box of frogs, where would I go and hide a bomb? Probably on one of those two bridges, because they see the most traffic and stand to make the most impact."

They looked between the High Level and the King Edward bridges and MacKenzie shivered as a gust of cold wind took her by surprise.

"I agree. But then, there's the Scotswood Bridge, too. It's not part of the seven main bridges in this stretch, but that sees a lot of traffic. And what about the A1 motorway as it crosses the Tyne?" she continued, as the possibilities began to spiral. "If that went up, you'd cut off the main road link between England and Scotland and grind things to a halt."

Phillips heard a note of panic in her voice and turned to give her arms a gentle rub.

"We'll do our best not to let that happen. That's all we can do."

MacKenzie thought of all the men, women and children travelling by car or rail, passing through the city and wondered whether they would remain unscathed by the time the morning was out.

They turned at the sound of the access door opening behind them and watched Ryan step out onto the rooftop, zipping up his all-weather coat against the frosty air.

"Temperature's dropped," he said, with a weather eye on the sky which had turned overcast as the morning progressed. "More snow is the last thing we need."

"Been a long winter," Phillips grumbled, while his keen gaze noted the lines of stress etched on his friend's face. "How'd it go with Tebbutt?"

Ryan made a show of turning up his collar and reaching for a pair of binoculars.

"She has more information than she needs," he said shortly, then bobbed his head in the direction of the river. "Any word from EOD?"

They turned back to the water, all business now.

"Nobel's team are down there in plain clothes and, since there's still a fair amount of traffic going over the bridges, they decided it was safe enough to do a quick pass over each of them to see if they could spot anything at a glance," MacKenzie replied. "Nobel's already looked over the Swing Bridge and he's down at the Millennium Bridge now. He's got two of his team on Redheugh Bridge and the Metro Bridge. Sue Bannerman's doing a walk over the High Level and Kevin Wilson's down at the King Edward, although it won't be easy to see much without making it very obvious that they're one of ours."

Ryan nodded as he fiddled with the lens on his binoculars and watched a couple of pedestrians. It wasn't until he looked again that he realised one of them belonged to the EOD Unit.

"They blend in," he murmured. "But let's hope nobody recognises any of them."

All three turned when the outer door was flung open again, this time to reveal one of the staff belonging to the Castle.

"Um, sorry, excuse me?"

A young man of around twenty-five emerged onto the roof wearing a cable-knit jumper emblazoned with the Castle's logo and a harried expression.

"I'm sorry, you can't be up here just now," Ryan said, and began reaching for his warrant card.

"I know—I'm sorry, it's just we need to know if it's true what they're saying on the news?"

Ryan's eyes turned flinty.

"What do you mean?"

The man blew a noisy breath of air between his fingers to warm them, and looked between the three of them with wide eyes.

"Moira down in reception told me it's just come on the news about there being another bomb on a bridge, only you don't know which one. Is it true?"

Ryan turned away and swore viciously, leaning both hands against the outer wall while he wondered who he should murder first: members of the news desk at *The Enquirer,* or the bigwigs in his own constabulary?

"Don't panic, son," Phillips stepped into the breach. "We've got it all in hand. But, if you need to get across the river to go home, it might be worth leaving early so your family aren't worrying about you."

The man needed no second bidding and spun around to clatter back down the stone steps in his haste to get away.

"Bloody brilliant," MacKenzie said, and put a hasty call through to alert the officers on the ground.

On the streets below, word began to spread like wildfire amongst the people of Newcastle and Gateshead. They scattered like ants, hurrying back to their homes and loved ones as the minutes ticked by, edging ever closer to midday. Details of the website where *The Alchemist* demanded payment were released and Ryan's small team watched with growing frustration as the online counter crept higher and higher as the public made donations to try to prevent another blast.

And as panic gripped the city, one person watched and felt invincible.

CHAPTER 12

Jack Lowerson watched the news report from the sofa in his parents' living room, with the sound turned low. He heard the words *bomb* and *terror* but couldn't seem to muster the energy to worry about it, or even to wonder what kind of warped personality might be responsible for striking fear into the hearts of his friends and neighbours.

"Jack?"

His mother came into the room carrying a tray laden with his favourite things from childhood; jam sandwiches, crisps, even a small pot of jelly. He watched her set it on the coffee table beside him.

"Aren't you hungry? You haven't eaten in hours," she said, coming to perch beside him on the sofa.

His head began to ache again, a constant pain at the base of his skull.

"No, thanks," he managed.

Her face fell in disappointment, but she nodded.

"Do you want some company?"

It was the last thing he wanted, but he could hardly refuse to have her near him when there was such a pleading tone in her voice, such a desperation to be near him.

"Yes, that would be nice," he said, robotically.

Wendy inched a little closer and reached across to take his hand, which she cradled on her lap. She looked down at the man's skin and remembered when it had been a tiny baby's hand that clung to her finger only hours after he had come into the world shrieking and crying, ready to make himself heard. Now, when she glanced across at her son's profile and saw how pale he had become, how shadowed his eyes were after months of unrest, she thought of the boy she had nurtured and wondered where he had gone.

"What are you thinking of, son?"

Jack felt his mother's soft hands holding his and almost succumbed to tears, but they did not come. As the television blared, he thought only of one thing.

Jennifer.

"Nothing," he lied.

They sat in silence for a few minutes, as he watched the images moving across the screen while she stared out of the living room window and watched the first snow begin to fall outside.

"We've missed you, Jack," she whispered. "We were so worried about you."

His chest tightened but he said nothing, and she began to rub soothing circles against the back of his hand.

"You've changed, love," she murmured. "You're not the same person you used to be."

Jack opened his mouth to deny it, but no sound came out.

"I don't know if we'll ever get the old Jack back again but, you know, that's alright," she continued softly. "That's okay, because nobody stays the same forever. Do they?"

He looked away from the television and into her tear-drenched eyes.

"Mum?"

She dashed a tear away and gave him a sunny smile.

"Yes, sweetheart?"

"I love you."

Her arms opened wide and she held him tightly, rocking gently as he poured out all the grief and the heartache, all the memories he'd never tell another living soul.

Outside, she watched the snow fall, covering the earth with a blanket of white.

* * *

On the other side of the city, Ryan faced a roomful of police and service personnel from inside the so-called 'Black Gate' of the castle, an area formerly used to enforce mediaeval law but more recently used as a museum, conference and events facility. Having commandeered one such meeting space, the room was populated by staff from the EOD Unit, Firearms and local police sergeants as well as members of CID in an attempt to manage a multi-taskforce approach to a threat facing two neighbouring cities and the many thousands of people who lived there.

"I've heard back from GCHQ," Ryan was saying. "They have confirmed what our internal tech team have already identified: namely, that the server hosting the website *www.savethebridges.org* is based out of the Ukraine. Our colleagues in GCHQ have already contacted the authorities over there to ask for details about the web host but, so far, have received no response."

"Sir? Can't we just ask them to take down the website?" Trainee detective Melanie Yates asked, from the corner of the room.

Ryan shook his head.

"GCHQ can take down the website by instigating a DOS attack—"

"Howay man, that's another Scrabble word," Phillips complained, eliciting a couple of snorts around the room.

"A DOS or 'Denial of Service' attack is where a host server is flooded with requests so that it becomes inoperative and nobody can access it," Ryan elaborated. "Unfortunately, the warning we received this morning explicitly forbade any such measure."

"Sneaky bastard, isn't he?" Phillips remarked.

"That he is," Ryan agreed. "*The Alchemist* is no fool; they know a bit about computers as well as something about explosives. Which leads me to my next update, concerning the ingredients we managed to extract from the debris left over from the first explosion. Nobel? Can you bring us up to speed on the type of device we're expecting to find?"

Ryan gestured the army captain forward to allow him to step through the components.

"Right, listen up," he said, with a ludicrous wink for MacKenzie, who eyed him with a dislike so intense it was almost comical. "We sent across the samples of circuit board, wiring and other residue we found to the lab and they worked on it all through the night. Turns out, our alchemist is a decent chemist, after all. It's likely he used an IED—"

"That's an improvised explosive device, for the dinosaurs amongst us," Ryan put in, and received a withering look from his sergeant.

"It works by marrying an explosive main charge with an electrical fusing system that contains components from a device used to detonate, such as a mobile phone or a garage door opener," Nobel continued. "It usually has four main components: a power supply, an initiator, explosive material and a switch. There are various designs, but our perp opted for a tried and tested rucksack, in this case. We found canvas material near the epicentre of the blast that would be consistent with the fibres of an ordinary rucksack."

"What about the explosive materials?" MacKenzie asked. "Can you give us some idea of what was used?"

"It gets a bit complicated," Nobel told her, and for a moment she expected to be patted on the head. "In this case, he used C-4 as the major component, which is a kind of white, pliable, military plastic-bonded explosive contained cyclonite. It's not easy to come by, and would definitely have flagged as a security alert with GCHQ if anybody searched for it online."

There were nods around the room.

"Anything else?" Ryan asked.

"We found ammonium nitrate, the remnants of wiring and circuit boards…it's all consistent with a combination-type explosive."

"What do you mean when you say 'combination'?" This, from one of the sergeants.

"I mean it's both an incendiary and an explosive device. For those of you who saw the blast last night, you'll remember there was a loud blast which blew a hole in the road tarmac and a small area of the bridge but there was also a fire, which lasted longer than the initial explosion. Our alchemist wanted the best of both, I'd say."

"Peacocking a bit," Ryan remarked, almost to himself. "Thanks, Nobel. We'll hand it over to our tech support team and GCHQ, to see if we get lucky and find that somebody ordered everything in one nice, easy delivery package."

"I think I just saw a pig fly," Phillips remarked.

Ryan huffed out a laugh.

"I can get on to GCHQ and ask them to start trawling through internet searches for those ingredients but it's unlikely our perp used Google or any other ordinary search engine. More likely, he went underground with it," Ryan said. "Besides, there isn't a cat in hell's chance that we'd find out anything helpful before noon today."

There were murmurs of assent around the room.

"Frank? Where are we with CCTV?"

Phillips rubbed a hand across his jaw and realised he'd forgotten to shave.

"I've spoken to the Council and a load of other local businesses around both entrances to the Tyne Bridge but it's going to take time we don't have to go through all the footage they're sending through. The worst of it is, they usually only keep the reels for a couple of weeks. It all depends how far in advance they planted the bomb, doesn't it?"

Ryan looked back at Nobel, who was lounging against one of the old stone walls.

"Gary? What's your assessment of the other six bridges in the vicinity?"

"Our lads have done a walk-over on each of them," he said. "They're still out there, now, circling back around for another pass over the bridges to be sure they haven't missed anything on sight. After that, I don't know what I can tell you besides what you already know. You need to evacuate."

Ryan gave a brief shake of his head.

"Again, that was expressly forbidden in the warning message. We're taking enough of a risk, as it is, allowing your team to check the bridges on foot."

Ryan checked the time, which read ten-thirty, and turned to his trainee, Melanie Yates, who had returned from her stint at the offices of *The Enquirer.*

"Yates? What can you tell us?"

She was becoming more accustomed to public speaking but, even so, pressure weighed on each person in the room and she could sense a degree of impatience while they waited for her to collect her thoughts.

She swallowed her nerves and forced herself to step up.

"Sir. I took statements from members of the news team at *The Enquirer* first thing this morning. A woman called Beverley Anderson, goes by the name 'Bev', was on the evening shift last night. She was responsible for keeping tabs on all incoming news alerts and that includes monitoring the e-mail inbox for general news desk enquiries, which is enquiries@enquirernewsdesk.co.uk."

"Did she explain why it took her twenty minutes to report a suspicious e-mail?"

"She claims that, at first, she thought it was just a hoax."

"Oh, really? How convenient that we were met with a full press junket when we made it down to the Quayside last night."

Yates nodded her agreement.

"I remembered what you told me about there being no real coincidences in our business, sir," Yates said. "That's why I asked to see her outgoing mailbox."

Ryan grinned.

"And?"

"She was resistant, at first, but I managed to persuade her it was the right thing to do," Yates said, with an air of deceptive guile. "I found several e-mails sent from her address to her colleagues within *The Enquirer*, as well as to local television broadcasters and wider nationals."

Ryan wasn't surprised.

"I hope you explained the gravity of withholding evidence," he said, and watched her eyes light up.

"Oh, yes, sir. I took the opportunity to remind her of the penalty for obstructing an investigation and lying to a police officer, too."

"Good," Ryan said, roundly. "I'll hazard a guess that our friend at the news desk also saw fit to leak the details of the second warning to the press earlier this morning, correct?"

"It would not be outside the realms of possibility."

Ryan ran an agitated hand through his hair.

"How much have people donated, so far?" he asked, of nobody in particular.

There were a few shuffles as people typed in the web address.

"Three hundred and seven thousand—no, three hundred and ten thousand now, sir."

Ryan looked across at the police constable who'd called out the total.

"You've got to be kidding."

But the faces around the room confirmed it.

"Number's rising every minute," MacKenzie told him, glancing down at the offensive bitcoin counter graphic, which showed a cartoon dragon breathing fire against a bridge every time the counter rose.

Ryan thought quickly and came to a decision.

"Yates? Get in touch with Bev from *The Enquirer*. Tell her I'm going to give a press conference and she can have the first scoop," he said, then, turning to the others, added, "That's sure to guarantee that every journalist within a thirty-mile radius will hear about it."

"What're you going to tell them?" Phillips asked.

"What they need to hear," came the surly reply.

CHAPTER 13

When Anna returned home to Elsdon, a sharp gust of wind followed her inside and scattered a stack of unopened mail from the previous day all over the flagstone floor. She bent down to scoop it up, nudging the front door closed with her hip and breathing a sigh of relief as it shut out the cold air blowing in from the hills outside.

"Freezing," she muttered, dumping the stack of assorted letters and junk mail on the kitchen worktop.

It wasn't until she had taken her first sip of hot tea that she thought about sifting through it all, and her fingers flicked through the paperwork with mild interest.

Then, stilled.

A postcard showing an artsy, black and white photograph of the Schönbrunn Palace in Vienna was nestled between a catalogue and what appeared to be an electricity bill. Carefully, she reached for a knife from the drawer beside her and used it to flip the postcard over, although she already knew what she would find.

It was blank, except for the stamp and postmark—and their home address, written in neat, black capital lettering.

Anna stared at it for long moments, then headed directly to Ryan's study where she knew he kept packets of unused nitrile gloves and fresh plastic evidence bags.

A moment later, she returned, suitably kitted out.

Using gloved fingertips on the extreme edge of the postcard, she scooped it into the evidence bag, then made sure to put the gloves in another one before setting both of them on Ryan's desk for him to look at, later.

Yes, she thought. She was learning a thing or two.

The tea had gone cold by the time she picked it up again, but she didn't care; she thought of the man who had sent the postcard, of a killer who knew their address. Oh, they hadn't been able to prove it was Nathan Armstrong who had sent the other cards; he'd been so careful. And when Ryan had taken them to Faulkner's team of CSIs for analysis, there had been no DNA match in the saliva from the stamp to any known person, either living or dead. What's more, the DNA had been different on each stamp.

But they *knew* it was Armstrong behind them.

Who else could it be?

Though she knew it was foolish, Anna set her tea down with a small splash and hurried back into the hallway to bolt the front door.

* * *

Back in the city centre, Ryan stood outside the gateway to the Castle Keep and faced a barrage of questions from the reporters who gathered in a huddle outside. As he had predicted, word had spread quickly, and it did not take long for them to arrive armed with mics, cameras and dictaphones.

"DCI Ryan! Can you tell us what progress has been made in finding the person responsible for last night's bombing? Is it true they're calling themselves *The Alchemist?*"

Ryan turned to face an eagle-eyed journalist from the local television news.

"We are taking every proper measure to find and apprehend those responsible for the attack last night," he told her. "We will continue to follow every avenue available to us."

"But what about the latest threat?" she threw back. "The bomber is moving very quickly. How can you hope to stop them in time?"

Ryan told himself to be patient.

"We are pursuing all leads."

More voices called out.

"What about paying the ransom?" somebody called out. "How do you know the bomber won't strike again? Isn't it better to pay the ransom now?"

Ryan sought out the voice in the crowd and found himself looking at a blonde-haired woman of around thirty-five matching the description of Beverley Anderson, the woman in charge of *The Enquirer* news desk.

"We do not accede to the demands of terrorists," he said, firmly.

He was cut off as more questions were called out and he held up a hand until they died down again.

"What I really want to do is make a personal appeal to every resident of Newcastle and Gateshead. I want to tell them that I understand how they might have felt as they watched an explosion hit one of our best-loved landmarks last night. I may not have been born in the North," he admitted, "but I've lived here for ten—nearly eleven years and I'm proud to call it my home. My wife is from your neck of the woods and can trace her family history back generations. I feel your pain, when you look at the scorched metal and tarmac on that bridge, believe me."

He paused to let that sink in, before continuing.

"But the fact is, this isn't about metal girders or steel arches. It's about the people who made them and moulded this landscape. It's about shared values and being able to trust our neighbours. It's about fighting for the things we believe in rather than giving in to a glorified bully. We can build other bridges on the foundations of the old, if we have to, and be proud that we stood up for what was right."

Ryan paused while his words carried on the air.

"I'm going to ask people not to donate their hard-earned cash to whatever monster is threatening our way of life. Don't log onto the website and donate bitcoins because you are only fuelling their greed."

"What can they do instead?" one woman called out. "Are they supposed to sit at home, waiting and worrying?"

Ryan paused before answering, considering his words carefully so they could not be misconstrued by anybody watching as an attempt to evacuate.

"They can trust their law enforcement agencies to act with their best interests at heart. They can receive regular updates on our progress via the extensive news coverage and we will, of course, work closely with you all to keep the lines of communication open."

"Is there any connection between these attacks and the death of DCS Jennifer Lucas?" Another intrepid reporter called out, and Ryan was not altogether surprised by the question. In fact, he was only surprised somebody hadn't asked it sooner.

"I speak on behalf of everybody in the Northumbria Police Constabulary when I say that we were very sorry to hear the news of our colleague's death yesterday. However, I have no knowledge of the progress of the investigation as the decision was taken, very properly, to enlist one of our colleagues from a neighbouring constabulary. Even if I were the Senior Investigating Officer, my answer would be the same: I do not comment on details pertaining to an active investigation."

Ryan was about to call the conference to an end when there was a final flurry.

"Isn't it true that the constabulary has suffered a series of setbacks during your tenure?" one man took pleasure in pointing out. "Some might think you're out of your depth, Chief Inspector."

Ryan turned to him with hard, unyielding eyes.

"Let them think it," he said bluntly. "I refer you to an exemplary record of public service over the past fifteen years. Now, if you'll excuse me, I have more important things to worry about than whether I'm the flavour of the month."

* * *

As Ryan finished his plea to the people of Newcastle and Gateshead, Ben Potter brought the train he was driving to a standstill on the south side of the High Level Bridge. He lifted his arms above his head and tried to stretch out the aches and pains, looking forward to the end of his shift when he could go out for a few beers with the lads.

He laughed at what his girlfriend would have to say about that, which dissolved into a coughing fit as his asthma kicked in.

"Bugger," he gasped, and rooted around for an inhaler.

He took a grateful breath or two from the little blue device, berating himself for giving in to the old habit of sneaking a cigarette after lunch. That was the culprit, he thought, as he watched for the green light that would tell him it was safe to cross the railway bridge leading into the station.

From his cabin at the front of the train, he had a perfect view of the river on both sides. Snow was falling and a shaft of light broke through the grey clouds swirling overhead, sending fingers of hazy light across the city. He watched it as he opened a bottle of Lucozade and took a long gulp of the lurid orange liquid, hoping the energy would see him through for another couple of hours until he made it home. His eye caught on the emerald green arches of the Tyne Bridge and he frowned, thinking of the bomb scare only last night.

Then, he shrugged it off.

If he worried about every bomb threat ever to face a train or a bridge, he'd never get out of bed in the morning. Besides, the company would have been in touch if they'd closed any of the other bridges.

Wouldn't they?

As the light turned green, he released the brake and began to guide the train slowly over the bridge.

* * *

A few hundred feet further north, Sergeant Sue Bannerman made her way back over the High Level Bridge. Thanks to the extensive news coverage, pedestrian and vehicular traffic had greatly reduced and Bannerman found she was alone inside the cavernous yet oddly claustrophobic interior of the old bridge. Long steel girders ran in symmetrical lines to support the railway track that was still in use on the level above, casting long black shadows when the sun burst through the thickening snow clouds in the skies overhead. To her right, the river ran out to sea and brought with it an icy wind which blew through the metal rods until they whined and creaked and, just for a moment, she fancied the bridge was a living, breathing thing.

Bannerman shook herself and glanced back over her shoulder, surprised to find she had almost reached the halfway point across the bridge. The south side seemed far away now, and she had the uncomfortable feeling she would not be able to make it out, should anything go wrong.

She turned back, and the heels of her boots echoed as she picked up her pace a little. Her eyes scanned the railings on either side of the pedestrian walkway which separated the pavement from the road in case she had missed anything the first time around, but she knew there was nothing there.

Without warning, the metal girders began to tremble overhead, nothing more than a gentle vibration at first and she realised a train must be approaching from the south. She checked the time on her watch and wondered if it would be one of the last to cross the bridge as the noon deadline approached, for it was already a couple of minutes shy of eleven.

She reached for her radio, intending to give the rest of her team an update on her whereabouts. She had already heard from Kevin and Gary, but Stevie and Paul were still out there somewhere, and it was time they were getting back.

But the words died on her lips as she looked up and spotted something stuffed into the corner where two steel rods converged on the roof, tucked directly beneath the railway line.

It was a dark navy canvas rucksack.

Her fingers grasped the radio and she tried to keep her voice steady as the rumble of the approaching train grew louder overhead and a bus turned onto the bridge from the north, loaded with passengers seeking to get home as quickly as possible.

"Control, this is Bannerman. Do you copy?"

No response.

"Control! This is Bannerman. *Do you copy?*"

Back at base, Nobel finished swallowing the last bite of a protein bar and reached for his radio receiver as Ryan re-entered the meeting room and began shaking out of his coat.

"Yeah, keep your hair on," he mumbled. "You found something?"

"*Yes!*" she almost shouted. "*It's—I've found a bag hidden between some steel girders, right beneath the railway line on the High Level, roughly in the centre of the bridge. There's a train coming, I have no idea whether the bag's attached to a trip wire—*"

"Sue, I need you to calm down," Nobel told her, with an eye-roll for Ryan, who had crossed the room to listen in. "How sure are you that it's a suspect device?"

At the other end of the line, Bannerman gripped her radio and wished it were her captain's throat. She raised her voice above the sound of the approaching train as it began its slow approach into Newcastle Central Station.

"*I'm as sure as I can be! We need to—*"

The line turned to white noise.

CHAPTER 14

On the stroke of eleven, Ryan heard the loud *pop* of a fresh explosion.

As Nobel tried to reach Bannerman on the radio, Ryan ran back outside to where several camera crews remained, ready to capture every second of the unfolding drama on film.

"Get back!" he warned them, and pushed through the crowd to reach the road which ran directly past the castle gates and continued all the way across the High Level Bridge.

Uncaring of the shouts from the journalists hovering nearby, Ryan ran down the street until he reached the darkened entrance to the bridge and raised his hand to shield his eyes from the falling snow. There, in the shadows, he spotted the amber glow of fire and smoke and, above it, the dark outline of a passenger train.

"Good God," he muttered, and was about to enter the bridge when Yates' urgent voice stopped him.

"*Sir!*"

Ryan spun around to see her sprinting towards him at full pelt.

"*Sir!* Don't—you can't go on the bridge! It'll go up!"

"What the hell do you mean?" he asked, when she came to a shuddering stop beside him, and automatically grasped her shoulders when her boots skidded slightly against the slippery ground. "The message doesn't say we can't go onto the bridge."

"He's—he's sent a new message," Yates said, gulping a couple of breaths of cold air into her lungs. "It went through to the news desk, but it's also been uploaded onto the website for everyone to see."

Ryan snatched up the phone she held in front of him and quickly read its contents from the internet browser.

My terms were clear.
I said there should be NO attempts to defuse or locate the bomb, or I
would detonate.
Now, there are new terms.
Nobody is to go on or off the High Level Bridge until the bitcoin total is
met, or I will detonate the main charge.
If my terms are not met, people will die.
You have all been warned.

As Ryan looked up again, he barely had a moment to process the new threat when he spotted a bus trundling along the road towards the bridge, laden with passengers rushing to return home.

He almost threw the mobile phone back at Yates as he leapt into the middle of the road and began waving his arms like a madman to stop it entering the bridge.

"*Stop!*" he shouted. "*STOP!*"

Luckily, the driver spotted him in time and they heard the hiss of brakes as the bus came to an emergency stop. Ryan retrieved his warrant card and jogged forward to exchange a word with the bus driver, who performed an awkward U-turn a few seconds later and diverted his passengers back to the city centre.

Once its tail lights rounded a corner, Ryan turned back to his trainee and was grateful she'd had the foresight to wrap up warmly.

"Mel? I need you to stay here until reinforcements arrive," Ryan told her. "It's crucial that nobody goes onto the bridge or comes off it, not until we know the level of threat if they do. I'll make sure there's somebody manning the south side, doing the same."

Yates bobbed her head.

"Yes, sir. Do you want me to contact the local police? I won't let you down."

Ryan hesitated for only a fraction of a second, then nodded. The only way to learn was to do.

"Alright," he said. "Keep me updated."

* * *

When Ryan muscled his way past the throng of reporters and re-entered the conference facility at the castle, he found the place in turmoil.

"Alright, settle down! This isn't the circus!" he roared, and watched their faces turn in shock. He didn't stop to worry about hurt feelings but strode into the room, already thinking of the next steps to take.

"Phillips?" He sought out his sergeant. "I need an impact assessment. Get onto the rail companies and tell them to radio the driver of that train."

"What train? There's a train—?" Phillips blustered.

"It was on the bridge when the explosion happened," Ryan replied. "It's at a standstill, with the first carriage just visible from the road, so I'd say it's stuck roughly halfway across the bridge. I need to know how badly the train was affected and if anyone's hurt."

"Leave it with me."

Phillips bustled away to make the calls and Ryan turned to the head of the EOD Unit.

"Nobel? Any word from Sue Bannerman?"

The other man ran agitated fingers through his streaky blonde hair and gave a sad little shake of his head.

"Nothing," he said. "I'll take a team down there to find her—"

"You can't," Ryan interjected, and the other man stood up to face him as if he were ready to square off about it.

"Look, feller, I'm in charge of my unit—"

"Check the website," Ryan said, brushing past him to bring it up onto one of the laptop screens with an angry click of the keyboard. When the website popped up, he spun the computer around and pointed at it. "The bomber has set out a new condition and it's simple— nobody is to go on or off the bridge, or he'll detonate."

Nobel leaned forward to read the message, noting that the bitcoin counter had jumped up to nearly a million pounds' worth of donations.

"I need an ambulance crew on standby," Ryan turned to MacKenzie, who was standing nearby. "They can't enter yet, but we don't know how this thing will play out."

"Done," she said, and turned away to speak in a swift undertone to their colleagues in the emergency services.

"What's your take on it?" Ryan turned back to Nobel. "What are we dealing with, here?"

"That might have been the initial charge," the man replied. "There could be a bigger one waiting to go off. It seemed to detonate at eleven o'clock or thereabouts, so there's a chance it was on a timer and was always intended to go off. On the other hand, it could have been manually detonated like the bridge last night. Either way, you're looking at something packing enough force to blow through steel."

Before Ryan could comment, Corporal Kevin Wilson hurried into the room with his remaining colleagues from the EOD Unit in tow.

"We heard the blast," he said, trailing slush as he came to stand beside them, wearing a concerned expression on his jovial face. He made a show of looking around the room. "Where's Sue?"

"Still on the bridge," Nobel said. "Instead of keeping calm like any one of us would have done, she found a rucksack and started panicking—"

"Oh, aye, and I'm sure you're just like Rambo in a crisis," MacKenzie's voice dripped sarcasm. "Ryan? The ambulances and hospitals are on standby. Yates has been in touch; she's working with the local police to divert traffic from the bridge."

Ryan nodded and turned to his sergeant.

"I've just spoken to the train operator," Phillips pocketed his phone. "They tell me that's a 125 HST Mark 3 train on the tracks up there. I haven't got a clue what that means, except that it's the big train from London to Aberdeen and it has nine carriages."

"How many people on board?" Ryan asked.

"Best guess is somewhere between five and six hundred. It's not at full capacity, today."

Ryan felt the blood roar in his ears as he thought of the potential toll, should anything go wrong.

"How badly was the train hit?"

Phillips tugged at his ear as he thought back to the garbled conversation with one of the train managers.

"The blast came mostly from below, so it hasn't caused any real damage to the train and there are no casualties, so far. The driver says people are getting restless and starting to panic but the train crew are doing what they can to keep them calm. The biggest problem is, they can't be sure how badly the line has been affected without getting some engineers up there to check the tracks. It's not safe for the train to continue crossing the bridge, even if *The Alchemist* hadn't already forbidden it."

Ryan realised it was time to make a judgment call.

"We know which bridge has been targeted now, so I'm authorising a full blockade on both sides," he said.

"Won't that make the bomber angry?" Wilson said. "I thought he wanted his instructions followed to the letter?"

"Why would he detonate now that he has hundreds of ready-made victims? The latest message warned nobody else to go on to the bridge. He has collateral, added to the fact his bitcoin counter is ticking higher and higher," Ryan said, and moved across to look down at the press gang outside.

"Whoever's responsible for this chaos must be loving every minute."

CHAPTER 15

Sergeant Sue Bannerman had been thrown to the floor by the explosion, scattering her radio across the pavement and into the gutter nearby. As her vision slowly cleared, her ears rang—one long *hum* as they recovered from the blast.

She fell heavily to her knees and when she lifted her head she inhaled the overpowering smell of smoke and burnt rubber. Coughing, she struggled to her feet and stumbled away from the blast site, noticing for the first time that her clothing was singed and torn and that her hands and chin were bleeding.

The blast had made a small hole in the metal separating the upper and lower layers of the bridge and she held an arm in front of her nose and mouth as she limped across to peer at the flaming edges.

Her toe kicked something solid and she almost wept as she reached down to pick up her radio.

"*Control? Are—are you receiving?*"

Her voice sounded ragged and she tried again, a little stronger this time.

"*Control. This is Bannerman. Do you copy?*"

Back at the castle, Ryan grabbed the radio before Nobel made it halfway across the room.

"*This is Ryan. Copy loud and clear. What is your position, Sue? Are you injured?*"

She let out a long, jittery breath and closed her eyes, never happier to hear another person's voice.

"*I'm—I'm okay,*" she said. "*A bit shaken up, but I'll live. There's a small hole between the upper and lower levels of the bridge, roughly halfway along. There's a train directly above me. I'm heading back now. Over.*"

Ryan prepared to tell her the bad news.

"I'm sorry, Sue, but you need to stay on the bridge. The bomber's new terms are that nobody enters or leaves until the bitcoin total is met."

Bannerman listened to Ryan's disembodied voice and watched wisps of ash float on the cold air, hovering in front of her face for a second before gushing out between the tall pillars holding up the eastern edge of the bridge. The wind was bitterly cold, and she was shivering badly now, but her army training had prepared her for worse conditions than these.

"Understood," she said. *"I'll await further instructions."*

There was a short pause before Ryan's voice came across the wires again.

"We won't forget about you, Sue. We won't forget about any of you. I promise."

After signing off, she limped a little further along the walkway until she found a dry spot before sinking to the floor to wait.

* * *

When Anna caught the late morning news, she felt her heart shudder against her chest in one hard *thump*. It was often this way, she thought. Fear and worry came as part and parcel of being next of kin to a man whose vocation demanded that he fight every day for what he believed to be right. It was simultaneously the most attractive and frustrating quality Ryan possessed.

She spent the first half hour telling herself that she needn't worry but, when she saw footage of him running past photographers and reporters towards the latest bomb site, she could stand the loneliness no longer and decided to call the one person whose need for comfort was greater than her own.

At first, she thought he wouldn't answer.

Eventually, he did.

"Jack?"

A pause.

"Hello, Anna."

She almost cried at the sound of his voice, at the sheer exhaustion she heard beneath the polite greeting.

"I hope you don't mind me calling you," she said, a bit nervously. She wasn't exactly sure whether she was supposed to be speaking to him, but he had been released without charge, so where was the harm in calling her friend? Besides, Tebbutt could have the phone records, if she wanted them.

"Of course not," he said, robotically. "Um, how are you keeping?"

She almost laughed.

"Jack, have you seen the news? Ryan's out there battling against time to stop another bridge blowing up, while I've been at home researching the various types of bird nesting on Holy Island. Much as I like birds, they aren't doing much to calm my nerves at the moment."

At the other end of the line, Lowerson smiled and when the skin stretched around his mouth it felt rusty and tight.

There was another pause, while he thought of something to say.

"How are you, Jack?"

Her gentle voice was his undoing and he sank down into one of the chairs in his parents' dining room to stare at the fussy floral wallpaper his mother liked, then over at something she called an 'accent wall' that consisted of a chimney breast painted in an unusual shade of pink.

"I'm not sure how I am," he answered, honestly. "I can't—I can't seem to wrap my head around things."

Anna cradled a mug of hot tea in one hand and the telephone receiver in the other, wishing she was there to give him a friendly hug.

"The feeling will pass," she said. "Right now, it seems as though it's the worst time in your life, but remember it will pass."

"Thanks, Doctor Taylor," he said, not unkindly.

"I'll bill you, later," she joked.

Another pause.

"So—"

"Ah—"

They spoke simultaneously.

"You first," Jack said.

"I was going to ask whether you'd heard any news," Anna said. "The sooner this is all behind you, the better."

In the quiet space of his parents' dining room, Lowerson closed his eyes and gripped the receiver, as if it were his friend's hand he was holding instead. Anna never questioned his innocence, never even suspected him, only asked when his ordeal would all be over.

But for so long as Jennifer's face haunted him at night, he wondered if it would ever, truly be over.

"Tebbutt isn't telling me much," he said, with grudging respect. "I can't blame her, for that."

Anna thought of the woman she'd met the previous day and was forced to agree. Justice meant nothing, if everything was not done by the book.

"At least you have Marbles to keep you company," she said, cheerfully clutching at something she knew would make him smile.

But there was a long, awkward silence on the line.

"She ran away," he said. Then, in an odd voice, "I'd better be getting off."

"Oh, right. Sure. Don't be a stranger, Jack. And remember, we're here for you, whenever you need us."

"Thanks," he managed.

As Lowerson set the phone down on the table in front of him, his mind swirled with flashing images, a constant reel of nightmarish memories he feared he would never forget.

CHAPTER 16

Ben Potter could feel his asthma getting worse. With every passing minute spent on top of the bridge, his anxiety rose and his breathing became more shallow and hoarse. He tried his inhaler again but, when he checked it, he realised the capsule had run out and he hadn't brought any more.

"Shit," he muttered.

He closed his eyes and focused on remaining calm, counting his breaths in and out as he'd been told.

One…two…three…

There came a sharp rap at the door and he almost jumped.

"Ben, it's Imran," came the sound of his train manager's voice.

He turned to unlock the door.

"Any news?" the other man said, squeezing into the cabin beside him. "People keep asking me what's happening."

Ben shook his head.

"You know the procedure," he said. "We can't tell them there's a bomb threat."

"But some of them who were sitting near the front will have seen the smoke, anyway," Imran said. "And it's splashed all over the news, look."

He produced his phone and scrolled through a selection of headlines, each more sensational than the last.

Ben sighed and rubbed a hand over the back of his neck.

"There isn't much we can do about that," he decided, looking away from the bitcoin counter. "Keep sending the trolley through and keep them hydrated and as happy as possible. Crack a few jokes. Just do what you can, mate."

Imran nodded, thinking of the people on board the train.

"I can tell they're stressed by the way they look at me," he said, and gestured to the beard he wore. "One minute, it's all smiles, the next they're looking at me and thinking 'terrorist.'"

Ben looked at his friend and put a hand on his shoulder.

"Most of them don't mean it. They're just scared and stupid."

Imran looked out across the snow-covered tracks and felt his own measure of fear.

"What kind of person does this?"

Ben felt his breathing hitch again and battled not to let it show.

"Somebody you probably wouldn't even notice walking down the street," he said. "They don't look any different to you and me, son, but they're rotten inside."

* * *

When Chief Constable Morrison stepped into the makeshift incident room inside the Castle Keep she had expected to find chaos but was surprised to find the place eerily quiet. Staff from several support divisions were seated at laptop computers and people spoke in urgent undertones on the telephone or huddled in groups, each focused entirely on their task. In the thick of it all, she spotted Ryan's dark head bent over a new report that had come through from the lab.

She crossed the room and, for once, nobody looked up or shuffled to attention.

"Ryan?"

He set the report aside and unfolded himself from one of the uncomfortable foamy tub chairs that had been laid on for their use.

"Ma'am."

He pulled out a chair beside him, which made her stop and blink. It had been a long while since a man had performed that small service and she wasn't sure how to feel about it. These days, it was unfashionable for a woman to admit to liking such things but, knowing Ryan as she did, she understood that the gesture did not come with any strings attached, nor was it intended as any slight upon her standing as a woman and his senior officer.

It was just the way he was made.

She murmured her thanks.

"You're here to tell me that the Commissioner wants us to pay the ransom." Ryan decided to take the bull by the proverbial horns. "You're getting plenty of flak and you're here to tell me that time's up. Correct?"

Morrison didn't bother to deny it.

"Ryan, things are getting out of hand. First, the bomb last night…now, this," she shook her head and, in the harsh morning light, he couldn't fail to see the lines of stress creasing her forehead.

"The bomber's last message has gone viral," she continued. "It's up there on the website for everyone to see. It's made international news; CBS, Fox, BBC World News…this isn't a local incident anymore, it's an international one. We need to put an end to it."

Ryan looked meaningfully around the room.

"What do you think we're trying to do, here?" he asked. "Nobody is happy about the situation, Sandra, but we've already discussed the alternative."

"And your view is, there is no alternative," she reminded him.

"I stand by it," he said.

She passed a tired hand across her forehead, trying to decide what was for the best.

"The counter has already reached well over a million bitcoins because people around the country and around the world are donating to try to keep the people on that train safe. We can't be seen to be doing nothing—"

"We're doing everything we can," he interjected.

"I know that," she said. "But I've already spoken to the Commissioner, who is liaising with the right people to put the remaining funds in place, if we need it."

Ryan said nothing.

"Look," she burst out. "It would cost more money to repair the bridge, if *The Alchemist* decides to detonate. It makes sense to just pay this bastard what he wants and get it over with."

"Do you think I haven't thought about it?" he asked, quietly. "I've never been more aware of how much this decision could cost us and, if it's the wrong decision, there's no coming back from it."

His stomach twisted, just thinking about the lives at stake

"We need to keep our heads," he said. "It's your call whether to pay the ransom but all I'm asking you to do is think about the bomber's motivation. We're dealing with a twisted individual, but I don't think he's a natural born killer. The small charge on the High Level Bridge wasn't intended to hurt anyone; the explosive wasn't packing nearly enough power to cause the train to derail. Even though they knew Sue Bannerman was on the bridge, almost directly underneath the device, it wasn't enough to cause serious injury," he added, then leaned forward, compelling her to listen.

"Everything about a bombing is hands-off, except the bomb-making itself. It isn't the same as shoving a knife into someone's belly or holding a gun to their face. On one level, our perp is squeamish and prefers to do things from a distance. If that's the case and the overriding motivation is money or power, then we've got something to work with."

"And if it isn't just the money?"

Ryan sighed.

"Either way you look at this, if you pay what *The Alchemist* is asking for, you'll be sending out a signal to every would-be bomber across the world stage that we're prepared to pay any price. It would open the floodgates to more and more incidents of the same kind."

Morrison was silent for a long moment, then looked him in the eye.

"And, if you're wrong about all this? What then?"

"I won't take that chance," he murmured, and quickly checked the time. "It's twenty-past eleven, now. Rail officials tell me it'll take around half an hour to evacuate the train and I've already spoken to Sentinel and the British Transport Police to smooth the way, when the time comes. If the counter hasn't hit two million based on individual donations in ten minutes' time, I'm not putting lives at risk."

"What will you do?"

"I'm taking people off that train," he said simply. "I won't have their lives on my conscience, Sandra."

"If that's the case, let's just take them off now—?"

Ryan had thought of that, turning the problem over and over in his mind but ultimately drawing the same conclusion each time.

"He or she is watching, Sandra. They knew Bannerman was on the bridge, that's why it blew. They'll be watching now and waiting to see if we breach another condition. We have to see if the counter reaches two million—it's not far off—before we risk it. Remember, the explosion just now was another warning. We don't know how much firepower might be hidden in the arches of the bridge, just waiting to go up if we break the rules again."

Morrison put a hand to her stomach, feeling sick at the thought.

"I-I'm not sure what to do," she confessed, and there were very few people she felt able to say that to. In all her years on the force, she'd seen and done a lot, but there had never been a terror threat of this scale and magnitude in the North-East.

Ryan felt for her and the burden she bore on her shoulders, but remained firm.

"Do what's right," he advised.

Just then, an e-mail pinged on her phone and she let out a mirthless laugh.

"Looks like I'll have to," she said. "The Commissioner says the Treasury won't grant the funds to make it up to two million. The UK government does not negotiate with terrorists."

She swiped a shaky hand over her mouth and then looked back at him.

"Looks like the Powers That Be agree with your strategy, Ryan. Let's hope that you're all right."

He reached across to give her hand a brief squeeze, then pushed back his chair and went to work.

* * *

Imran pasted a weak smile on his face as he walked through the carriages of the train, looking at the faces of the people he passed with a growing sense of unease. Some were tearful, others were angry, but these strangers were all united in one emotion that trumped all others.

Fear.

It crawled over the walls and doors, snaking its way into the hearts of these strangers who had been thrown together and were now trapped inside a metal box, unable to leave.

"Why isn't the train moving? Why can't we go backwards and get off the bridge?"

"I'm afraid I don't have any further information, ma'am, please try to remain calm," he told them, while his own nerves jittered.

"We're all going to die," one man kept saying, causing those around him to fly into vitriolic outbursts of rage and panic.

"Shut up! Stop saying that—you're frightening my little boy!"

"We're all going to die, I know it. We're all going to die—"

"Please, sir, try to remain positive. The emergency services are working hard to resolve the situation—"

"I want to get off this train! Let me off! I want to get off!"

Several people jumped up, demanding to be let off the train so they could fend for themselves. But, if it was true what the warning said on *www.savethebridges.org* and they tried to leave now, then the whole thing could blow up. Besides, all his training told him that passengers were almost always safer on the train than on the tracks.

"Please, sit down," he begged them. "I need you all to stay calm, this isn't helping—"

There were more threats, more wails and cries, and he heard the same reports from his colleagues in the other carriages.

The situation was becoming volatile.

* * *

Less than twenty feet beneath the train, Sergeant Sue Bannerman felt time slipping away while she shivered against the hard metal railing of the pedestrian walkway. All around, the wind howled and sent the metal quaking but if she turned her head in either direction she could see light at both ends of the tunnel.

Safety.

It shamed her to admit that, over the past half hour, she'd thought once or twice about making a dash for it, consequences be damned.

But that would be tantamount to going AWOL and she was better than that.

"I'm 'enry the eighth, I am, 'enry the eighth I am, I am…I got married to the wido' next door…" She sang a silly song she'd heard on a movie somewhere and checked the time on her mobile phone.

Nearly half-past eleven.

She blew out a long breath which clouded on the air in front of her, then sang a little louder as the minutes ticked on.

CHAPTER 17

At precisely twenty-five minutes past eleven, Ryan made a final check of the online counter, which read £1,846,321 in bitcoin donations made by people around the world. Morrison caught his eye and nodded, acknowledging that she had made her decision and would abide by it.

"Be careful," she said.

Ryan put a hand on her shoulder in silent support, then turned to address the room.

"Can I have everybody's attention, please?"

The space became so quiet, they might have heard a pin drop. He looked around the faces of his friends and colleagues and felt a mixture of emotions; pride mingled with resolve.

"I don't need to state the obvious, but I will," he began. "It's nearly half-past eleven and we haven't been able to trace the person responsible for terrorizing our cities."

"If I only had more time," Phillips said. "The CCTV has just come through. If I just had a bit more time to check it—"

"There's no more time, Frank," Ryan said, gently, then carried on. "I want to thank everybody for their hard work and dedication this morning. I'm as sorry as you are that we haven't been able to bring this madness to an end before now."

He drew in a breath.

"The first thing I need to remind you is that there are absolutely no assurances that the bomber isn't still watching the bridges—all of them—or that they will fail to detonate simply because the counter has *almost* reached its target. That may not be good enough. We simply don't know what they will choose to do; all we do know is, they are watching

113

and they gave us a clear instruction that nobody should go on or off the bridge."

Ryan paused to allow his warning to sink in.

"Having said all that, there are hundreds of lives at stake. We've given it as long as we can but now we need to act. I have liaised with the relevant train and transport officials who, together with the EOD Unit, are on standby to give us access to the tracks via the railway station."

He watched the penny drop.

"Eh? Lad, you can't go in there," Phillips was the first to say. "It's too dangerous."

"And what about the five or six hundred people trapped on that bridge, unable to move? It's too dangerous for them, too," Ryan shot back, then held up his hands to stave off any further comment. "I'm going up there to start evacuating people, in direct contravention of what this bomber has said. Given the gravity of the situation, I will not be ordering any of you to come with me."

They looked amongst themselves, and then MacKenzie's lilting voice broke through.

"Would you take volunteers?"

Ryan gave a funny half-smile.

"Yes," he said quietly. "I'll take volunteers so long as they know the risks."

"Aye, well—don't think you're gannin' up there and takin' all the credit," Phillips sniffed, in a courageous attempt to lighten the mood. "You're not bloody Superman, y'nah. Me 'n' Denise'll go with you."

"And me," Yates said, followed by several other voices.

From her position on the sidelines, Morrison felt tears rise unexpectedly, lodging somewhere in her throat. Ryan never had to use force or threats, he hardly even needed to ask for their support because it was freely given. Their loyalty came from knowing that this tall, irreverent man was more than simply their boss or a Senior Investigating Officer; more than the bloke who signed off their sick leave.

He was their friend.

Ryan glanced at the clock, which struck the half hour.

"Let's go."

* * *

While Ryan and eight other volunteer members of CID covered the short distance between the Castle Keep and Newcastle Central Station, Detective Constable Jack Lowerson walked through the automatic doors of Police Headquarters.

The duty sergeant recognised him instantly.

"Jack?" she hissed, looking around to see who might have noticed his arrival. "You shouldn't be here—"

"I want to speak to DCI Tebbutt," he said, very clearly. "Can you tell me where she is?"

There was an odd note to his voice that made her frown.

"Why? Have you got an appointment or something? Where's your solicitor?" she added, trying her best to dissuade him from doing anything foolish.

"Where is Tebbutt?" he repeated.

The duty sergeant was torn, but eventually nodded.

"Alright, Jack. I'll call up and see if she's in."

Lowerson refused the offer of a chair in the waiting area and stood beside the main desk until he spotted Tebbutt buzzing herself through the security doors.

Her eyes were deceptively placid as she strolled across to meet him.

"Hello, Jack. I understand you wanted to see me?"

"Yes, I—I did," he said, and willed himself not to lose the little courage he had.

"You're sure you wouldn't like to contact your legal representative?" she asked, within earshot of the duty sergeant. She could never be criticised for not giving the lad every opportunity to cover himself.

"No, I don't need anyone."

115

"Would you like to go into a meeting roo—"

"I killed her."

The words came out in a rush, spilling over one another in their haste to break free. Sweat coated his forehead and his eyes darted around the room, unable to hold hers for more than a second or two.

"I think you should sit down," she said, after an endless moment.

"I killed her," he repeated. "I want to make a statement."

Tebbutt gestured towards the interview suite and the sound of their receding footsteps echoed like the beat of an executioner's drum against the tiled floor.

* * *

Unaware of the latest development unfolding at Police Headquarters, Ryan and a small party of police volunteers arrived at Newcastle Central Station less than two minutes after leaving the Castle Keep. Since all roads leading to the High Level Bridge had been closed and traffic diverted to a minor bridge much further west, the streets were deserted as they made the short journey.

"It's like a ghost town," Phillips remarked, as they approached the tall sandstone columns outside the station.

"Look," MacKenzie murmured, pointing to a shop window as they passed. Faces peered at them from the relative safety, customers and sales assistants alike waiting for the worst to be over. Many were unable to travel home, with the roads and all major forms of public transport having been locked down.

Ryan glanced at their pale faces.

"They look like mannequins," he muttered. *Or bodies.*

"It's like something from a dystopian horror movie," Phillips said. "I keep expecting to see them break through the window, like a zombie apocalypse."

"You've been watching too much late-night telly again," Ryan muttered, then fell silent as the station manager hurried across to greet them.

"Thank God you're here," he said.

The station had been emptied too, with passengers and pedestrians having been evacuated to nearby shops and waiting rooms, a safe distance away from the platform giving access to the High Level Bridge.

"Normally, the King Edward VII carries most mainline traffic through to Scotland," he continued, as they hurried towards the end of Platform 2. "But the High Level is still very much in use. Sorry, I'm babbling."

When they reached the end of the platform, Ryan found a small group of railway officials and transport police waiting. He also spotted Gary Nobel and Kevin Wilson standing nearby, presumably discussing the best approach.

"Have you spoken to Bannerman?" he asked.

"I just got off the radio, as it happens," Nobel replied. "I told her to keep looking for any other devices from the underside. If there's a ladder connecting the upper and lower levels of the bridge, I've told her to be on hand in case we need her to come up and help."

Ryan nodded.

"How's she holding up?"

Nobel looked at him as if he'd grown two heads.

"What d'you mean?"

Ryan almost laughed.

"Never mind," he muttered, and turned to the rest of the crowd. "Who has the T-key?"

He referred to the implement that would allow them to open any window or door on the train; an innocuous piece of metal that wielded so much power.

An engineer from Network Rail stepped forward.

"I do."

"Alright," Ryan said. "You've all been briefed about the dangers. Anybody who's having second thoughts about coming onto the tracks, speak now or forever hold your peace."

There was complete silence.

"Good. Let's get this show on the road, as quickly as we can. The time is"—he looked up at the large iron clock hanging from the rafters of the station—"eleven thirty-three. I want everybody off that bridge before the clock strikes noon."

With that, he shrugged a high-vis jacket over his body armour vest and stepped off the edge of the platform.

CHAPTER 18

Ben Potter undid another button on his shirt collar and turned up the air conditioning in the driver's cabin at the front of the train. A set of enormous wipers swooshed back and forth across the windscreen, scraping away a layer of snow that was growing heavier by the minute, and yet he felt as though he was burning up; one minute hot and bothered, the next, so shivery he might faint.

He pressed shaking fingers against his temple as black dots swam briefly in front of his eyes.

"Ben? Open up, it's me!"

Behind him, there came another knock at the cabin door and he leaned across to unlock it after hearing Imran's voice calling out to him.

A moment later, the train manager's head appeared.

"How's the mood out there?" Ben asked.

"Volatile," Imran replied. "There's only five of us on shift today and it's just not enough to manage. I've got Carole and Will doing walk-throughs of the carriages so they stay visible and we're taking three carriages each. But the minute our backs are turned, the passengers are up in arms again. Kids are crying, people are really panicking. I had one woman nearly pass out in Carriage E."

Ben swiped his sleeve over his clammy forehead and Imran cast a concerned eye over him.

"Hey, mate, you alright? You don't look so good."

The driver waved it away.

"I'll be fine," he said. "Just stressed, like everybody else."

Imran started to say something, then heard a commotion behind him.

"Shit," he muttered. "It's kicking off again. I'll be back in a minute—"

"Wait," Ben grabbed his sleeve and pointed out of the wide convex window. "Look over there."

Both men narrowed their eyes against the mist of the falling snow and then broke into broad smiles for, up ahead, they spotted a line of men and women in high-vis jackets walking carefully towards them.

"They're coming to get us," Imran said, happily. "I'll go and get things ready."

As he hurried back out into the carriage, Ben felt a twinge in his arm and gave it a hard rub, thinking it was time he got up and moved around. As soon as all this was over, he was going to go on that diet his girlfriend had been none-too-subtly nagging him about. The doc said the extra weight he was carrying didn't help his asthma but, well, what was a bloke to do? He sat on his arse driving trains all day long; he wasn't an Olympic runner. When he got home from work, all he wanted to do was sit down and relax with a nice chicken curry and a few chips to dip in. Where was the harm in that? He was a hard-working man.

But the twinges kept coming, stronger this time, and he resolved to change his ways.

Just as soon as he got off the train.

* * *

Ryan had eight volunteers from CID including himself and an engineer from Network Rail, plus three members of the British Transport Police joining him on the north side of the bridge. At the same time, he'd arranged for local police to access from the south to evacuate passengers from the carriages that were closer to that end of the bridge and numerous ambulances and paramedics waiting to stretcher people away, should the need arise. The EOD Unit were already combing beneath the train, checking for any sign of a device hidden beneath its underbelly while their colleague Sue Bannerman did the same on the road and pedestrian level of the bridge, below. They had already checked the tracks for any sign of trip-wires and had pronounced it clear.

Ryan banged a fist on the reinforced glass door of the first carriage and showed his warrant card.

"DCI Ryan, CID! Open the door, please!"

As the train manager nodded and released the internal mechanism with a loud hiss of compressed air, Ryan turned to Phillips and MacKenzie.

"Mac, start unloading passengers from this carriage. I want it done in a safe and orderly fashion; I don't want people rushing in a stampede. Nobody should try to bring their luggage with them, either. We've got the transport officers waiting at intervals from here all the way back to the platform acting as marshals to guide them along."

"Leave it to me," she said, and turned to help Imran unfold a ladder that would allow people to disembark the train.

"The rest of you, fan out and take a carriage each," Ryan said. "Phillips? I need you to oversee the front end of the train, I'll run down to the back end. Yates? You're with me."

Suddenly, they heard the roar of a helicopter engine, its whirring propellers tearing through the clouds until it was directly above them. It hovered in the sky like a giant winged insect, buzzing around their heads. Ryan realised it must be a media helicopter, as he had already expressly forbidden the use of the police helicopter.

"They shouldn't be up there—" Phillips began.

"It's too late to stop it!" Ryan called out, above the roaring noise. "If they're streaming live footage, the bomber could see this, if he hasn't already. Let's move! Move! *Move!*" Ryan shouted to his team, then broke into a run as the carriage doors were opened, one-by-one.

* * *

It was a sad truth that, in a crisis situation, most people reverted to their most basic selves and looked out for Number One. Unfortunately, this resulted in a mad, thoughtless dash towards the train doors as soon as they were opened and, in their haste, several people sustained minor injuries.

Ryan's team worked together with the onboard train crew and other transport officials in a seamless conveyor belt, grasping the hands of each person who stumbled down the ladder and onto the gravelled walkway. They saw every type of person, a blur of faces and a stream of colour as they worked against the clock to clear the train.

In the middle carriage, a man with an arthritic hip began to lower himself down and was jostled from behind by an impatient crowd. He cried out in pain, clutching a hand to his leg as he fell forward.

"Woah, lad! I've got you!" Phillips cushioned the man's fall and found himself winded in the process, but there was no time to worry about that. He set the man on his feet again. "You alright, feller? Course, you are," he said, when the man shook himself off. "Just follow the crowd in that direction and keep going as fast as you can, alright?"

Further down the train, Yates held a toddler in her arms while its mother lowered herself down the ladder clutching another baby to her chest.

"Careful, now," she warned. "Watch where you tread."

The most able-bodied passengers fled the train like rats leaving a sinking ship, moving in a silent exodus along the outermost edge of the train line. Where they would have tried to run, officers shouted warnings and tried to reduce the constant and overriding threat of panic taking over.

Ryan knew the feeling; he could feel his heart beating too fast, could feel the tightness growing in his chest as the minutes slipped by.

"This way," he said to a woman of eighty or ninety, who stood in the doorway of the train paralyzed by fear. He tried not to think about the wasted seconds and instead reached up to hold out a hand. "Take my hand, I've got you."

"There's an offer," the train stewardess joked, to make the woman laugh.

"Best one I've had in forty years," the woman replied, and Ryan flashed a smile as he took her weight and lifted her down onto the walkway.

"There, now," he said. "You see that handsome chap over there?"

He pointed to one of the marshals standing further down the walkway.

"Mm, not bad," she agreed, and made him smile again.

"Keep to this pathway and head towards him," Ryan told her, pressing a gentle hand in the small of her back to nudge her along. "He'll show you where to go after that. Take it nice and steady."

To his shock and surprise, the old woman gave his backside a none-too-gentle pat.

"See ya, handsome!" she said, with a wink.

As Ryan reached up to help the next passenger off the train, he marvelled at the tenacity of the human spirit, which seemed able to find humour in even the most extreme situations.

* * *

"Let's run through this, one more time."

DCI Tebbutt set her pen back on top of her notepad and folded her arms comfortably across her chest.

Jack Lowerson ran restless hands through his hair. How many more times did he need to say it?

"Turning back the clock, tell me again when you first met the late DCS Lucas."

Lowerson closed his eyes, feeling sick and weary of all her questions.

"I've already told you," he said. "I met her about five months ago, when she transferred up from the Met to be our new superintendent."

"And, what did you think of her?" she asked, to throw him off guard a little.

"What?" He ran an absent hand across his eyes. "What did I think of her?" he repeated, a bit distractedly.

Smart. Attractive. Seductive.

"I thought she was…I thought she was everything I'd been looking for in a woman," he said, out loud.

"But she was older than you?"

"Yes, but I never noticed." *Until later. Until she chose to remind me, every day,* he almost said.

"She was also your senior officer. Your boss."

"Yes, she was."

"How did you come to work with her, day to day? You were previously assigned to work with DCI Ryan, weren't you?"

Lowerson thought of how easily he had allowed himself to be manipulated, how he'd yearned to believe every honeyed word she'd spoken.

"DCS Lucas offered me a promotional pathway, on condition that I went to work for her."

Even saying it out loud, he felt such a fool.

Tebbutt continued to regard him with a patient, unthreatening expression while she took her time drawing him out.

"Did that come as a surprise?"

"Yes, it did," he remembered. "I thought—I chose to believe her, when she told me it was on account of my previous work record."

Tebbutt raised an eyebrow.

"No reason why not," she remarked, to put him at ease. "You have an exemplary work record, Jack."

He said nothing, biting down hard on the soft flesh of his inner lip. There would be no more shining work record, no gold watch at the end of thirty years' service. This would be the end of all that, but he'd made his choice freely.

"How did you find it, working for DCS Lucas? How would you describe her management style?"

Subversive. Manipulative. Divisive.

"Business-like," he said.

"But you began a personal relationship with her, didn't you?"

Lowerson closed his eyes again, hardly able to keep them open all of a sudden. The adrenaline it had taken to drive himself down to the station was wearing off, leaving him tired and hollowed out.

"Yes," he muttered. "We had a personal relationship, almost from the start."

"You never felt that was…awkward?"

"Not at the time, no."

"Who instigated the relationship, in the very beginning?"

"She did," he admitted. But honesty compelled him to add, "I was very willing."

"How did you feel about her?"

"I loved her." *I love her still,* he thought, with self-loathing. It would take a good, long while for that old feeling to diminish and for his heart to catch up with his head.

"I see," Tebbutt murmured. "So, this went on for a number of months. Were your colleagues aware, to your knowledge?"

"If they were, they never said anything," he replied. He didn't bother to add that he'd found himself more and more isolated from his friends. Each time he'd suggested seeing one of them, Jennifer always seemed to have arranged something else so he couldn't go. That's how it had begun.

"Turning to the events of last night, then," Tebbutt watched him closely. "Can you walk me through your movements once again, please?"

Lowerson swallowed and reached for the glass of water on the table in front of him, finishing it in several gulps to ease the scratchy, burning sensation in his throat that came from a night spent crying.

"I had the day off," he said. "I'd spent Friday night with J—with DCS Lucas, at her home, but when she went to work in the morning I left and went back to my flat, in Heaton."

"Go on," she urged him.

Lowerson swallowed again.

"I-I didn't really do very much. I stayed at home watching some TV—"

Thinking things over, he added silently.

"—and then I went for a walk."

"Where? At what time?"

"Oh, until around one, one-thirty," he mumbled. "Nowhere in particular. Just around the streets. Jesmond Dene. The park. The church."

"The church? Are you a church-going man, Jack?"

"Not usually, no."

"What made you go in, yesterday?"

"I-I suppose I felt like I needed somewhere quiet to sit for a while."

Tebbutt rolled her pen between her finger and thumb, while she thought.

"Then what?"

"I walked home again and stayed there until…ah, until I knew Jennifer's shift would have ended and she'd be back home. I drove across to her house around four-fifteen and let myself in."

"You had a key?"

"Yes."

"What happened once you were inside?"

"We argued," he said, in a low voice.

"What about?"

Lowerson looked up with dazed eyes.

"Sorry?"

"I asked what you argued about."

"Oh," he said, and thought back to the ugly row they'd had, only the previous day and yet it might have been years, decades. The memory of it had taken on a sepia-hued quality, like an old movie reel he had consigned to the recesses of his mind.

"We argued about my cat, Marbles."

Tebbutt scratched her ear and thought that this read like a classic case of a coercive relationship gone bad. She'd lost count of the number of times a cherished pet had been collateral damage, used as an emotional weapon.

"What happened to the cat?" she asked, although she could have guessed.

"Jennifer killed it," he said, matter-of-factly. It helped to say it that way, or he'd break down again and never be able to go through with what he needed to say. "She was always insanely jealous because it was something I loved before her."

Tebbutt took a moment to gather herself together, having been moved by his last sentence more than she liked to admit.

"You accused her?"

"Yes," he said. "I thought about it throughout the day and I knew, in my gut, she'd done it. The cat went missing when I was at work but Jennifer wasn't. She had access to my flat, in any case."

"And when you accused her, she denied it?"

"At first," Lowerson said, with a sad little smile. "Once she really got into the swing of things, she didn't bother to deny it. She said the cat was a mangy, flea-ridden creature and that she wouldn't touch me again if I continued to own it. She'd said that before but…well, I loved that cat. I kept her and looked after her and Jennifer didn't like it."

"What happened during the argument?"

Lowerson gathered his thoughts, not wanting to make a mistake.

"I—ah, I guess I saw red. I shoved her, I think."

"One hand, or two?" Tebbutt put in, mildly.

"Ah, I think it was one," he said. "I can't really remember."

"Okay. You shoved her. Then what?"

"She fell hard and hit her head on the radiator. I, ah, I grabbed her head and hit it against the metal, to be sure."

The words made him sick to his very core and Tebbutt watched his skin turn an unnatural grey.

But not as grey as Jennifer Lucas, who now lay dead inside a refrigerated drawer.

She hardened herself.

"How did you grab her, Jack?"

"What do you mean?"

"I mean, how'd you grab her? By the sides of her head, by the hair, by the neck…how?"

Lowerson looked blank for a second, then he reached for another glass of water.

"By the hair," he said, and hoped that was right.

Tebbutt scribbled something on her notepad and then circled it. Lowerson frowned, wishing he could read what she had written, then decided it didn't matter.

"Up until now, you've been adamant that you didn't hurt her," she said, after a pause. "What changed, Jack? Why the sudden change of heart?"

His eyes welled, but he held himself together.

"It's the right thing to do."

CHAPTER 19

By eleven-fifty, hundreds of people had been safely evacuated from the train. Ryan watched them shuffling along the walkway, their heads bent against the wind and snow, and wondered how many had made it safely off the bridge. There had been no time for a head count and, in fact, the train crew hadn't been able to say with any certainty how many passengers were on board. People got on and off all the time, some with railcards, some with advance tickets and some with no ticket at all.

His radio crackled, and he heard that seven out of nine carriages were now empty, with the remaining two almost empty but for a wheelchair user and a man who was refusing to leave.

Ryan hauled himself onto the train, passing through the empty carriages strewn with bags and half-eaten food until he reached Carriage C, where he found Phillips crouched beside a man of around twenty who was refusing to move from the vestibule area. His face was pale and drawn and he had the skinny, malnourished look of somebody who hadn't seen a good meal in days. One of the stewards stood beside them, casting frequent glances over his shoulder towards the open doorway beyond.

"Get going," Ryan barked. "We'll take it from here."

Phillips glanced across and Ryan saw concern writ large on his sergeant's face.

"What's the trouble?"

The man looked away, clinging with both hands to the edge of the wall.

"This lad says he wants to stay on the train because he hopes it blows up," Phillips said, sadly. "He says his girlfriend's left him and taken the baby with her. He lost his job a couple of months ago and he's just been rejected for another one. His name's Luke."

Ryan looked away briefly, trying to manage his own sense of rising panic. There was no time to have the kind of careful, in-depth discussion that Luke needed, much as he might have liked.

There was simply no time.

"I'm sorry you're feeling so low, Luke, but however you're feeling now will pass," he said, as time slipped through his fingers like sand. "I need you to understand that the decision you're making affects more than just yourself."

"I want to die," he muttered. "Can't you just leave me on here?"

He turned to Ryan with such a look of appeal, he felt his heart shatter.

But there were others to think of.

"No, Luke. I can't."

With that, he reached across and simply hauled the man to his feet. It was such an unexpected action, Luke had no time to protest.

"Listen to me, Luke. I know you're a good bloke and you want to do the right thing," Ryan grasped his shoulders and hoped he was right. "After all this is over, we'll sit down with a pint and you can tell me all about it. But, right now? I need you to help me. *I need your help*. Do you think you can do it?"

The man struggled with himself.

"I-I don't know how I could possibly help. I'm no use to anyone."

"Yes, you are," Ryan told him, and led him towards the ladder leading off the train. He cast a quick glance in both directions and then stuck his fingers in his mouth to emit a loud, ear-popping whistle that caught the attention of Yates, a little further along the tracks. He gave her a hand signal and a moment later she was hurrying towards them. Ryan turned back to the young man hovering beside him. "See this lady? She's a police officer and she needs you to help guide some of the older passengers along the tracks. I need you to make sure people are safe, Luke. Can you do that for me?"

As Yates approached, Ryan gave her a meaningful look.

"Luke wants to help us to make sure everybody makes it off the bridge safely. Including himself," he added, as a warning as much as anything else.

Yates was a quick study.

"Thank God," she said, with hardly a pause. "I could use another pair of hands. This way."

Once she had led him away, Phillips put a hand on his friend's shoulder.

"You soft git," he said, affectionately.

"Yeah, well. Don't let it get about."

* * *

At five minutes before noon, the world watched.

They tuned in from their homes and offices and waited with bated breath, unwilling to look and yet unable to look away until they knew whether *The Alchemist* would make good on his promise to burn up another bridge. Ryan had, by now, assumed that whatever device had been rigged had been set to a timer rather than manual detonation, otherwise there would surely already have been a second explosion in punishment for breaking the rules. On that analysis, the bomb had always been scheduled to detonate, regardless of whether or not they stumped up the cash in bitcoins.

Either that, or their bomber had a heart, after all.

Ryan wasn't holding out too much hope.

Passengers had been fully evacuated and all official personnel had been ordered to leave the bridge other than himself, Phillips and MacKenzie, who were checking the carriages one last time to make sure nobody had been forgotten. He was striding through Carriage A, at the front of the train, when he was met by the train manager.

He looked ashen.

"What is it?" Ryan demanded.

"It's Ben—the driver. I think he's having a heart attack and we need to get off. We have to get off—"

"Alright, try to stay calm. Where is he?"

Ryan hurried after him towards the driver's cabin and put an urgent radio call through to his team to make sure everyone else was off the bridge. With only a couple of minutes before noon, it was getting too near to the deadline for an ambulance crew to come onto the tracks; that would risk more lives than they'd save. Their best hope was to get the driver off the train and closer to the station, away from the blast zone.

In the fleeting seconds it took them to cross from one end of the carriage to the other, it flashed through Ryan's mind that, by staying on the train to help a stranger, he was risking his own life, too. In the past, it hadn't seemed to matter so much because he'd been alone. He'd felt less constrained, less frightened about taking decisions that needed to be taken because he had been accountable only to himself. But now, there was someone he had vowed never to hurt and who he'd promised to protect—whether she needed him to or not—because he loved her more than anything or anyone else, including himself.

There was Anna.

He experienced a momentary twist in his stomach, a slow roll of nausea as he thought of what it must be costing her to watch events like these play out on television, or even to hear about them on the radio. It was true that he'd never lied to her and that she had known from the start what his job entailed. But there was knowing and then there was *knowing*.

Ryan shoved the thought aside.

It was too late for self-recriminations, too late for doubts that could cost lives. He needed to focus on the task ahead.

As he and Imran reached the driver's cabin at the front of the train, they were met by MacKenzie, who climbed the ladder leading up to the first doorway.

"What's happened? Ryan, we need to get off the bridge—"

"It's the driver," he said, and wasted no more time before ducking inside the cabin. There, he found Ben Potter half-sitting, half-lying in his seat clutching his left arm. Sweat poured down his face, which was contorted with pain.

"Where's the First Aid kit?" Ryan demanded of the train manager, who looked as if he might keel over himself. "Is there a defibrillator, if we need it?"

Imran hurried off to look for it, while Ryan leaned across to loosen the man's clothing a little to make him more comfortable.

"My lass," Ben gasped. "Tell her—tell her—"

Ryan cut him off.

"It won't come to that," he assured him, because it was the right thing to do. They all needed to remain positive, not to start saying their goodbyes, as if the fight was over. "You're going to tell her yourself."

The man panted, drawing in vast gulps of air, but nodded.

"We need to get him out," Ryan turned to MacKenzie. "You get his arms, I'll get his legs."

She didn't hesitate and reached beneath the man's arms to clasp her hands in a sturdy grip around his upper chest.

"Ready?" Ryan asked her.

She gave a short nod.

"On three…"

It was an awkward job given the cramped space, and was made more difficult by the fact that Ben Potter was carrying quite a few extra pounds. With a monumental effort, they lifted him out of his chair and into the vestibule, where they paused to catch their breath.

"S-sorry," the driver gasped. "It's my chest, I can't—"

His face turned white with pain and then his eyes rolled back in his head. His hand fell limply to the floor as he stopped breathing.

"Mac—"

"You pump his chest, I'll do the airways," MacKenzie was a more experienced First Aider, and fell to her knees beside Potter's collapsed body.

133

Ryan did as he was bid, muscles working as he compressed the man's chest beneath the breastbone, pausing at the right times to allow MacKenzie to breathe air into the man's lungs.

"Come on," she muttered. "*Come on.*"

She cocked her cheek against his face and felt shallow breathing, while Ryan took his pulse and found it thready but still there. When Imran hurried back from the next carriage with a small canvas bag, they strapped a portable oxygen mask to his face.

"It'll have to do," MacKenzie said.

"Time to go," Ryan muttered.

"What time is it?"

"Just turning noon," he said quietly. "Our time's up."

* * *

It would take more than a few veiled threats from the British Transport Police to stop DS Frank Phillips helping the woman he loved. It made not a blind bit of difference that Denise MacKenzie was his senior officer, nor that she could handle herself in any situation. He would not stand by and watch her struggle, and the same applied to his friend. As far as he was concerned, he wouldn't be losing his fiancée and his best man in one fell swoop.

Not on his watch.

As the iron clock in the railway station chimed the hour, Phillips ran faster than he had in years, spurred on by a healthier diet since meeting MacKenzie and an abiding need to be with her. When he reached the train door, he summed up the situation immediately.

"Holy shitballs," he said.

"Frank, grab his legs," Ryan ordered.

The four of them manoeuvred the driver off the train with a series of grunts, each of them straining with the effort, but they weren't home and dry, yet.

"I don't know how we're going to get him the rest of the way," MacKenzie said, brushing snow from her eyes. "He's too weak to walk—"

Phillips exchanged a glance with Ryan, who nodded.

"We'll get an arm each. No point in this 'un having all those muscles if he's not prepared to use them," he jerked a thumb in Ryan's direction, then draped one of Potter's arms around his shoulders.

"Times like these, I wish I'd eaten more spinach when I was a kid," Ryan muttered.

"It's not spinach you need," Phillips panted. "It's a corned beef pasty."

They moved off as quickly as they could along the narrow pathway towards the station, to the sound of Potter's shoes dragging against the gravel as they tried to hold him upright. MacKenzie and Imran followed, and with every passing metre they put a safer distance between themselves and the train, but they had no idea of knowing where a device may be hidden. EOD had checked all the obvious places where explosives might have been planted but there was a margin of error in all things.

"Nearly there," Phillips puffed.

Paramedics waited by the edge of the platform to transfer Potter onto a stretcher but there was still a way to go.

"Keep looking forward," MacKenzie said, and put a hand on Imran's back in a show of silent support. "Don't look behind, just keep going."

Ryan and Phillips gritted their teeth as Potter passed out again and, in a final show of strength, they had almost reached the end of the bridge when the explosion hit them from behind.

CHAPTER 20

As the paramedics rushed to save Ben Potter's life, Ryan and his team stood in an exhausted line on the farthest edge of the platform to watch another bridge go up in flames. The blast had thrown the rails into the sky with a deafening twist of metal and asphalt, blowing a hole in the mezzanine structure of the bridge that separated the upper and lower levels, somewhere near the second or third carriage from the front of where the train stood. The wind carried with it the strong stench of smoke and burnt chemicals, and they held their hands across their mouths to stave off the worst of it.

"Exactly on time," Phillips eventually broke the silence.

"No, it wasn't," Ryan replied, turning to face him. "The blast came three or four minutes after noon. I know, because I was thinking—"

He broke off. He didn't need to tell them what they had all feared as they'd made their desperate run along the edge of the tracks.

Any second now, they'd thought. *Any moment now, there'd be an explosion.*

Wiping a hand across his dirty face, Ryan pulled himself together and turned to look at the men and women who had volunteered to come to the aid of others. A short way off, the EOD Unit were slumped on a metal bench, the team rallying around Sue Bannerman to praise her stoicism in getting through that first explosion and gathering her strength to help the evacuation effort. Even her captain could not find it in himself to denigrate the woman, for which Ryan was grateful. Not far off, officers from British Transport Police were talking to the train crew, who were clutching foil blankets around their shoulders to keep warm. Ryan would need to speak to them—to all of them—but first, he had something to say.

"I want to thank all of you, for what you did out there," he said. "It went above and beyond."

MacKenzie smiled.

"Beats going over Cold Cases, any day of the week," she quipped.

"Aye, well, it's tuna casserole in the staff canteen t'day," Phillips reminded him. "That's enough to get me out of the door, bomb scare or no bomb scare."

"I've always said you were a man of refined tastes," Ryan said, and then excused himself. He found a relatively sheltered corner and made an important phone call.

Anna answered after the first ring.

"Ryan? Oh, thank God. I was so worried—"

"I know," he murmured. "I'm so sorry you had to go through that. But I wanted to call to let you know I'm safe. You're still stuck with me for another fifty years or so, if you'll have me."

At the other end of the line, Anna's lips curved into a smile, which dimmed as she thought of what might have been.

"It looked bad out there," she said.

"It was," he admitted, but decided against telling her just how close they'd been to the wire. It would serve no purpose other than to make himself feel better and would only cause her pain.

Instead, he lightened the mood.

"You had some competition today," he told her.

"Oh?"

He smiled at the sudden chill in her voice.

"Yeah, from a blonde with a lovely smile. She got a bit handsy, too."

Back at home, Anna tucked her feet up onto the sofa and savoured the sound of his voice, deciding to humour him.

"Well, it's good to know you're not past it," she agreed. "Have you set a date for the elopement?"

Ryan chuckled.

"It might take some special planning, since she's nearly ninety."

Anna's soft laughter came down the line.

"You old flirt," she said. "I hope it made her day."

"It made mine," he replied. "Until I heard the sound of your voice."

From his position a few feet away, Phillips made kissy-kissy sounds and Ryan flipped him the bird.

"Gotta go," he said, as manfully as he could muster. "Duty calls."

"Take care, Chief Inspector."

"You too, Doctor."

* * *

"Sir?"

Ryan's smile died when he was flagged down by Yates, who looked anguished.

"Is it another one?" he asked, and was terrified of the answer she might give. There had been no time to regroup and recover from the last two bombings, which had been only hours apart. They had a task of monumental proportions on their hands and were badly under-resourced.

When she shook her head, his relief was short-lived.

"No, sir," she said. "It's—I've just had a text from Jack's mum. She knows me," Yates explained, babbling a bit. "It's bad news. She says Jack's gone missing and she can't find him. She's worried he might have hurt himself or done something stupid."

"I'll call the hospitals," Phillips said, already pulling out his phone.

"I'll call Tebbutt," Ryan began, but then caught sight of Chief Constable Morrison weaving through the crowds of people, craning her neck to look for him. "Hold that thought."

He ran across to meet her.

"Sandra?"

Morrison spun in the direction of his voice and hurried through the hoard of passengers. Her first thought was that he looked even worse than she felt, but she couldn't possibly feel any worse and therefore retracted the comment even before it was said.

"Ryan. There's been a development."

"Another bomb?"

Morrison sucked in a breath and her forehead furrowed at the acrid smoke riding on the breeze.

"Not in the way you mean. It's Jack."

Ryan's heart slammed against his chest in one hard motion and his eyes became shuttered as he prepared himself to hear the worst news. It had been a hard few months for his friend and an even harder twenty-four hours. If he had gone missing from home, there was no telling what he might have done…

"Say it quickly, please."

Morrison looked him in the eye.

"He's confessed to Lucas's murder," she said.

Ryan's elation that the man was still alive was followed by total disbelief.

"*What?* You can't be serious," he said, angrily. "He'd never kill anybody."

Morrison had been prepared for his reaction; it was the same reaction she expected to receive from every member of the constabulary. Jack Lowerson was a gentle young man, the kind who watered the ailing plants on the window-ledge in CID and cared about his fellow man. There was not a violent bone in his body, except insofar as the line of duty demanded and, even then, the slightest hint of force upset him for months afterwards.

"I'm sorry, but it's true. I've just heard from Tebbutt and I thought you should hear it from me before you find out through the grapevine, or the papers."

"And who would have told them?"

"Come on, Ryan. You know these things have a habit of finding their way out."

Ryan was shaken to the core, unable to accept what she had just told him. He would be lying if he said the possibility of Jack having killed Lucas hadn't crossed his mind; he was a murder detective, so the prospect of foul play was never far from his thoughts. But the idea had been so ridiculous, so far outside the character of the Jack Lowerson they all knew, as to be almost unthinkable.

"All last night, Jack consistently denied any involvement in her death," Ryan argued. "Why has he changed his story?"

"Tebbutt doesn't think he's changed his story," Morrison told him. "She thinks he's come around to admitting guilt out of a sense of basic decency."

There was a pause while Ryan considered the likelihood of that, then his brows drew together in one dark line.

"I want to speak to him," he demanded.

"I can't allow it," Morrison said.

"Under full guard, properly recorded, whatever you want," he insisted. "But I need to hear this for myself."

Morrison looked across at the smoky trail rising into the sky following the blast and thought of the simmering threat that another bridge would be targeted. Then she thought of how this man and others had put themselves in danger to save others.

She owed him. They all did.

"You get five minutes," she said. "I'll clear it with Tebbutt, although she won't like it."

"Neither would I," Ryan said, evenly. "But I'm still going to speak to him."

Ryan began to turn away to tell the others, when Morrison stopped him again.

"There's one more thing."

"What else? Don't tell me Lowerson's being blamed for a bunch of unsolved cases, now that he's apparently turned into a killer overnight."

She ignored the sarcasm because she knew it came from a place of hurt, and raised her phone to show him the screen.

"The counter's just hit two million."

He looked down at the bomber's website and watched a cartoon dragon dance across the screen blowing a speech bubble containing the word, 'CONGRATULATIONS!'

"Whoop-de-doo," he snarled, before striding away to break the news to the rest of his team.

CHAPTER 21

Ryan left MacKenzie in charge of overseeing the aftermath of the bomb on the High Level Bridge and headed back to CID Headquarters with Phillips in tow. Both men were physically and mentally exhausted but there was no opportunity to take stock, not when their friend had confessed to murder.

The moment they stepped inside Police Headquarters, they were intercepted by DCI Tebbutt, who wore an expression of extreme displeasure.

"I'd like a word with you, please."

Ryan turned to look at her.

"Let me say it for you, shall I? You find it both overbearing and inappropriate that I've requested to see my colleague and friend, especially in light of the fact he's confessed to the murder of our former superintendent. You're concerned it will appear incestuous within the police hierarchy and it bothers you that I called on the Chief Constable for a special favour. Is that about it?"

Tebbutt folded her arms.

"In a nutshell."

"Good, so long as we understand one another," he muttered, and would have headed off again but paused long enough to ask an important question.

"Tell me something, Joan—off the record, just one detective to another. Do you think he did this thing? Do you truly believe it?"

It was on the tip of her tongue to give him another ticking off, to tell him to go to hell and not bother asking any questions she was not at liberty to answer. But she knew him to be an honourable man and there were times in life when there was more to be gained by giving a little.

"Before I answer your question, do me a favour and answer one of mine," she said.

Phillips eyed her with suspicion, but Ryan gave a brief nod.

"Go on. What do you want to know?"

"Why would a man confess to a murder he didn't commit?"

"It's your job to find out the answer to that," he shot back. "There must be DNA evidence on the body that isn't Jack's—"

"It's being analysed," she went so far as to say. "I'm expecting to hear back from the lab today. They've been held up a bit, for obvious reasons."

Ryan nodded. It was true that their technicians had been working flat out to determine the components of the bomb used on the Tyne Bridge the previous day and would be called upon again to find out whether the same ingredients were used in the double explosion on the High Level Bridge.

"Have you contacted his family?" he asked. "They're worried sick."

Tebbutt shook her head.

"Lowerson didn't want them to be told straight away and he declined a solicitor," she said. "It's up to *him*," she added, when he would have argued. "I gave him the opportunity several times; listen to the tape, if you don't believe me."

Phillips took a step closer, lowering his voice so that only they would be heard.

"Now, look here, Joan. Tell the CSIs to put a rush on it," he said. "They might be run off their feet, but the lad's life is hanging in the balance and he's one of our own. We need to know. *You* need to know."

"Don't tell me how to do my job," she snapped, but a flush crept its way up her neck. Perhaps she could have hassled the forensic team a little more, she thought. "You're forgetting that he's the one who made a confession. It isn't for us to disprove…"

"Excuse me," Ryan interrupted her, and brushed past them towards the custody suite.

He'd heard from everybody aside from Lowerson himself, so he decided it was time to go and get it from the horse's mouth.

* * *

They found Jack sitting on the edge of a narrow bed, lost in thought as he counted the breeze-blocks on the wall of his cell.

Twenty-eight, in total.

It was the same cell he'd occupied the night before and there was a funny sort of comfort in that, as if he were coming home.

There came a rattle at the door, followed by the sound of metal brushing metal as the bolt was released and it swung open.

"Got some visitors," the custody officer told him, and nodded to Ryan and Phillips. "Make it quick, mind. Morrison said five minutes."

"Haddaway, man," Phillips muttered, and waved him away with the kind of authority that came from knowing everybody across four command divisions, and beyond.

Lowerson looked up at them with a pitiable mixture of joy and sorrow.

"Budge across," Phillips said, before the silence could grow awkward. "I'm knackered, after the morning we've had."

Lowerson shuffled across the bed so Phillips could perch beside him, then cast a wary glance towards Ryan, a man he had looked up to throughout his career on the force. He'd always wanted to be like him, to walk in his footsteps and, he supposed, to make him proud.

But Ryan remained silent, looking at him as though he could see inside his mind and read what was hidden there.

"Why, Jack?" he asked. "Why are you saying you killed her?"

Lowerson said nothing and turned away from Ryan's eyes, which saw altogether too much for comfort.

When no answer was forthcoming, Phillips stepped in.

"You know you can tell us anything, son. We're not here to judge, we're here to help you, if we can."

Jack swallowed painfully, and his Adam's apple bobbed precariously as he fought his own emotions.

"I don't need any help," he said. "It's all taken care of."

"Nothing's over yet," Ryan cut in, and in a couple of long strides he covered the distance between them and dropped to his haunches, so they were on a level. "D'you hear me, Jack? Nothing is done and dusted yet. If you made a mistake, you can sort it out—explain why you would say…"

Ryan trailed off, struggling to understand. He searched the younger man's face for any clue of what might have led him to make a false confession, never believing that it could be real.

He stood up again to pace away, turning his back on the pair of them until he had gathered the strength to say what he needed to say now, in front of two of his closest friends.

"Jack, I never really told you—I never told you what happened, between Jennifer and me."

Lowerson rubbed his hands up and down his upper arms to warm them.

"You don't need to."

"Yes, I think I do. But I'll save the details for another time, when all this is behind you. For the moment, I want you to know just one thing," Ryan said, turning around again to face them. "I understand that you might have *wanted* to kill her, even when you thought you loved her."

Lowerson's lips trembled.

"I understand you might have felt as though you couldn't break free, that you were trapped. I understand these things because I've been there myself. It's worse because we stepped through the hoops to get there, inviting her into our lives so she could turn us inside out, chew us up and spit out whatever was left."

Phillips sat beside the two younger men and could not have felt for them more deeply had they been his own kin. He wished he could have done something, anything, to protect them from the pain that was still so fresh, but there was nothing. It was an old scar for Ryan, one that had healed but had been scuffed and bruised over these past five months, like a phantom ache in his chest that gave him discomfort every now and then. But for Jack, it was still an open, bleeding wound that would take time and care to heal.

Time that he would not be given behind bars, where every criminal worth their salt would be gunning for him from the outset.

"I'm telling you this, Jack, because I don't want you to feel guilty for imagining what might have been, or what you *might* have done, given the right provocation. But thinking about killing someone is a long way from doing it."

Lowerson didn't trust himself to speak, so remained silent.

Ryan shook his head in frustration and Phillips reached across to put a hand on Lowerson's shoulder.

"What happened, lad? Why'd you say that you did it?"

"You came to my home, shocked, shaken," Ryan reminded him. "But the one thing that never wavered was your story. You said you hadn't hurt her, that you *couldn't* hurt her. I believed you, Jack," Ryan finished, and his voice almost cracked. "I believed you would never lie to me."

"I haven't lied to you," Lowerson whispered.

The door opened to reveal Tebbutt, who tapped a finger against her watch.

"Time's up."

CHAPTER 22

It was almost two-thirty by the time Ryan and Phillips climbed the stairs and headed along to the incident room, having first made a pit stop for some essential provisions. It had been one of the most difficult days on record and their need for sustenance was great. The owner of the legendary Pie Van had come through in their hour of need, filling two large cardboard carriers with all manner of favourites, ranging from sandwiches to Scotch eggs and from pease pudding stotties to quinoa salad, which had elicited a suspicious glare from Phillips.

"Don't know why everything's got to be *organic* this and *vegan* that," he muttered, as they headed down the corridor towards CID. "Whatever happened to good, old-fashioned cholesterol?"

"I think they call it progress," Ryan said, dryly.

Phillips gave an eloquent snort.

"Half the vegans I know sneak a sausage sarnie after a big night out," he said. "I've never seen anybody hoover a lamb kebab as fast as a drunk vegetarian."

"You give them a run for their money."

"Waste not, want not," Phillips replied.

They shouldered into the incident room and watched heads slowly rise from computer screens as the appetizing scent of a late lunch carried across the room.

"Grub's up!" Ryan called out. "Refuel yourselves before we sit down and talk about what happened today."

Phillips watched several younger members of the task force tuck into the quinoa salad and sent Ryan a pained look.

"Younger generation," he said, sadly. "They don't know they're born."

* * *

After his team had eaten their fill and taken the time to splash some water on their faces after a long shift, Ryan moved to the front of the room to begin a briefing. On the front row, Phillips had been joined by MacKenzie, who was polishing off the remainder of a Scotch egg. On Phillips' other side, Melanie Yates balanced a clipboard on her lap and was sipping an extra-large mug of tea emblazoned with a motif which read, 'CANNY GOOD.' Sitting at the end of the row, Gary Nobel represented the EOD Unit and Tom Faulkner, the senior CSI attached to Northumbria Police, slipped in to join them and took a seat beside Jasmine Patel, head of computer analytics.

"Thank you for showing up," Ryan said. "I don't need to tell you it's been a bloody hard couple of days and I'm sure everybody is ready for some shut-eye. That's going to come but, before I let you all go home for a few hours, we need to be sure that we've made the cities of Newcastle and Gateshead as secure as possible."

There were nods around the room.

"We've had a total of three explosions across two bridges in as many days," he said, "causing massive disruption to all concerned. You're all aware that *The Alchemist* asked for two million pounds worth of bitcoins to be donated via the website *www.savethebridges.org*. As of the last count, we had over two million in donations from the general public, which was reached shortly after the last bomb went off."

"Does that mean it's over?" Yates asked.

"On the face of it, the bomber has got what he wanted but I've already heard from GCHQ, who tell me none of those bitcoins have been drawn down yet. When they are, they'll do their best to trace where they've been cashed in but, for the moment, there's no movement. That could mean something, or nothing," Ryan said. "In the meantime, all we can do is hope that's an end to it and make the bridges safe again."

He turned to Captain Nobel.

"Gary? Tell us what's being done by EOD."

Nobel was sprawled at the end of a row, his legs splayed an anti-social width apart in a classic 'alpha' gesture that generally had the opposite effect to the one he intended.

"I've got the team out there now combing the bridges, checking and double checking for any other devices. We can use the sniffer dogs this time, since we don't need to keep a low profile. We've also been joined by another unit from Catterick, down in Yorkshire, so if there's anything to find, I'm as confident as I'll ever be that we'll find it. We know the kind of device our perp prefers to use, so we can be on the look-out for anything similar."

"Morrison wants everything operational again by tomorrow morning," Ryan said, with a degree of irritation. "It's the start of the working week and she wants to put the whole thing behind us. I agree, but only if it's safe to re-open those bridges."

"On the face of it, there's no reason why not. The threats were only a few hours apart, so if our perp wants to hit another bridge and ask for more money we'll probably hear about it pretty soon. If we don't hear anything and my team confirm there's nothing suspect on the remaining major bridges, we have to make a decision and move on."

Ryan happened to agree.

"Were you able to salvage anything from the bomb site on the High Level Bridge?" he asked.

"Yeah, we've collected a load of samples," Nobel said. "They've been sent across to Faulkner's team but I dunno how long it'll take them to process. Faulkner seems a decent bloke but he's—"

"Fastidious? Professional?" Faulkner suggested, from a couple of rows back, and Nobel turned in surprise.

"Sorry, mate, didn't know you were with us. I just meant—"

"Yeah, I think I understand what you meant."

The temperature in the room dropped several degrees and Ryan stepped in quickly.

"You won't find a better forensic specialist," he said, and his tone brooked no argument. "On that note, can you tell us anything yet, Tom?"

Tom Faulkner was a quiet, academic man with a natural flair for forensic science. He could step into a crime scene and tell at a glance what the blood spatter and configuration of a body meant and whether it spelled murder. As a chemist, he had a natural interest in the components of improvised bombs and, privately, he could admit to a degree of professional excitement at the prospect of poring over the evidence to help discover who was responsible.

"I've sent through a report of our preliminary findings about the first bomb," he said. "I've been liaising with Captain Nobel and his colleagues to discuss the most likely construct and I've included a diagram in there."

Ryan flicked through the pages of the report until he came to the back sheet, which showed an improvised device sitting inside the cross-section of a rucksack.

"The bomber gave specific deadlines for each explosion which might suggest a fixed timer," Faulkner continued. "But, in reality, the explosion was delayed by a few minutes each time. We have to assume it was rigged up for remote-controlled detonation, which would be consistent with the evidence we have."

Ryan frowned, thinking back to their most recent encounter on the High Level Bridge.

"If the bombs rely on manual detonation, why did they wait to detonate? The smaller charge went off as a warning or a punishment because they'd clocked members of EOD scouring the bridges and that was against the rules. If they weren't afraid to press the button when people were on the bridge then, what stopped them from pressing the button later, when they could see us taking hundreds of people off that train?"

The room was silent as each person mulled it over.

"If I've said it once, I've said it a thousand times," Phillips' rumbling voice broke the silence. "You can never second-guess a nutter."

"Words to live by," Ryan muttered.

"Maybe you were right before," MacKenzie suggested. "Maybe this person doesn't want to kill anybody, so they waited."

"They might have killed Sue, or anyone else who happened to be around when that first charge went off," Nobel argued. "There was a bus crossing the bridge—they could have been caught up in it. Who knows? The explosion might have hit a weak point and taken out more of the tracks than intended. What if the train had been a little further along? It could have been derailed."

"Nobel is right," Phillips agreed, though it pained him to say it. "There are too many 'ifs', 'buts' and 'maybes' in all this. I've managed to get my hands on the CCTV footage from the Council's cameras around the entrances to the Tyne Bridge on both sides and I'll hunt out the same for the High Level by the end of the day. The bloke from Network Rail tells me there aren't any cameras on the tracks—they just don't have the money for that kind of coverage—but there are a couple in Central Station, so we'll see if they've captured anything interesting."

Ryan hitched himself up onto a nearby desk while he listened.

"There's been no time to sit and look through the CCTV footage but that's a task for the coming days," he said. "It's a mammoth job because we don't know where or when the bridges were accessed to plant the devices. Frank? I want you to get in touch with our colleagues in the British Transport Police and enlist some volunteers to help go through it all. We need plenty of eyes on this."

"Aye, good idea."

Ryan ticked off the mental checklist in his head, thinking through what needed to be done.

"Jasmine? Any news from your team?"

Her eyes flicked towards Nobel, no doubt fearful of another outburst from the man who had undermined her publicly last time they'd been at a briefing together. Ryan noted the action and was ready to step in, if necessary.

"Ah, well, we're still stuck with the Ukraine," she said. "We hit a wall when we trace it that far and I've been speaking to GCHQ to see if there's any way of putting pressure on the authorities over there. But the fact is, it's a very different jurisdiction and they're not co-operating, sir."

Ryan just nodded. It was no more than he had expected.

"What about internet searches for the bomb components?"

"We've been working with them to cross-reference any leads they've generated on a national level with any known offenders locally, but there's just been no time, sir. We need a few more days because, at the moment, they've got thousands and thousands of searches for things like circuit boards but nothing that stands out as being potentially relevant."

She paused, then gave them the bad news.

"Our best guess is, the bomber used the Dark Web to order the things they needed and that will take more than a few days to trace— maybe even months. Even then, there are no guarantees."

Ryan thanked her and considered the next move as he looked around their shattered faces. Local police were managing the infrastructure in Newcastle and Gateshead and, in true northern style, the residents of both cities had chosen to rise to the occasion. They followed the long diversions to travel where they needed to go and thanked their lucky stars that nobody had been seriously injured. If there were grumbles, they were no more than the usual grumbles of a city-dweller who would rather not be inconvenienced by something as piddling as a major bomb incident. The media continued to report the high drama of the day and pseudo-experts talked about this being the product of the Digital Age and how, without the internet, this might never have happened.

Ryan was more inclined to think that people were always people, flawed or otherwise. If some arsehole wanted to threaten an entire population, they'd figure out a way to do it, internet or no internet. That was just human nature.

Outside, the snow had stopped falling to reveal clear blue skies and the sun shone bright beams of light through the rain-washed windows, so that the storm of the morning might never have happened.

"Go home and get some rest, all of you," Ryan said. "Nobel? Let me know when the bridges have been cleared and are deemed safe to re-open but, in the meantime, the rest of you catch forty winks. I'll see you back here tomorrow morning, eight a.m. sharp."

As they began to disperse, Yates took him to one side.

"Sir? I wanted to ask what was happening with Jack. Have you heard anything more? I've been getting texts from his parents and I don't know what to tell them."

Ryan sighed.

"He's in custody," he said. "Jack confessed to Lucas's murder, as you know. Tebbutt is still investigating."

He watched tears spring into the young woman's eyes and cleared his throat.

"Jack didn't want his family to be told straight away but they'll have to know soon enough. Tebbutt will keep them informed, even if Jack won't."

Yates blinked a few times and nodded.

"They'll be crushed," she said softly. "Jack is so close to his family."

As she walked away, Ryan stuck his hands in the back pockets of his jeans and thought of his friend.

CHAPTER 23

David Lowerson helped his wife out of the car and locked it with a trembling hand before taking her arm.

"I can't stand not knowing," Wendy whispered. "I just can't stand it any longer."

"I know, love," he murmured. "But DCI Tebbutt says she's got some news for us; maybe it'll be good. They probably just want to confirm Jack's whereabouts, so they can eliminate him from their enquiries."

David looked across at his wife and felt protectiveness wash over him. She looked so frail, all of a sudden; as if a gust of wind could carry her off at any moment. He'd made sure she wrapped up warm before they left the house, bundling her into a "Big Coat" and looking out a pair of rubber-soled shoes so she wouldn't slip on the icy ground, but she was still shivering.

It was the shock of it all.

"We'll get you a nice hot cup of tea, just as soon as we're inside," he promised.

He told himself to stay strong, to go through the motions for all their sakes, but whenever he thought of his youngest son, he wanted to crumble. He wanted to cry out, to hit something, anything to dispel the dreadful cocktail of anger and disappointment festering inside his belly that told him that, just maybe, his son had done a dreadful thing after all.

Last night, he'd been unable to sleep thinking of Jack as a boy, as a cute little bundle of mischief he'd carried on his shoulders. He'd watched both of his sons play together at the park or on trips to Bolam Lake, watched them kick up leaves there in autumn. He'd seen Paul grow up to marry and become a father himself, while Jack had gone on to excel as a first-class policeman and murder detective.

How he'd bragged about his clever son, David thought. How he'd bored his friends down at the snooker club about Jack's heroic exploits.

What would he tell them now?

"This way, love," he muttered, as he took his wife's arm and guided her through the automatic doors.

* * *

"Mr and Mrs Lowerson? Thank you for coming so quickly."

Wendy and David looked up to see DCI Tebbutt crossing the foyer in a pair of smart chinos. They could read nothing from her face, which was both comforting and concerning.

"Where's—where's Jack?" Wendy burst out. "What have you done?"

Tebbutt didn't flinch at the outburst.

"If it's alright with you, I'd like to speak to you both individually."

"I'm not going anywhere without David," Wendy said, and looked perilously close to tears.

"She's overwrought," he explained, apologetically. "I'm afraid everything's come as a huge shock—to all of us."

Tebbutt thought of how to get around it, then held out an arm to guide them towards the nearby family room.

"Why don't you come and sit down, both of you, and we'll have a chat."

"Aye, alright. This way, pet," David helped his wife out of her chair, her legs no longer seeming to function as they used to.

On the wall beside the family room, they passed a small poster which had recently been put up alongside a number of other notices and signs warning people not to smoke. It was printed in colour and showed DCS Jennifer Lucas as she had been in life, smiling coyly for the camera in her dress uniform. Beneath it were the simple words: 'R.I.P. Jennifer Ann Lucas, 1972-2018.'

David jerked his eyes away from the sight of it.

"Take a seat," Tebbutt invited them, before closing the door. "Can I offer you a coffee, some tea?"

"I don't want anything," Wendy snapped. "I just want to know what's happened to Jack."

"Well, now," Joan said, pleasantly. "Before I go into it any further, I'm sure you understand I need to caution you both. It's just standard procedure."

David nodded, and they listened while Tebbutt recited the formal police caution.

"…anything you do say may be given in evidence. Is that all clear?"

They both agreed, and she placed a small recorder on a low coffee table laden with business cards and a bowl of potpourri that had lost its scent long ago.

"The time is three-oh-seven on Sunday, 11th February. Detective Chief Inspector Joan Tebbutt with Wendy and David Lowerson at Police Headquarters. Both have been cautioned however they understand this is not a formal interview, they are here to discuss the present situation regarding their son, Detective Constable Jack Lowerson and to provide any useful information in connection with the investigation into the death of Detective Chief Superintendent Jennifer Lucas."

She paused to ask them one final, important question.

"I'm required to check. Would either of you like to call a solicitor?"

"I don't think we need one," David replied, and Wendy nodded her agreement.

"Alright. Let me start by bringing you up to date, as I understand you've been concerned for the past three hours about Jack's whereabouts. I can assure you that he is safe and well and is in one of our custody cells, downstairs—"

"You've arrested him, again?" David burst out.

Tebbutt held up a hand, requesting that he allow her time to finish.

"Jack came down to the station of his own accord, asking to see me. I met with him and he voluntarily confessed to killing DCS Lucas. Accordingly, I have placed him in custody while our investigation is ongoing."

She let that hang on the air for a moment, watching their faces crease with twin expressions of shock.

"He *what?* No. No, that can't be right," Wendy whispered.

"Jack tells me the situation was one of self-defence," Tebbutt continued. "There was a heated argument which became physical and he was in fear of his own safety. He tells me he was forced to act or be hurt himself."

His parents stared at her, dumbfounded.

"Now, it's my job to investigate the veracity of the statement he has given to me, and we're looking at all the available evidence including DNA found at the scene," she said. "I'm hoping you'll assist me by confirming some of Jack's movements—and your own. Let's begin with yesterday morning."

"I—wait a minute, I can't believe this of Jack," his father said. "I don't care how *heated* the argument was, Jack doesn't have a violent bone in his whole body. I should know, I'm his father," he said, and his voice broke on the last word.

Tebbutt waited until he'd recovered himself, looking between the pair of them.

"I understand this is difficult," she said. "Take as long as you need."

When they seemed to have composed themselves, she continued.

"Did you see Jack at all, yesterday?"

David rubbed a hand across his forehead, trying to remember.

"Wendy, what time did I go across to see Paul and the kids?"

"About eleven," she murmured, and looked across at Joan. "David went to entertain the grandkids while I had some shopping to do."

"Those would be your other son's kids?"

"Yes, they live over in Low Fell. I took them down to Whitley Bay, for a run-out," David said.

"Nice spot," Tebbutt murmured. "How long were you there?"

"Ah, just a couple of hours because Leila had a dance class in the afternoon. I got home just after three."

"What about you, Wendy? Did you get home around the same time?"

"I think you were a bit after me, weren't you, love?" David turned to his wife. "Maybe five-ish?"

"Yes," Wendy said, vacantly. "I went to the library to exchange some books, then had a look around the shops."

"With a friend?"

"No, just on my own."

Tebbutt smiled.

"Neither of you saw Jack yesterday, other than when he was arrested in the evening?"

"No, we hadn't seen him in a few weeks," David said.

"Oh?"

Tebbutt pasted on her 'listening face', the one she had cultivated over the years to put people at ease, so they felt comfortable enough to tell her whatever popped into their heads. It was remarkable, really, what could be learned from saying nothing at all.

"Jack was like a different person," his father said, and Wendy nodded.

"He used to come over for his dinner every Wednesday night. But his new girlfriend didn't like it. We invited her to join us, but she never came. Maybe we weren't good enough for them anymore."

"That new girlfriend was DCS Lucas?" Tebbutt put in, and Wendy nodded, tight-lipped.

"He thought we were common."

"Now, love," David chided. "I'm sure that isn't what Jack thought."

"How do we know *what* he thought, Dave? I feel as though I hardly know my son anymore." She looked up at Tebbutt with wide, glassy eyes. They were of an age and, in other circumstances, Wendy could almost imagine herself sharing a glass of white wine and a scone with the woman.

Tebbutt made a sympathetic sound.

"It's hard, sometimes, when they grow up."

"It wasn't just that he had a new girlfriend," David said. "To tell you the truth, we'd have been happy for him. It was the fact she was his boss…the fact that Jack never sounded happy. He was forever cancelling plans, never spoke to us on the phone for more than a couple of minutes, it was like he had no family any more. We were worried."

"I'm sure," Tebbutt murmured, and then sighed deeply, preparing to round things up. "That's about all the questions I have, at the moment. I'll be in touch."

"That's it?" David asked. "Isn't there anything else we can do to help? Can't we—can't we see him?"

Tebbutt didn't answer directly.

"There is one thing you can do," she said, confidentially. "I understand Jack has a cat—Marbles, is it? Somebody will need to look after it. Perhaps you could do that?"

But David gave a sad shake of his head.

"Jack *did* have a cat, but I'm surprised he didn't mention that it's gone. He says it went missing but…who knows what happened. It's not around anymore, so there's no need to worry about that side of things," he said.

Tebbutt feigned surprise.

"Sorry to hear it. I suppose that's one less thing to worry about," she said, and reached across to stop the tape.

"Thank you both for your help."

CHAPTER 24

When Ryan arrived home just after four o'clock, he found the place empty, but Anna's car was still on the driveway, so his wife hadn't ventured far. The thought of curling up in bed was a tempting prospect after the day he'd had but, instead, he changed into a pair of sturdy walking boots and went in search of his wife. The wind was bracing when he stepped back outside, and he made a mental note to start planting some trees to provide a bit of shelter through the winter months. The skies were clear, though, and that first gulp of cold, crisp air into his lungs was a balm after the smoky air of the railway station. They'd built their home on high ground above the village of Elsdon and its position made it vulnerable to the elements but that was the price they paid to live somewhere that looked like a scene from an oil painting, with snow-tipped peaks spreading out across the quiet valley all the way to the Rothbury Hills and beyond.

His feet crunched against the melting snow as he followed a pathway leading him down into the valley, stepping carefully to avoid tufts of grass and mounds of partially-frozen sheep dung until he rejoined the road that ran through the centre of the village.

Almost immediately, he was spotted by one of the locals.

"Saw you on the telly, last night!" they called out.

It was disconcerting to be recognised on the street and Ryan found himself returning an awkward half-wave. When further conversation was forthcoming, he made a polite, non-committal sound but didn't stop to chat. It might be deemed anti-social, but he was in no mood to pass the time. Instead, he kept a look-out for Anna, in case she should pass him on the way, but if he was any judge he knew exactly where she would be. In times of stress, some people turn to drink or drugs, others overeat or gamble away their money.

His wife liked to learn about local history.

He took a left turn and followed the road past the village hall—which, he noted, was advertising a night of 'murder and mayhem' with a local crime writer—and followed a single-track lane leading to what looked like a dead end. However, at the end of the road there was a small heritage plaque and Ryan let himself through a wooden gate before making his way up another sharp incline that would take him to Elsdon Castle, the ancient motte and bailey fortification that overlooked the village.

There was another set of footprints in the snow and he smiled as he reached the brow of the hill to find Anna standing at the top, taking a few snaps on her smartphone. Ryan stopped a few feet short, indulging himself in a private moment so that he could admire the tall, slender woman with long, dark hair blowing in the gale. She wore a pair of bright red earmuffs he'd given her for Christmas, ones that doubled as headphones, so she could listen to her favourite power ballads from the eighties without offending the rest of society.

Whatever she was listening to at that moment must have been good, judging by the way her hips were jiggling.

Sensing his presence, she turned and her face broke into a smile.

"Hello, stranger."

"Hello back," he said, and covered the distance between them.

Anna's arms wound around his neck as he caught her up against him, burying his face in her hair, breathing in the scent of her.

"I missed you," he said, his voice muffled against the side of her neck.

Her arms tightened, holding him close. They stood there for a long moment, two living statues amongst the ancient landscape. Then he speared his fingers through her hair, pushing back the ear muffs with a lopsided grin before lowering his face to hers to kiss her mouth, her face and finally the tip of her nose.

She chuckled, nudging him away to take his hand and look out across the quiet vista.

"Lovely, isn't it?"

He nodded, turning his face up to the breeze and taking several deep breaths before he spoke again.

"Jack confessed to murder," he said, quietly.

The words were suspended on the air while Anna went through the processes of shock, all the way through to acceptance.

And back around to denial.

"I don't believe him," she decided.

Ryan turned to look at her, searching her face.

"Why do you say that?" *He'd thought the same thing, himself.* "In my experience, almost anybody is capable of extreme violence."

"I could believe that she'd accidentally fallen in the course of a struggle," Anna said. "But to take her head and smash it against a radiator? That's cold-blooded and it's personal. It shows a level of contempt. Jack isn't that person."

Such simple reasoning, he thought, but it mirrored his own.

"What's going to happen to him now?"

Ryan took her hand again and they started ambling back down the hill towards the village. He could feel the tiredness seeping into his bones and knew it was time to rest.

"Jack's in custody at the moment but, strangely, Tebbutt hasn't charged him yet."

"Even though he's confessed?"

"Mm," he said.

"Do you think she's onto something?"

Ryan opened the wooden gate for her and shut it behind them.

"Put it this way," he said. "If the roles were reversed and I was in Tebbutt's shoes, the only reason I would have for failing to charge Jack Lowerson at this point would be if I had other, more compelling evidence pointing towards a different suspect."

With that, he draped an arm around her shoulders, tucking her against the warmth of his body as they headed home.

* * *

Phillips had just closed the blackout curtains in their bedroom when he heard MacKenzie's sharp cry of pain. He rushed across the room to the small en-suite bathroom and found her lying on the floor, clutching her leg.

"Denise! What happened, love?"

He hurried over to help her, kneeling beside her on the tiles to run gentle hands over the exposed skin.

"It's just the old scar tissue," she managed, and her face was deathly pale and sweating as she fought the shooting pain that ran through her leg and up to her hip and back.

A year ago, she'd been the victim of a notorious serial killer who'd kidnapped her and held her for days before she'd escaped. Since then, she'd worked hard, every day, to rebuild her strength both physically and mentally. But though the physical scars were healing, she bore invisible scars that would never heal, memories that would never be forgotten.

Just when she thought she was winning, her treacherous body would suffer a setback like this to remind her that she would never be the same woman again.

"Let me help you up," Phillips said, gently.

"I can do it," she started to say, but she'd hurt her elbow and her lower back when the cramp had taken hold and she knew there'd be bruises in the morning. "Alright, if I could just take your hand—"

Phillips lifted her up into his arms without another word and she was too surprised to argue. For all his love of a bacon butty, her fiancé was a keen boxer and had been since childhood. He was constantly active and, judging by his sudden show of strength, he could still pack a decent punch if he wanted to.

"You've been holding out on me," she murmured.

Phillips let out a rumbling laugh as he deposited her on the bed.

"I'm just saving myself for the honeymoon," he told her, with an outrageous wiggle of his bushy eyebrows.

MacKenzie laughed, just as he'd hoped, and tugged him down onto the bed beside her, where he rubbed firm, soothing circles on her bad leg as the physiotherapist had shown them.

"I'm looking forward to it," she said. "Not long to go, now."

"You're right," he agreed, thinking of the wedding they'd planned.

She reached up to cup his cheek, running the pads of her fingers against the stubble on his chin.

"I can't wait, Frank. I never thought I'd find my soulmate in my forties."

He looked across at the vibrant, beautiful woman who had—to his endless amazement—agreed to become his wife.

"You're no spinster yet," he joked. "Besides, who says there's a time limit? Some folk meet each other when they're just kids and end up spending the rest of their lives together. Some folk only meet each other in their eighties. And, even if you'd never met me, you'd have been just fine."

MacKenzie nodded.

"I agree that I would have carried on and been happy because I'm too stubborn to do otherwise," she grinned. "But, all the same, I'm thankful every day that I met you, Frank."

"Aye, me n'all, love. I'm a lucky man."

He leaned across to bestow a gentle kiss.

"How's the leg feeling now?"

"Much better," she whispered, and took hold of the lapels of his pyjamas to give them a firm yank so that he tumbled forward into her waiting arms.

CHAPTER 25

The sun had not yet risen in the sky by the time Kayleigh-Ann Dobson made her way down to the riverside from her apartment on the south side of the Tyne. Usually, she didn't mind the early-morning twilight because it made her feel so alive to join all the other men and women making their way into the city, making their way in life.

Like in that old movie, *Working Girl.*

She was no Melanie Griffith, and this was hardly New York City, but she was still proud to join the ranks of those in paid employment, unlike so many of her generation. Besides, working at the courthouse was an interesting job. She'd seen so many people come and go over the past two years since she'd started there, people accused of crimes ranging from the most heinous to the downright bizarre. It couldn't help but make her wary of people and frightened of who might be sitting next to her on the bus or brushing past her in the street. After all, they said one in five people were psychopaths, didn't they? She was sure it was something like that.

She paused to swap her takeaway coffee cup from one hand to the other, letting the hot liquid warm her fingers. It was only a five-minute journey to work via the Millennium Bridge, which spanned the river from the Baltic Art Gallery on the south side to the courthouse on the north, but already her hands were numb.

She stopped as she reached the art gallery, a towering old converted flour mill that was now a sprawling space for new and established artists to exhibit their creations. She'd gone in once or twice but, since she'd met her feller, there'd been less time for mooching around galleries. He was the kind of man who preferred the big outdoors and they'd spent plenty of time braving the wind and rain on the beaches further north, not to mention plenty of time rocking the bedsheets inside most of the hotels in between.

She started to wonder how long it would be before they could live openly and freely, without worrying about who might see them. She wondered when he would get the divorce he'd been talking about and marry her instead.

She watched a mother hurrying along the Quayside with a little girl in tow, rushing to drop her off at nursery before she went on to work, no doubt. It reminded her of the constant juggling act her own mother had been forced to do, after her father had left them.

It made her wonder whether his wife would be forced to do that, when the time came, and Kayleigh felt a vicious stab of conscience.

Home-wrecker, it whispered.

She tried to distract herself from thoughts of what her love life might be costing others and took a hasty gulp of her coffee, burning her tongue in the process. Why should she care? She was happy—deliriously happy—and that's all that mattered. Besides, his wife was a bitch, she reminded herself. Hadn't she been miserable and unfeeling, all these years? At least, that's what he'd told her. They didn't live as a couple anymore and they hardly spoke, that's what he said.

Why then, did they have such a young child? Things couldn't have been all bad, could they?

She didn't want to think about any of that, not today.

Maybe tomorrow, or the day after.

The sun was rising as she looked out across the water and she watched the morning come alive in all its splendour, relieved to see that the bridges had been re-opened after being declared safe. Still, she waited until she'd seen a few other people crossing before she decided to take her chances. Yesterday, the courthouse had been shut down thanks to the terror alert and it had taken *hours* to get home, despite the fact she could see her apartment from the entrance to her workplace.

She yawned, then made her way towards the entrance to the bridge. It was a swing structure, elegant and curved so that when a boat passed beneath it, the underside of the bridge rotated upwards in a delicate arch. There was a bin situated halfway along and, if she timed it right as she usually did, the coffee would be finished, and she could dump the cup in there as she passed by.

Funny, the habits people developed.

She couldn't leave her front door without checking the lock at least ten times, and she couldn't step on a particular paving stone outside her apartment block without worrying that it would bring her bad luck. She didn't know why; it was one of those things, she supposed.

As Kayleigh stepped onto the Millennium Bridge, her only concern was whether she would finish her coffee by the time she reached the centre.

It would be bad luck, otherwise.

* * *

Just before eight, Ryan awoke to the sound of his mobile phone bleating out a metallic rendition of the *Indiana Jones* theme tune, wakening him from a very pleasant dream. At around six, he'd been dimly aware of Anna leaving for work in Durham and of her leaning across to kiss him, but he'd fallen into a dead sleep the moment she'd left. It was unlike him to sleep for longer than a few hours, but he acknowledged that his system needed to catch up on the deficit, otherwise he'd be of no use to anybody.

He threw out a hand and felt around the bedside table until he located the source of the offending noise and stabbed his finger on the green button to take the call.

"Ryan."

His body and mind went straight to full alert as he listened to the message from the Control Room and, within the space of ten minutes, he'd left the house and was driving back towards the city.

He put a call through to Phillips using the hands-free.

"Frank?"

"Mornin', lad," he said, between mouthfuls of toast. "I'm on my way into the office, I'll be there in time for the briefing—"

"There's been another explosion."

Phillips swallowed the bread and leaned back against the worktop in his kitchen for support.

"Where?"

"Millennium Bridge," Ryan said, and activated the blue light on his car to get past the traffic leading into the city centre. "I'm on my way now."

"We'll meet you there," Phillips said, as MacKenzie walked back into the kitchen to join him. "When did it happen?"

"Ten, fifteen minutes ago."

"There was no warning e-mail," Phillips said. "The online counter hit two million and the bridges were thoroughly checked. How—?"

"We'll find out," Ryan said. "This is worse than before, Frank. There were people on that bridge; I don't know how many. Get on to the Underwater Search and Rescue Team because we're going to need divers down there. I'll alert EOD."

* * *

A short while later, Ryan drove past his old apartment building on the Quayside and followed the narrow roads leading down to the river until he reached the courthouse, where a crowd of people had already gathered. A couple of squad cars had arrived at the scene and were doing their best to keep people back, but several bystanders had witnessed the blast and were suffering from shock, while others were in the throes of panic.

Ryan slammed out of his car and hurried towards the crowd, pushing past them until he reached the flimsy police barrier that had been erected beside the north side of the Millennium Bridge. He could feel his phone vibrating inside the pocket of his jeans and a quick glance told him it was Chief Constable Morrison.

"Ma'am?"

"Ryan, I've just heard. What's being done? I need you to get down there—"

"I'm on the scene now," he shouted above the din. "We need to close all the bridges again and put the city back on full-scale alert."

"Yes. Yes, I'll get onto that. I thought it was over," she added, brokenly. "I thought they had what they wanted—"

"We were wrong," Ryan said. There would be time enough to think about motivations later but, for now, he had a job to do. "I'll be in touch."

He slipped the phone back into his pocket.

One of the local constables spotted him and started to say something but Ryan didn't hear it. He ducked beneath the barrier and simply stared at the destruction that had been wrought, unlike anything he'd dealt with before.

It was like a war zone.

Dust and debris floated on the morning breeze like cherry blossom before falling to the earth to join the mound of detritus and human flesh that lay scattered across the narrow walkway of the bridge. Even standing a few dozen feet away from the entrance, Ryan could see the twisted remains of bodies lying broken and burned amongst what was left of their possessions; a handbag, a shoe and, in one case, a child's school bag.

Tears flooded his eyes and Ryan took several deep breaths, ordering himself to remain detached.

"…sir?"

He looked around at the first responder hovering beside him, looking to him for instructions.

"Are there any survivors?" Ryan asked.

"Just two," the constable replied, pointing towards a couple of ambulances parked further along the road. "The paramedics are helping them now. It wasn't safe for them to go onto the bridge to check the others, so we don't know for sure but, judging by the look of them, there's nothing… I don't know how many people were killed, sir, I couldn't—I couldn't tell…"

The man faltered, visibly struggling with what he'd seen, and Ryan put a hand on his arm.

"Take a breath," he advised. "Focus on action, for now. I need you to push this cordon right back and close the road in both directions, for starters."

The man nodded vigorously and hurried off to make a start.

Ryan looked across the faces of the crowd, sensing their fear and mistrust, and wondered if a murderer was amongst them. He wondered if *The Alchemist* had come down to get a front row seat and watch as they shattered lives.

And then he spotted Phillips and MacKenzie making their way towards him.

"We got here as quickly as we could," MacKenzie said, ducking beneath the barrier to join him. "What's the status?"

"I'm waiting for EOD to arrive so we can access what's left of the bridge," Ryan said. "On the face of it, there are no survivors still on the bridge. You can see that at a glance."

She looked past him towards the bridge and swallowed.

"What did we miss?" she whispered.

Before he could answer, Ryan spotted the EOD Unit arriving, fully kitted out in protective gear. Nobel had called in Sergeant Bannerman and Corporal Wilson, the other members of his unit having been dispatched to help secure the southern side of the bridge.

As Nobel approached, Ryan steered him to one side.

"I thought these bridges had been thoroughly checked," he began, working hard to rein in his anger. "You personally checked that bridge yesterday afternoon and declared it safe, then this morning there's a massacre—"

Nobel stepped forward to push his face into Ryan's and, although the man was a few inches shorter, Ryan frowned at the level of aggression swimming so close to the surface.

"Firstly, you can address me as *Captain* from now on—"

"Careful," Ryan warned, in a low tone. "Watch yourself, Nobel. You're not at the barracks, now."

"I'm not answerable to you—"

"Wrong," Ryan cut across him. "As long as I'm the Senior Investigating Officer in charge and there's a memorandum of agreement between the army and civilian law enforcement, you *are* answerable to me. And I'm asking you to provide an explanation for how this was missed."

Nobel held up a hand and paced away for a moment, seeming to bring himself under control, and Ryan realised suddenly that the man looked shaken.

He moderated his tone, to take account of it.

"Look, Gary. Mistakes can be made but I need to know what happened, here. People have died."

Nobel ran his hands through his hair and turned back with over-bright eyes.

"I don't know how it happened, okay? Is that what you want to hear? I don't bloody know how the hell this could have happened. I checked the bridge myself with one of the lads and we combed every inch of it. The local police stayed on through the night to make sure nobody tried to access the bridge between then and now, so I haven't got a clue how this could have happened."

"You must have missed it," Ryan thought aloud.

"I'm *telling* you, I checked every inch of the bridge," Nobel reiterated. "Look, Ryan. I have a wife and kids myself. If I thought we'd dropped the ball on this, I'd tell you, believe me."

Ryan searched his face and gave a brief nod.

"Then somebody slipped beneath the radar and accessed the bridge after it was checked, yesterday afternoon. Who checked it with you?"

"I had Kev with me," Nobel said, gesturing towards his corporal who was talking to Phillips. "He knows his stuff, Ryan. We all do."

"Alright, Gary. I need you to make the area safe so that we can access it and make a start identifying the victims."

Nobel looked across at the bridge.

"I've seen worse when I've been on tour," he said, bleakly. "You're taught to expect that, to prepare for it, because you're on active duty. Nobody goes to Afghanistan and thinks they'll come home without having seen some shit. But at home?" He shook his head. "Up until now, we've always disposed of any threat before anybody was hurt. We got complacent," he said, with a catch to his voice.

Ryan put a hand briefly on his shoulder, then moved off to deal with the fall-out.

CHAPTER 26

While the EOD Unit went to work on the bridge, Ryan went over to speak to the two survivors who were being treated for minor cuts and bruises inside an ambulance before being transferred to hospital.

"Can I have a minute?" he asked the senior paramedic.

"I need to get them over to the RVI," she said, referring to the closest hospital. "They have shrapnel injuries. You can speak to them later."

"I only need a minute," he said.

"That's all you've got."

Ryan thanked her and followed the ramp onto the back of the ambulance, where he found a woman and her young daughter being tended to by another paramedic. Despite the gash on the woman's face and the cuts on the little girl's arms and legs, his heart soared to see them.

"Hello," he said. "I'm DCI Ryan, from the Criminal Investigation Department."

The woman's eyes flickered briefly over the tall man with the jet-black hair, then fell away again as she bore down against the pain at her temple. The little girl stared at him with wide green eyes, and then pointed to her leg.

"I've got a Frozen plaster on my leg," she told him, tapping the large bandage covering her calf that was emblazoned with the cartoon likeness of two princesses from the Disney movie.

"I can see that," he said, coming a little further into the ambulance. "You're very brave. What's your name?"

"Amelia," she told him, shyly. He did, after all, resemble so many of the cartoon princes she'd seen in her favourite films.

"Hi Amelia," he said. "I'm a policeman. Do you mind if I ask you and your mum some questions about what happened?"

She looked across at her mother's face, which was still drawn with shock.

"I think my mummy's poorly," she said.

"I'll tell you what I can," her mother said, in a voice barely above a whisper.

"Thank you," Ryan said, putting his hand on hers for a second. "Is there anyone I can contact for you?"

"Her husband's on his way to the hospital," the paramedic put in. "She's not critical but he's meeting us there, so I don't want to wait too long."

Ryan nodded.

"I understand, and I won't keep you. I only want to ask one thing, for now. Did you see anyone acting strangely as you were crossing the bridge? Anyone who seemed out of sorts?"

The mother, whose name turned out to be Carole, closed her eyes and shook her head.

"There were just a few other people walking over the bridge, mostly from the Gateshead side towards Newcastle. There couldn't have been more than four or five people, including us."

"Alright," he said. "Do you remember if any of them were wearing a backpack, or carrying a large bag of any kind?"

"I lost my bag," Amelia complained, and Ryan thought of the little school satchel he'd seen lying amongst the debris. He'd thought the child it belonged to might be counted amongst the dead, so to find her sitting there chatting to him was an overwhelming relief.

"I'm sorry to hear that," he said softly. "Maybe you'll get a new one. Do you remember seeing anyone else carrying a satchel or a big bag?"

The girl screwed up her face as she tried to remember, then shook her head.

"No, just normal bags like my mummy's."

"Okay. Do you remember seeing anybody running away from the bridge?"

But the little girl had lost interest and her mother just shook her head.

"It was still dark, you see, and I was in a hurry. I wasn't really paying attention."

Ryan thanked them both and wished them well, promising to return to the hospital to check up on them. He was making a mental note to purchase a new school bag for the little girl when her mother called out to him.

"Do you know if the woman in the red coat survived?"

Ryan frowned, thinking of the remains he had seen on the bridge.

"Was she a friend of yours?"

"No, no. I don't even know her name, but I see her almost every morning around the same time because we both use the bridge each day to get to the north side."

"And she was there today?"

"Yes, I saw her sipping a coffee outside the Baltic," she said. "She's always got a coffee in her hand, too. We passed her, so I was wondering if she was on the bridge behind us as we were reaching the north side."

"I don't know," Ryan said, honestly. "But I'll try to find out."

* * *

By the time Ryan finished speaking to Amelia and her mother, the EOD Unit had dispatched a robotic device to check over the remains of what had been the Millennium Bridge and pronounced it safe to cross. Ryan decided against making any snide remarks about that and joined Faulkner, their senior CSI, and Captain Nobel in a walk-through of what was now a major crime scene in addition to being a national incident.

They wore protective polypropylene suits over padded vests and helmets and when they took their first steps beyond the police barrier they could only be grateful that the weather was not warm. Their rubber boots skidded against the slippery metal floor of the bridge, which was coated in a layer of melting ice and rubble and, through the dust, they could see the sharp ends of the nails and ball bearings that had been packed into the explosive device.

"The bomb was designed to cause serious damage, this time," Nobel said, as evenly as he could. "Not only was the blast zone much larger but you've got all this crap packed inside it."

He scuffed the toe of his boot against the nails coating the floor.

"Where was it hidden?" Faulkner asked.

"We're fairly certain it was inside that rubbish bin in the middle of the bridge," he said, pointing a gloved hand towards a burnt-out shell. "We emptied it yesterday and checked it inside and out, so something had to have been planted sometime after four o'clock, yesterday afternoon."

"Watch where you step," Ryan murmured, and all three men fell silent as they entered the main blast site. They stopped to allow Faulkner to photograph each section from different angles, moving carefully so as not to disturb too much or to stand on anything that looked as though it had once belonged to a person.

Ryan's system wanted to revolt, to reject the sight of torn flesh carpeting the floor beneath his feet but he continued, boxing away his feelings, for there was work to be done here, and a killer to be found.

He'd counted three separate bodies, so far.

"Two male, one female," he murmured, and Faulkner nodded, stooping down to capture a close-up of one of the victim's faces to be used for identification.

"There were eyewitness reports of at least one person falling into the water," Ryan said, pausing again to allow Faulkner to photograph the third body of a man whose face was covered in nails. "The woman who survived—Carole—tells me there may be another woman in a red coat. I haven't seen anyone matching that description, so far. Have you?"

Nobel said nothing, but made as if to hurry ahead.

"Wow! Gary, we take each section at a time," Faulkner reminded him, with a measure of irritation. The man was surely used to their procedure, by now.

"Sorry," he muttered. "I thought I'd go ahead and check to see if we'd missed anyone."

"The divers are suited up," Ryan said, and bobbed his head towards a boat moored off the south side of the river holding a team of five or six police divers from the Marine Unit. "They'll start searching to see if there's anyone to find."

"I don't envy them going down there at this time of year," Faulkner said.

"They're used to it," Ryan murmured, and raised a hand to acknowledge the sergeant in charge of the unit, who he had worked with several times before.

"Careful," Nobel warned them, as they neared the epicentre of the blast. "The bridge is holding but it's much smaller than the others and there are no guarantees it won't buckle. The bomb took a chunk out of the centre."

Ryan and Faulkner stepped to one side as they neared the centre of the bridge, swaying a bit in the strong wind that blew in from the seaward side and swirled up small clouds of dust. They could see a jagged hole where the bin once stood and, if they edged closer, they could see rippling water beneath.

"Why this bridge?" Faulkner asked. "There was nothing to be gained from it."

Ryan disagreed.

"The explosion went up this morning at eight-oh-nine. It's an odd time to pick, if the bomber had set a timer. That has to throw up the possibility of a remote-controlled device. What do you say, Nobel?"

"I agree," he said. "We've taken what was left of the device and we'll do our best to reconstruct a diagram, with Faulkner's help, but it makes logical sense that it would be manually detonated."

Ryan had already asked Phillips to speak to the security staff at the courthouse, to see if their CCTV cameras had picked up anything from the bridge that morning, or last night, and would do the same with all the local businesses that might have footage of what happened.

He turned to Nobel and Faulkner but, just as he opened his mouth to speak, he felt a buzzing in his jacket pocket and pulled out his phone to check the caller ID.

"Yates?" he said, stepping away from the others to find a more secluded spot.

"I've just had a call from Bev at *The Enquirer*," Melanie said. "She was absolutely distraught, and it took a while to calm her down enough to understand what she was talking about. They've just received another e-mail from *The Alchemist*. I'm sending it through to you now."

"Thanks," Ryan ended the call, and then waited for what felt like the longest five seconds of his life until the e-mail pinged into his inbox. His eyes narrowed at the content:

> *You were warned not to interfere with the website.*
> *Did you think I wouldn't notice that you rigged the bitcoin counter?*
> *The Millennium Bridge is the price you must pay.*

Ryan read, then re-read the e-mail before placing an urgent call to Chief Constable Morrison followed by his contact at GCHQ. To his knowledge, nobody had tampered with the website or the bitcoin counter; nobody had dared. But, if some trumped-up Whitehall bigwig had gone over his head and fiddled with it, they'd have him to answer to.

CHAPTER 27

By one o'clock, there were four confirmed victims of the Millennium Bridge Attack, as it had come to be known in the press. All seven bridges connecting Gateshead and Newcastle via the city centre remained closed while the threat was ongoing and the transport network ground to a halt once again, forcing people to revert to an earlier time when cars and trains had not been available. They walked or cycled through the streets, bundled into woollen coats and scarves as the temperature remained steadily below zero.

There was an uncomfortable silence in the two cities as people waited, trapped in a kind of purgatory where they were unable to continue with their ordinary lives and yet could do nothing to help themselves. As the situation dragged on, businesses closed their doors and the police were stretched to their limits as complaints of theft and looting began to trickle in and they were called upon to keep the peace.

Phillips ruminated on the subject as they drove the short distance from the Quayside to the mortuary.

"Now, just hear me out," he began, and Ryan rolled his eyes. "If I were the kind of low-life degenerate who decided to go looting the minute my city was in trouble, why the bloody hell would I go and nick off with a pair of Nike high-tops?"

"Maybe it was the first thing they saw."

Phillips carried on.

"All I'm sayin' is, if you woke up and thought, 'whey aye, I'll gan' doon the toon and nick a few bob's worth of stuff while nobody's lookin',' why wouldn't you choose a jewellery shop? Or one of the fancy department stores? Why the chuff would anybody go and steal a pair of trainers?"

"Maybe they needed shoes," Ryan suggested.

"Aye, but if you needed to steal a pair of shoes you could do that any time," Phillips argued. "This here is prime time for thieves, at the moment. It's an opportunity to have their pick o' the lot and they're still goin' for neon green high-tops. Some people have got no idea."

Ryan turned into the hospital car park and brought the car to a stop inside one of the bays before turning to his sergeant.

"There's no accounting for taste."

Phillips let out a *harrumph* and followed him towards the service entrance.

* * *

They descended into the bowels of the hospital basement and followed a long, stifling corridor towards a set of security doors operated by a digital keypad entry system. Ryan stopped to type in the passcode and swore when he realised it was out of date.

"Do you remember what the new code is?"

Phillips tugged on his lower lip and screwed up his face in an ostentatious manner, before shaking his head.

"Not a clue, son."

"Right," Ryan muttered, and raised a fist to bang on the double doors. Sometimes, the old-fashioned methods worked best.

A moment later, Doctor Jeffrey Pinter's long face appeared around the doorway.

"Forget the code, did you?" he exclaimed.

"Obviously," Phillips muttered, a bit irritably. He didn't mind Pinter so much, these days, but he had an unfortunate manner that was prone to rub him up the wrong way.

They followed the pathologist inside the open-plan mortuary and scribbled their names in the log book before fastening themselves into a couple of visitors' lab coats. They looked around the room at the line of metal gurneys and then back into Pinter's expectant face.

"Where are they?" Ryan asked.

"Given the unique circumstances in which they were found, I took the decision to assign each victim to a private autopsy room," he explained. "I've got my best people working on them."

"Give us an overview, Jeff."

Pinter tucked his hands into the pockets of his lab coat and rocked back on his heels, as though preparing to deliver a speech.

"Well, as you know, there are four in total. The first three—two men and a woman—were found on the bridge, I understand, while the fourth body of a woman was recovered from the water about an hour later. Dreadful business," he said.

"Cause of death?" Ryan asked, though it seemed an obvious question.

"Naturally, we haven't had nearly enough time to complete full post-mortem examinations and the cause may be slightly different in each case. However, given the nature of their injuries, I'll venture to say that each victim suffered massive cardiac arrest and cerebral aneurysm following multiple injuries to major arteries and organs including the heart, liver and lungs."

He paused to look at each of them in turn.

"I must warn you before we go in that their bodies have been, quite literally, torn apart by nails and other jagged metal objects. It does not make for pleasant viewing."

"We didn't come down here for the laughs," Ryan pointed out, while Phillips shuffled his feet. All his years as a murder detective hadn't made him any less squeamish when it came to viewing cadavers.

"I'm sure we can handle it," Ryan was saying. "It's important to see what we're dealing with."

Phillips made a weak sound of agreement and followed the two taller men towards a side-wing of the mortuary, keeping his eyes straight ahead and focused on the white-washed wall at the other end of the room.

* * *

"This man has been identified as John Edward Walsh," Pinter said, as they entered the chilly interior of Examination Room A and came to stand around the shrouded figure of a man of average height and build.

"Dental records?" Ryan queried.

"Yes, we were able to do a fairly quick match. He's a barrister, originally from Middlesbrough. There's an address on file, so it should be straightforward informing his next of kin."

He made it sound so clinical, Ryan thought. But then, that was the man's vocation. He supposed it was necessary to maintain a degree of professional detachment to get the job done.

"There've been hundreds of calls coming in already from relatives wanting to know if their loved ones are safe," Ryan said. "Most will have heard from them, by now, but there's bound to be somebody we'll need to call back."

Informing the next of kin was an unenviable task, one he dreaded and felt obligated to perform in equal measure.

"John suffered the most trauma to his back, as is the case with most of these victims, because he was facing away from the blast when it happened," Pinter told them. "Shall we take a look?"

Before Phillips could steady himself, the paper blanket was peeled back to reveal a man covered in a series of serrated tears. It was a hard sight to behold but, remarkably, the man's face had escaped unharmed.

Ryan looked down at his serene expression and felt immeasurable sorrow for a man who could not have been much older than himself—somewhere in his mid or late thirties—and wore a wedding ring. Anger followed swiftly as he thought of whoever had snatched away this man's life, before he had even truly lived. He would not grow to be an old man and look back upon his youth with the wisdom of age. That privilege had been stolen away by a person who put their own desires above all else, and consigned the lives of those who got in the way to the scrap heap.

"Show me the rest," he said.

* * *

It was half an hour before they reached the final examination room and, when they stepped inside, they found a mortuary technician already working on the body of a woman somewhere in her mid-twenties.

"This is the only one we haven't been able to identify through online dental records," Pinter told them. "It may be that she hasn't been registered in a while, or it could be a glitch on the system, but we'll keep trying."

Ryan nodded. "No ID or mobile phone found on the body?"

Pinter shook his head. "We didn't find anything in her pockets, so my best guess is she had a handbag that hasn't been recovered yet."

"Let me know when the dental records come through," Ryan said, coming to stand beside her bloated body while Phillips chose to remain at a respectable distance. It was a wise man who knew himself and his own limitations, and Frank Phillips was a very wise man indeed.

"As you can plainly see, this young lady suffered the worst damage of all," Pinter said. He took out a retractable pointer and used the tip to show them a series of burns, heavy contusions and lacerations to her face, neck and torso. The wounds were deep, slicing through her body like bullet holes.

"It looks as though she was directly in the blast zone," Ryan remarked.

Pinter nodded.

"I'd say so, judging from the extent of her injuries. She's also the only victim to really suffer serious damage to her face and torso, whereas the others sustained injuries consistent with an entrance wound through the back, or the kidney region."

"It would explain how she fell in the water," Phillips added. "The force of the blast near the centre of the bridge would have been enough to throw her back and over the barrier."

Ryan agreed.

"Any word on the CCTV in the area?"

Phillips nodded.

"The head of security at the courthouse is sending the footage directly to me by the end of the day, as are several local businesses. Haven't had much joy getting hold of the security person at the Baltic Art Gallery but I'll chase them up. The Council bloke is already feeding me through everything from the past few days, so he says he'll get straight on to the cameras beside the Millennium Bridge as soon as he can."

Ryan turned back to look down into the ravaged face of the young woman lying stiffly before them and remembered something.

"Pinter, what was she wearing when she came in?"

He crossed the room to bring up a computer record on the screen.

"The clothes have been transferred to Faulkner's team for testing but I've got pictures of them on file, here," he said.

Ryan leaned across to look at the images and his eye was drawn immediately to a water-damaged and heavily torn red wool coat.

"I think this could be the woman that Carole—one of the survivors—was telling me about," Ryan said. "She may be able to tell us more about this Jane Doe."

"I can tell you one other thing," Pinter said, sadly. "She was pregnant. About six weeks gone, I'd say."

"Poor lass," Phillips muttered.

"She may be the key," Ryan said, channelling his emotions into action, as he so often did. He wasn't sure he'd cope with the work that they did, otherwise.

"Why do you say that?" Pinter asked.

"Because she had a routine. If a bomber wanted to kill somebody specific, they would need to know if the target had a regular routine to maximise the chances of an attack being successful. She's the only one, so far as we know, who had a routine like clockwork."

Ryan took one final look at the woman, committing her face to memory, before turning back to the other two men in the room.

"So we don't have any of the woman's personal effects?"

"As Jeff said, there was no phone or purse found in her pockets," Phillips replied. "Nothing found at the scene we can tie to her either."

"Guess we'll have to do some proper detecting, Frank."

"'Bout time," Phillips joked. "I'm gettin' too old for running from one bridge to the next, carrying folk off trains…"

"Keeps you fit," Pinter said.

"Aye, so does a quality night in with the soon-to-be Mrs Phillips."

On that note, Ryan made a hasty beeline for the door.

CHAPTER 28

Since they were already at the hospital, Ryan and Phillips made a detour to the Accident and Emergency Ward which was a department they had come to know very well over the years. As they stepped inside its familiar entrance, they recognised the sights and smells of illness that were as familiar to the doctors and nurses of the hospital as the scent of tuna casserole was to the officers of Northumbria CID.

"Hello," Ryan said, as they reached the reception desk. "I wonder if you could tell me if a patient has been admitted by the name of Carole Fentiman. She has her daughter with her, Amelia."

He showed her his warrant card, which she took the trouble to read.

"Just give me a moment, Chief Inspector, and I'll see where she's been taken."

She tapped a few keys and then directed them to one of the observation rooms, down a corridor to their left.

They thanked her and followed the corridor around until they reached the right door. After a brief knock, they heard Carole calling out for them to enter.

"Hello again," she said, and Ryan was pleased to see her looking considerably better than she had done in the back of the ambulance.

Her husband rose to his feet and crossed the room to greet them.

"Euan Fentiman," he introduced himself and ran an eye over their warrant cards. Ryan could hardly blame him; in the space of a morning, he'd almost lost his wife and daughter.

"Where's Amelia?" Ryan asked.

"They're checking her over in the Paediatric Department," Carole explained. "They did an x-ray and found there was still a fragment of nail lodged in her hip area, so they may have to operate to get it out."

Ryan watched her battle tears.

"She's sleeping at the moment," her father added. "I'm going to head up to see her again in a little while."

"She's a very brave little girl," Ryan said, and was sorry he hadn't had a chance to find a new satchel for her. Instead, he'd made a quick stop by the gift shop on their way across and had managed to find a colouring pad and pencils featuring a variety of Disney characters.

He held out the carrier bag to the girl's father, feeling awkward.

"I—ah, I got these for Amelia," he said. "I hope she likes them. Tell her we wanted to say, 'thank you' for all her help, earlier today."

Her parents smiled while Phillips looked at him as though he'd sprouted three heads.

"That's so kind of you to think of her," Carole said. "It'll distract her from the pain in her legs."

Ryan stuck his hands in his pockets and dragged himself back to the point.

"I hope you don't mind but I need to ask you some more questions, if you're feeling up to it?"

"She's very tired," Euan began, but Carole reached across to take his hand.

"I'm alright for a little while longer," she said, giving his hand a quick squeeze to remind him she was all there, in one piece.

She turned back to the two detectives.

"I'm one of the lucky ones," she said quietly. "But I know that there were others who didn't come out alive. How many were there?"

The media had already reported there were four victims, so Ryan felt able to confirm that much.

"Four people lost their lives today," he said quietly.

Carole's eyes welled up.

"Was the woman in the red coat one of them?"

Ryan nodded.

"We believe so, yes."

Carole continued to grip her husband's hand and he covered her fingers with his own in an instinctive, protective gesture.

"May I ask how you knew her? Did you happen to know her name?" Ryan had already asked her the same question before, but she'd been traumatised after a recent shock, so it was always worth asking again.

"No, I never knew her name, but I saw her every Monday, Wednesday and Friday for the past five months. Those are the days I drop Amelia off at pre-school," she explained. "I think she worked at the courthouse, though, because I seem to remember seeing her walking up the steps there once or twice after crossing the bridge."

Ryan's spirits lifted. Here was something they could use.

"That's great," he said, encouragingly. "Just carry on telling me anything you can remember."

"Alright," Carole said, and reached across to take a sip of water while she thought back to the young woman she'd seen almost daily. "She always wore that coat or a light beige anorak, if the weather wasn't so bad. Both of them looked designer, to me, and she was always very smartly turned out. I remember feeling like such a mumsy frump, by comparison," she confessed.

Her husband lifted her hand to his lips and kissed it.

"A few months ago, she wore her hair in a much longer style," she continued, getting into the swing of things. "But recently, I'd say in the past two or three months, she had it styled shorter and it was coloured blonde. I thought it suited her; fun but professional, you know? She looked as though she worked in an office somewhere and, as I say, I'd seen her going into the courthouse once or twice."

"Did you always see her around the same time?" Phillips asked.

Carole nodded.

"Yes, I tended to be at the bridge for around eight-fifteen because by the time I walk the rest of the way to Amelia's nursery I'm right on time and don't need to wait around outside with her. I always saw the woman in the red coat on the bridge or just walking towards it around then, too."

"Was anyone ever with her?" Ryan asked.

"Not that I remember," Carole said, doubtfully. "But I can't be sure about that because I wasn't really looking out for it, if you know what I mean."

"I do. Don't worry," Ryan reassured her. "You're being very helpful. Did you ever happen to see anyone acting strangely around her, or do you remember seeing her arguing with anyone?"

It was a long shot, but he had to ask.

"No, I'm sorry," she said. "I only ever saw her walking over the bridge and sometimes stopping to chuck her coffee cup in the bin."

Their ears pricked up.

"The bin in the middle of the bridge?"

"Yes, she often seemed to carry a takeaway coffee as she was crossing," Carole said.

"Starbucks, Nero?"

"No, it didn't have a logo, so I guess it might have come from one of those little artisan places."

"Another one," Phillips muttered, and wondered if the place sold quinoa salads, too.

"You've been a real help," Ryan told them. "Thank you both and, Carole, take care of yourself."

"I just keep wondering why it wasn't me," she said, huskily. "I feel so guilty walking away from that, when others didn't."

"You have nothing to feel guilty about," Ryan told her. "Don't question why, just be happy that things have turned out the way they did. You have a beautiful daughter and a lovely family. Thanks to whatever lucky star, you'll be going home with them very soon. That's exactly as it should be."

Her husband rose from his chair and shook their hands.

"I hope you find whoever did this," he said.

"Never fear," Ryan told him. "It's only a matter of time."

* * *

Before they left, Ryan made another minor detour to the Intensive Care Unit, where he knew Ben Potter had been admitted following emergency bypass surgery. They spoke to the consultant on the ward, who told them Potter had a strong chance of survival, and they were satisfied that was the best news they could hope for.

When they stepped back outside into the chilly February afternoon, the sun was already slipping back into the horizon, leaving a blazing trail of amber-red light in its wake. They paused to watch the sunset for a moment, rubbing their hands together for warmth while they thought of all the misdeeds and tragedies that went undetected beneath the moon and stars.

"Helps, doesn't it?" Phillips said, as the first star popped into the cardinal blue sky above their heads.

"To watch the stars? Yeah, it gives a bit of perspective."

"We're all nothing, really, in the grand scheme of things," Phillips mused. "Not in comparison with the stars and planets. But, all the same, I've been thinking about what you said earlier."

"Which bit?"

"The bit about the girl in the red coat being the only one to have a regular routine. When we were in there chatting to Carole and Euan Fentiman, it struck me that she's another one who had a regular routine, isn't she?"

Ryan had thought of that.

"Yes, she is. And if, for whatever reason, she was a target, then our bomber will be angry that he missed the mark."

"Worth putting some surveillance on her, just for a couple of days?"

Ryan thought of the money and resources, then nodded.

"Make the call, Frank. I'd rather be safe than sorry."

CHAPTER 29

It was after dark by the time they arrived back at Police Headquarters and its cheap strobe lighting cast an unflattering, garish light over the tired faces of the task force assigned to Operation Alchemist.

"At first, our perpetrator was a terrorist," Ryan said, once they had reconvened. "Now, he's a killer."

Ryan moved to stand beside the long whiteboard at the front of the room, which now displayed images of the victims of the Millennium Bridge Attack as they had been in life, with their names written in bold black lettering beneath. Pinter had come through with the dental records for the woman in the red coat, whose name turned out to be Kayleigh-Ann Dobson, and Ryan added her name beneath an image of her taken from her driver's licence.

"If we assume that the same person who bombed the Tyne and High Level bridges is also responsible for killing four people and injuring two others today, they now have these people on their conscience," he said, rapping a knuckle against the wall. "First off, we have John Walsh. He was a thirty-eight-year-old barrister, husband and father. Next, there's Pritesh Joshi, a forty-one-year-old IT consultant, who was also married with children. Thirdly, we have Anouk Paradis, a twenty-one-year-old translator who was single, as far as we know. Finally, this was Kayleigh-Ann Dobson, a twenty-three-year-old receptionist at the courthouse."

He turned to them with serious eyes.

"Remember their faces," he said. "Because these are the people we're fighting for."

"Do you think it's the same person?" MacKenzie queried. "The MO is similar, especially coming so soon after the other bridges went

191

up, but there was no advance warning message, no demand for bitcoins. There's no motive."

"Other than the e-mail *The Enquirer* received after the event," Ryan said. "That's why I want us to focus on these four people, and to add another name to the list."

He tacked up a picture of Carole Fentiman, set a little apart from the others.

"Carole Fentiman is a thirty-nine-year-old, married mother of one, a little girl called Amelia who also survived the bridge attack," he told them. "They're both recovering in hospital but it's down to pure chance that they came out of that alive when the others didn't. That means they were potential targets and I believe they should be counted."

"You think the target was one of the people on the bridge?" This, from Corporal Wilson.

"I think we have to consider that as a strong possibility," Ryan said. "The attack is a departure from the other bridges and it's an escalation in behaviour. Remember, our bomber hadn't hurt anyone before—"

"Sue might have been more badly hurt," Phillips pointed out and glanced across at Sergeant Bannerman, who had a small bandage on her left cheek and similar patches on her knees which were hidden beneath a loose pair of trousers.

"I've had worse injuries taking my niece to the soft play," she joked, and got a few laughs from around the room.

Ryan smiled.

"Besides, I assume our bomber would have known the first charge was not enough to cause serious damage because it was intended as a warning. The bomb this morning had a very different purpose."

There were nods around the room.

"It's still possible that we've got a copycat on our hands," MacKenzie thought aloud. "It wouldn't be the first time somebody has taken advantage of an existing crisis to further their own ends."

"Aye, but to make a bomb like that, they'd need to have the components already at hand and that's no easy job," Wilson replied.

"There's no way a copycat could have put together a nail bomb like that overnight without some forward planning."

Ryan agreed.

"There's something else to bear in mind, too. I've had a word with GCHQ, who've been looking into the bitcoin website and monitoring any movement there. In their opinion, the website is not genuine. Our own team agrees."

There were a few frowns around the room as the team considered the new information that had come to light.

"You're telling us the e-mail about the counter being rigged was correct?" MacKenzie said, leaning forward to rest her forearms on her knees. "It never hit two million?"

Ryan shook his head.

"I asked my contact at GCHQ whether they had gone over my head on this and falsely inflated the counter to make it look as though it had reached two million, to prevent another explosion. They say they didn't and I'm minded to believe them."

"It wouldn't have helped," Yates muttered. "It would only have made the bomber angry when he found out the bitcoins weren't there and that would risk repercussions."

"Exactly," Ryan said. "I asked them whether it's possible that some misguided hacker tried to alter the counter to make sure the target was reached, but they're telling me the website hasn't been interfered with from outside; they're telling me it's been manipulated from *within*."

"Hold on," Phillips held up his hands. "Just hang on a minute, here. You're telling me the bomber fiddled about with his own website? Why would he want to do that? I thought they wanted to get their hands on the cash?"

"Perhaps that's only what he wanted us to think," Ryan said, and the light began to dawn. "What if everything that happened on the Tyne Bridge and the High Level Bridge was just an elaborate cover for what they always planned to do on the Millennium Bridge?"

The clock on the wall ticked loudly in the ensuing silence.

"By making it look as though the counter hit two million, *The Alchemist* let us believe the conditions had been met and the threat was over. The bridges were checked and re-opened, business as usual," Ryan said. "We were lulled into a false sense of security because we believed it was over and, in any event, he'd send us a warning before anything else happened. That was our mistake."

Ryan turned and walked back to look at each of the faces on the wall.

"We need to look at these five people because, if I'm right, one of them's the reason for all of this."

"In that case, let's get to work," Phillips said, and rubbed his hands together.

* * *

As the room disbanded to begin working on each of the tasks Ryan had assigned, Tom Faulkner took his chance to have a private word.

"I've got the team working on the samples we took from the bridge this morning," he said, and Ryan nodded as he added a few significant timings to the murder board.

"Mm, yeah, thanks, Tom. Just let me know when you find anything important."

"Right."

Faulkner still lingered there, and Ryan sent him a sideways glance.

"Something else on your mind?"

Faulkner tapped his fingers against the side of the folder he held in his hand and shuffled from side to side, looking extremely uncomfortable.

"Spit it out, man," Ryan told him. "You're making me sea-sick."

Faulkner took a quick glance around the room to check nobody was listening and then lowered his voice to a stage whisper.

"You, ah, you know I've been working on the Lucas case," he said. Ryan nodded.

"I…well, I shouldn't—"

Ryan held up a hand to stop him.

"Tom, I don't want you stepping outside professional boundaries…"

"We found another set of DNA," Faulkner said, in a rush of words. "Tissue and hair found on Lucas' body that didn't belong to her."

"Who—?"

"We're running it now. But, Ryan, if another person was there, Lowerson might not have done it."

Having already said too much, Faulkner tapped his nose and then scurried from the room, leaving Ryan to mull over the news.

The question remained: if not Jack, then who?

CHAPTER 30

John Walsh Esq. had lived in a very comfortable home in South Shields, close to the seafront. When Ryan and Phillips parked on the kerb outside, they could see the remains of a thawing snowman on the front lawn and wondered if he had made it with his kids over the weekend.

"Ready?" Ryan murmured.

"Aye, best get it over with," Phillips replied, with a heavy heart.

They steadied themselves while they waited for somebody to come to the door, preparing the right words to say, if there were any 'right' words that could be used to convey the worst possible news.

When the door opened, a boy of around ten or eleven stood in the doorway wearing an *Avengers* t-shirt and a pair of scuffed jeans.

"Who are you?"

"Alfie! Wait, I'll get the—oh."

His mother hurried downstairs but stopped on the bottom step as she saw them framed in the fizzy orange glow of the streetlamps outside.

"Alfie, go and look after your sister," she said, in a dull voice.

"I don't want—"

"For once, please do as you're *told*," she snapped, and then put a hand to her eyes as he stormed off towards the lounge and shut the door with a slam.

"Mrs Walsh?"

She nodded, and tears began to spill from her eyes as she clutched the bannister rail.

"My name is DCI Ryan, and this is DS Phillips," Ryan said, as gently as he could. "We're very sorry to inform you that your husband, John, was killed in an explosion on the Millennium Bridge earlier today. Our sincerest condolences."

It didn't matter how many times he'd said the words, nor how trite they sounded, his sympathy remained real.

She said nothing at first, just continued to stare at them while tears flowed freely and silently down her cheeks.

"I can't let the children—I can't let them see me like this," she lifted trembling hands to her face and tried to stem the flow of tears.

"Can we come in, love?" Phillips asked, and simply stepped inside to take her arm while Ryan shut the door behind them. "Let's go into the kitchen and sit down, shall we? Is it this way?"

She nodded helplessly and leaned against his arm, allowing herself to be led through to a room away from the children, for now.

Once they stepped inside the bright family kitchen, Phillips settled her into one of the antique pine chairs and Ryan grabbed a box of tissues he spotted on the countertop, which he offered to her.

"I don't believe it," she whispered, after long minutes. She looked between them with pleading eyes. "Are you sure it's him? It could be someone else."

"We're sure, love," Phillips told her. "But you'll need to come down and make a formal identification, when you feel able."

Her whole body shuddered as she succumbed to grief and Ryan put a hand over hers.

"Is there anybody we can contact? Perhaps one of the children's grandparents could come?"

"My—my parents are in Kent and John's are too old; it'll kill them, when they hear... There's my sister. She lives in Alnwick," she mumbled.

"Do you have the number?"

Ryan put a call through to her sister, who promised to come down straight away.

"She's on her way now," he said. "Mrs Walsh, I'm sorry, but I need to ask you some questions. Do you think you can manage it?"

She pressed her fingers to her lips.

"Will it help?"

"It might."

She nodded.

"Thank you," he said, and came to sit beside her.

"Can you tell me, was it usual for your husband to cross the Millennium Bridge every morning?"

She dabbed her face with a tissue and then clutched it in her hands as she thought.

"Yes, I think John liked to park his car on the south side and walk the rest of the way into work because it saved him having to drive through the centre of Newcastle on his way home."

"Was he due to be in court this morning?"

She seemed not to hear him at first, and Ryan was about to ask her again, when she finally answered.

"Ah, I'm not sure. He's in court most days, but his chambers are right next door to the courthouse, so he didn't have far to travel most of the time."

"I see," Ryan murmured, and exchanged a glance with Phillips. Here, they had found another victim with a regular routine and it made their job all the harder.

"Would you say your husband had any enemies? Was there anyone who might have wanted to hurt him?"

Her eyes were red and swollen when she looked up, but they were fierce.

"John was a good, kind man. He never made an enemy in his life—"

"Alright," Ryan murmured, ever mindful of the fact she was in the throes of grief and required careful handling. "Did John ever mention any cases that gave him cause for alarm? A difficult client, perhaps?"

She pinched the bridge of her nose between thumb and forefinger and tried to think clearly.

"John never really spoke about his cases," she whispered. "I'm sorry, I-I can't take it in."

"Alright, Mrs Walsh," Ryan said. "We'll leave it there."

Just then, the door to the kitchen opened and two children looked on at them with frank suspicion. They saw their mother's tears and hurried across to her.

"Mummy! What's the matter? Where's Daddy?"

She wrapped her arms around them and buried her face in their soft hair, holding them close as she wondered how she could say the words that would change their lives forever.

"Daddy's gone to heaven," she managed. "A bad person hurt him, and he's gone to heaven."

Ryan and Phillips left them to their grief but waited on the kerb outside her house until the woman's sister arrived, twenty minutes later.

Only then did he start the engine.

"It probably isn't real to them," Ryan said, angrily. "To the person who killed those kids' father, he wasn't real. They just pressed a button and, *boom!* John Walsh is gone, alongside three other people."

"If they thought about it too much, they wouldn't be able to go through with it," Phillips agreed. "It's a coward's way."

Ryan released the handbrake.

"Time to make our next stop," he said, grimly.

* * *

Pritesh Joshi had lived in a smart area of Newcastle known as Gosforth, not far from the racecourse. As MacKenzie and Yates pulled up outside his large, newly-built property they found it brimming with people and cars, which spilled out of the driveway and onto the paved cul-de-sac outside.

"Shit," MacKenzie muttered. "This is all we need."

"Do you want to come back later?" Yates suggested, peering through the windshield. "It looks like they're having a party."

MacKenzie drummed her fingers on the steering wheel, then shook her head.

"His wife needs to be told, today."

They made their way across the darkened street and up to the front door, where they heard the sound of merriment coming from within.

"Here goes," MacKenzie said, and rang the doorbell.

It took several attempts before anybody answered and, even then, it was not Mrs Joshi but a much older lady who looked them up and down, then shouted back into the house in a stream of Hindi.

They stood awkwardly on the doorstep for long seconds until a stunning woman with a fall of black hair came to see what the fuss was about. Her wide, almond-shaped eyes flicked between them with the beginnings of something like fear, before she leaned down to kiss the old woman's cheek and direct her back into the house.

"Can I help you?" she asked, keeping one hand on the doorframe.

"Mrs Joshi? My name is Detective Inspector Denise MacKenzie, and this is Trainee Detective Constable Melanie Yates. I'm afraid we have some bad news. Is there somewhere private we could talk?"

"Bad news? What do you mean?"

MacKenzie met her eyes and steeled herself to keep going.

"I regret to inform you that your husband, Pritesh, was killed earlier today in a bomb explosion on the Millennium Bridge. We're terribly sorry for your loss."

She watched the woman's knuckles turn white on the doorframe, and her skin drain of all colour.

"No. *No*," she repeated, daring them to argue. "Pritesh is working late tonight; he told me he would be home late."

When they said nothing, only continued to look at her with compassion, her eyes filled with tears and the noise from the party dimmed in her ears.

"I'll call him," she decided. "I'll call him, and you'll see."

She looked around with dazed eyes searching for a telephone, and MacKenzie judged it was time to step in.

"Mrs Joshi, let's go upstairs, where it's quiet."

The old woman had come back to hover in the hallway and Yates beckoned her forward.

"She needs you," she said, and although the woman spoke no English, she needed nobody to interpret the meaning.

Something terrible had happened.

Mrs Joshi looked up as her mother rushed to help and reached out a hand.

"*Maata*," she wailed.

They went upstairs, walking slowly behind the two women until they reached what looked like the master bedroom. A man's clothing was folded across the back of a chair and they spotted a pair of glasses on a bedside table, beside a bottle of aftershave.

They waited while Mrs Joshi explained the situation to her mother and felt tears clog their own throats as the old woman's face creased into lines of profound sorrow.

"Mrs Joshi, the last thing we want to do is disturb you at this distressing time," MacKenzie said. "But there are one or two very important questions we need to ask you."

"You're—you're *sure* it's Pritesh and not some other man?"

"Your husband was identified by his dental records," Yates said, quietly. "I'm so sorry."

The woman raised a slender hand to her face, covering her eyes as her mother held her close and sang what sounded like an Indian lullaby amid her own tears.

"I saw it on the news," she said, dazedly. "I said to my mum, 'Who would do such a thing?' But I never thought...I never even thought—"

"Don't blame yourself," MacKenzie told her. "The only person to blame is the one who set the explosives."

"What was he doing there?" she burst out, turning to them with wild eyes. "I don't understand why Pritesh would be on that bridge, at all."

"He didn't work around there?"

"He goes from place to place," she muttered. "He's an IT consultant, so he works in various offices. On Mondays, he's supposed to be in Ashington."

"Long way from there," Yates murmured, and made a note on her pad.

But MacKenzie had years of experience and, sometimes, the truth wasn't so hard to find.

"Did your husband have any financial difficulties, Mrs Joshi? I realise, it's a difficult question to answer, but take your time."

Mrs Joshi looked at her mother and then spoke in a low tone.

"He—yes, we're in some credit card debt," she said, shortly. "Why? You think—you think he was in court today and never told me?"

MacKenzie nodded and made a mental note to check the court list that morning, for any civil proceedings brought against the late Pritesh Joshi.

"We'll look into it," she murmured. "I have one final question to ask you, Mrs Joshi. Was your husband in trouble with anyone? Did he tell you about anyone he feared or was worried about?"

The other woman simply shook her head.

"He was my life," she said, in a slurred voice as her body went into shock. "We didn't move in those kinds of circles. All we ever did was spend too much on a credit card. Is that enough to be punished like this?"

MacKenzie and Yates had no answer to give her, and soon afterwards they took their leave.

When they returned to the confines of MacKenzie's car, they sat quietly for a few minutes thinking about a man they had never known.

"In the normal course of things, Pritesh Joshi wouldn't have been on the bridge," MacKenzie said, uncapping a bottle of lukewarm water she found in the side compartment. "I think Ryan's right that we should focus on the victims who regularly passed over the bridge, rather than the one-offs like Pritesh but, all the same, let's not forget about him."

Yates nodded.

"If he never told his wife he was due in court today, what else did he keep from her?"

MacKenzie offered her a swig of water.

"My thoughts exactly. People who get up to their eyeballs in debt tend to get desperate, too. And with a family and kids to support, maybe our man started to get desperate and went to the wrong people for help."

She started the car.

"Come on, Mel. One last stop before we call it a day."

"It's been a bloody long one."

"You're tellin' me, kid."

CHAPTER 31

Anouk "Nookie" Paradis had lived in a flat share on the south side of the river, just beside the Baltic Art Gallery. It was an expensive part of town for a young woman of twenty-one, but she'd chosen her career wisely and was putting her linguistic skills to good use as a court translator. She earned a tidy living and was able to afford a few of the finer things in life. Her parents still resided in Lyon and had been informed by local French police, but MacKenzie and Yates had decided to pay her flatmate a visit in lieu of close family.

They pressed the illuminated intercom buzzer for the secure apartment block and, when nobody answered straight away, they were on the verge of turning around again when a young woman with a fall of platinum blonde hair and eyebrows deserving of their own postcode walked up to the front entrance with a bag of grocery shopping in each hand.

"You forget your key?" she asked, setting the bags down at her feet while she rooted around in her voluminous designer bag for the entrance fob.

"No, we're from the police," MacKenzie told her, producing her warrant card. "We were hoping to speak to the lady in 4B."

The girl paused and scrutinized the badge closely, eyes widening at the title of *detective*.

"I live in 4B," she said. "Are you looking for Nookie?"

MacKenzie's eyebrows raised, before she realised the double entendre was not deliberate.

"You're Maisie?" Yates enquired.

The girl nodded. "You said you were from the police. Has something happened? Look, if this is about me clipping the corner of that car the other day, I left a note and everything—"

"We're not here about that," MacKenzie was quick to nip any parking dramas in the bud, and casually leaned down to pick up one of the woman's shopping bags. "Let's go inside, out of the cold, and we'll talk."

"Okay," the girl said, worriedly.

They made their way through a gleaming foyer and up to the fourth floor, where there were only two apartments on each level.

"Very nice," Yates couldn't resist commenting, and earned herself a swift frown from MacKenzie. It was not their place to comment on anyone's living arrangements, nice or otherwise, especially given the purpose of their visit.

It did beg the question of how two young girls could afford to live somewhere so glamorous, but they'd get around to that.

Once they'd deposited the bags in the kitchen, Maisie turned to them.

"It's your flatmate, Anouk," MacKenzie said. "I'm sorry to tell you she was killed earlier today in the explosion on the Millennium Bridge. I'm very sorry."

Maisie raised both hands to her mouth and sank onto the armrest of a nearby sofa.

"But—I saw it, I saw it happen this morning," she whispered. "You can see the bridge from that window," she said, raising a trembling finger to the large floor-to-ceiling windows in their living area. "I watched it happen and thought of all the poor people who were hurt. I never thought Nouk would be one of them."

"But didn't she use the bridge every day?"

Maisie nodded.

"I texted her twice to see if she was okay."

"She never replied?" Yates pressed her.

"No, but she never did when she was at work. They're not allowed to use their phones in court and she was due to be doing some case or other. I just—I assumed she was tied up."

Two tears ran down her face in perfect white tracks.

"Have you told her parents? I can probably find their number, if you need it…"

"It's alright, Anouk's parents have already been informed but thank you for the offer," MacKenzie said, with a smile to put the girl at her ease.

It was an interesting phenomenon that, sometimes, the most innocent of witnesses displayed the most suspicious of behaviours because they were nervous or upset. It didn't help them for Maisie Smith to be too intimidated to tell them what they needed to know.

"Do you mind if we sit down?" MacKenzie asked, and the girl shook her head.

"Go ahead."

"We'd like to ask you some questions about Anouk, if you don't mind. I know this must have come as a dreadful shock but the sooner we find out as much as we can about her, the quicker we can find whoever killed her."

Maisie nodded, using the sleeve of an expensive-looking cashmere jumper to dry her eyes.

"What do you want to know?"

"When did you first meet Anouk?"

Maisie seemed flummoxed, even by such a simple question, and the two detectives looked at each other in mild confusion.

"I just mean, when was it and how did you meet," MacKenzie repeated herself, using slightly different language to see if it would help.

"Um, a friend introduced us at a party," Maisie said, carefully. "They knew I was looking for a flatmate after my old one moved out."

MacKenzie smiled again.

"Can I ask what you do for a living, Maisie?"

The girl flushed deeply and crossed her legs, defensively.

"I—ah, I'm a student."

Yates made an obvious show of looking around the room with an expression that seemed to reek of disbelief.

"Great! What do you study?"

"Geography," the girl muttered.

"Good for you," MacKenzie said, and summed the situation up immediately. "Does the escort work pay well?"

Maisie's eyes flew up to hers and filled with tears again.

"I only did it once—"

"I'm not here to judge, Maisie, so don't start telling me any lies. Was Anouk an escort, too?"

Maisie nodded.

"She really did work as a translator as well, though. She had a degree in Modern Languages from some place in France and got a job working for the Courts Service when she came over here. She did a bit of escort work in the evenings to pay for extras."

"Thank you for being so honest," MacKenzie said, and meant it. "Now, I need you to tell me if Anouk was ever worried about someone, a client maybe, who bothered her? Or perhaps an old boyfriend?"

Maisie re-crossed her legs and was momentarily distracted from her grief by the prospect of being useful.

"You always get a couple of perves," she said, frankly. "Every girl gets them, after a while. She had her regulars who liked to take her to dinner but there was this one bloke who found out where we live and kept turning up at all hours, demanding to come up. It was scary, actually."

"Do you know his name?"

"I don't think he gave his real name. Not many do," she said. "This one called himself Kevin. I can't remember his last name."

MacKenzie took down some further details, including the name of the escort agency both girls were registered with.

"Had she seen this man lately?"

"No, not after, ah…"

"After the agency had him roughed up a bit?"

Maisie nodded again.

They stayed a while longer to see if there was anything else they could learn from Anouk's former flatmate, but the two women had not been close and, for the most part, had lived separate lives.

As they stepped back outside into the cold evening air, both women shivered and walked briskly back towards MacKenzie's car, pausing briefly beneath the shadow of the Baltic Gallery to exchange a word with the constable posted on the south side of the police cordon which remained in place to protect the Millennium Bridge.

"Anouk had a semi-regular routine, but she wasn't at court every day," Yates remarked. "If somebody wanted to target her, they'd have to be sure she was due in court on that day."

"I agree," MacKenzie said. "It would mean ringing around the court, which is risky in itself. If somebody wanted to follow her routine, it would most likely be from her escort work. And then, I have to ask myself, why would your garden variety stalker go to all the trouble of blowing up a bridge? It's not their usual style."

Yates sighed.

"So, I guess we keep looking?"

"Tomorrow's a new day," MacKenzie said. "Let's hope it doesn't bring any more nasty surprises."

* * *

It was just before eight when Ryan and Phillips made their last stop of the evening, this time to the village of Heddon-on-the-Wall, west of the city. It stood on high ground overlooking the valley and consisted of a few streets of old stone houses, a couple of village shops and a petrol station, which made it larger than most villages of its kind.

Rosehip Cottage was a tiny, two-up, two-down affair which, despite its name, had seen better days.

"This is the one," Ryan said, bringing the car to a stop on the road outside.

"I could murder a pint," Phillips muttered, and Ryan wouldn't have turned one down himself. It had been an unprecedented three days and informing close relatives that their loved ones had died in a freak terror attack did not rank highly on their list of 'fun things to do.'

But this was the job they'd signed up for, and it required a steady pair of hands.

"After all this is over," Ryan said. "It'll taste all the sweeter."

"Promises, promises," Phillips replied.

In the light of the single downstairs window, they could see the door had once been a cheerful pillar box red but was now peeling badly and in need of repair. It was accessed straight from the pavement and, on the other side, they could hear a television blaring. Ryan raised his hand to the iron knocker, which had been fashioned in the shape of a rabbit.

Within seconds, the television was turned down and they heard a lock being unbolted. The door opened to reveal a woman of around fifty.

"Mrs Dobson?"

Phillips happened to know that Kayleigh-Ann's mother was not married but he was of the old school and had been brought up to address any lady of a certain age as 'Mrs.'

"Yes?"

"My name is Detective Sergeant Phillips, and this is Detective Chief Inspector Ryan," he said, and both men produced their warrant cards for her to check. "We're sorry to intrude on you at this time of night but I'm afraid we have some very bad news. I regret to inform you that your daughter, Kayleigh-Ann, was killed this morning in an explosion on the Millennium Bridge in Newcastle. We're very sorry."

Cilla Dobson just stared at them, her tired brown eyes not seeming to have registered the meaning of the words he'd just spoken.

"Kayleigh-Ann?"

"Yes," Ryan said. "I'm so sorry."

She raised a trembling hand to her head, but the tears did not come. Not yet.

"C-come in, for a minute," she said, and stepped aside to allow them to pass.

"Thank you," Ryan murmured, taking care to wipe his feet on the small mat just inside the doorway which read, 'IT'S ALWAYS GIN O'CLOCK!'

The front door opened directly into the living room, which was very small but crammed with furniture of all kinds. An extensive collection of porcelain animals had been arranged inside a small glass cabinet and an empty birdcage had been stuffed into the corner of the room.

They stood politely while she cleared away several stacks of glossy magazines from the tiny sofa and offered them a seat, which they accepted.

"I'm trying to—I can't believe what you've told me," she said, sinking into the single armchair. "Kayleigh's dead?"

"Yes, I'm afraid she is," Ryan said, trying not to notice when Phillips took a seat beside him and the two men found themselves crammed onto the miniature sofa like a couple of sardines.

"I saw the news today, so I knew another bridge had gone up and that people had died," she said, numbly. "I rang the emergency number because I was worried Kayleigh might have been hurt. I knew. I just...*knew*."

She rested her head on her hand and stared at the television screen while she thought of her little girl, and the first tears started to fall.

"She's all I have," Cilla whispered. "She was all I had left."

Ryan got up briefly to fetch some tissue from a bathroom down the hall and then chose to remain standing, rather than sit on his sergeant's knee.

"Was it the Muslims?" she asked, and they sighed inwardly. Grief did little to dispel the wrongheaded opinions some people held.

"No, Mrs Dobson. As far as we know, there was no religious motivation of any kind," Ryan told her, firmly. The last thing they needed was a grieving mother giving interviews to the press inciting racial hatred; they had enough to deal with already, and minority communities in the area had seen more than their share of violence and vandalism fuelled by their small-minded neighbours.

"Who was it then?" she said, angrily. "Have you found them yet?"

"No, not yet. That's why we need your help, Mrs Dobson," Ryan said, keeping an even tone to counteract her rising anger. "We need you to tell us everything you can about your daughter's general life and routine. We understand she lived alone?"

"She has a flat down on the Gateshead side," Cilla said. "It was one of those repossession auctions, that's how she got it. Somebody overextending themselves on credit, no doubt."

They made a polite sound of agreement.

"Did she share it with anyone?"

Cilla let out a tearful snort and blew her nose.

"She had her new bloke around all the time," she said. "I told her that he was no good for her, but she wouldn't listen to me. Never listened to me," she added, to herself.

"Do you remember his name?"

But Cilla shook her head.

"I only found out she'd met somebody when I happened to see them over at the Black Bull in Matfen," she said, referring to another picturesque village a bit further west. "Looked very cosy together, too. You should have seen her face, when she saw me."

"She wasn't happy?" Phillips asked.

Cilla's lip curled.

"I told her afterwards, she was making a mistake. She had guilt written all over her face and it's no wonder she never told anybody about him. She was too ashamed."

"He was married, then?" Ryan surmised.

"You can spot them a mile off," Cilla said, forgetting for a moment that her daughter was dead as she moved onto a pet topic of hers. "I told Kayleigh she should've had more self-respect, especially after her dad left us for that slut from the docks in North Shields."

Both men remained diplomatically silent. Sometimes, it was for the best.

"You'd think, after she'd seen how heartbroken I was, after she'd seen how we struggled for years after that, she'd never want to be the one to do that to someone else. I told her, straight out, I told her, 'Kayleigh, I never thought I'd raise any child of mine to be a grubby little bitch like you.' "

Ryan and Phillips exchanged an awkward glance. Clearly, mother and daughter had not been especially close.

Phillips cleared his throat.

"So—"

"I told her something else as well, mind. I told her, 'Kayleigh, that man will never leave his wife.' If she thought he'd marry her instead, she was more of a fool than I thought," Cilla carried on, her voice growing more and more heated.

"Do you know anything else about the man? His profession, perhaps?"

"I can tell you what he looked like but that's about it. He looked like a right *poser*," she spat. "Must've been forty if he was a day but walking around in those skinny jeans like he was some sort of pop star. I'm sure his hair had been highlighted, too."

"What about build, eye colour?"

"Bit above average height," she said, thinking back. "Can't remember his eyes and I never found out what he did for a living; the little weasel scuttled off as soon as Kayleigh spotted someone she knew. Typical rat."

"Okay. Let's turn to Kayleigh's general lifestyle," Ryan said, steering her gently away from what was obviously a sore spot. "She worked for the Courts Service?"

"Mm-hmm. She worked as a receptionist, although the way she put on airs, you'd think she was one of the bloody judges."

Ryan looked at her for a long moment and her eyes dropped to the floor, filling with tears again. He had seen behaviour like hers before; relatives who would rather focus on anger than sadness, would rather pretend they'd hated their loved one than face up to the reality they would never be coming back.

"Is there anything else you can tell us about Kayleigh, Mrs Dobson? Did she ever mention being frightened of anyone, or of seeing anyone strange?"

Cilla's eyes strayed to a small frame hidden amongst a hoard of other trinkets on the bookshelves behind the television. It was old and faded now, but it was an image of herself and Mark with Kayleigh sitting on her lap. She couldn't have been more than a year old and was dressed in a pretty pink dress and matching sun hat.

All three of them were smiling for the camera.

Never again, she thought. They would never be together again and now she was the only one left.

"She didn't tell me anything," she said, tiredly. "We hardly spoke."

"Did Kayleigh keep in touch with her father?"

Cilla heaved a sigh.

"No, neither of us had seen him in twenty years," she said. "I hear he's onto his fourth, now."

Ryan and Phillips let themselves out a short while later and headed back to the car with stony faces.

Once they were inside, Ryan turned on the heater to thaw the frosted windshield but didn't start the engine.

"We see all kinds of people in this job, don't we, Frank?"

"That's putting it mildly."

Ryan gave a short laugh, then sobered again.

"The fact is, we're getting nowhere fast. Any one of the victims today could be connected to the bomber and, since we don't know what kind of nut-job we're dealing with, it could be something completely innocuous that set him off."

"If it was a 'him'," Phillips was bound to say.

"Indeed," Ryan said, thoughtfully. "The phone companies are sending through their data first thing in the morning and we've still got a team going over the CCTV—and more keeps rolling in."

"I've told the analysts to focus on footage around the entrances to the Millennium Bridge from yesterday afternoon all the way through to the explosion this morning. Surely one of the cameras will have captured the bomb being planted."

Ryan nodded.

"There's always a chink, somewhere, Frank. We just have to find it."

"Well, if anyone can…"

"MacKenzie can," Ryan finished for him, with a grin.

"You're not wrong, son. What that woman doesn't know about policing isn't worth knowing."

Ryan smiled and started the car.

"Which reminds me. After all this is over, we need to have a serious discussion about your stag do."

Phillips had been afraid of that.

"No rush," he said, casually. "I'd be happy with a few drinks down at my local—"

"I wouldn't dream of it," Ryan said, with a roguish smile. "After all the trouble you went to for my send-off, the *least* I can do is to return the favour."

Phillips could already feel his liver wincing in anticipation.

"Now, you know I'm getting on a bit," he said. "I'm not as young as—"

"Don't think the geriatric card will work with me," Ryan said. "I've seen you in the boxing ring, remember?"

Phillips twiddled his thumbs.

"Just promise me one thing."

"What's that?"

"Don't have me in any unitards or onesies. Think of the general public, if you won't think of me."

Ryan sucked in a deep breath and pretended to consider it as they joined the motorway.

"Sorry, mate. I can't rule it out."

CHAPTER 32

Ryan pulled up outside the entrance to Police Headquarters so that Phillips could collect his own car. He was about to drive off again when he spotted a van parked near to the custody entrance at the side of the building. With a muttered expletive, he left the car where it was and jogged across the tarmac to confirm what he already suspected.

Tebbutt was moving Lowerson into general custody, at one of the prisons nearby.

He rounded the side of the van and saw two of his colleagues having a quick smoke while they waited for the paperwork to be completed.

They stood up a bit straighter when they heard his footsteps approaching.

"What's going on here? Who's your transfer?"

"Lowerson," one of them answered. "He should be coming up any minute now."

Ryan was rarely one to use any kind of physical advantage or to pull rank, but desperate times called for desperate measures.

"You don't leave this car park until I come back down. Is that understood?"

"But, sir, we have orders from DCI Tebbutt," they argued.

"And now you have orders from me," he ground out. "I repeat: if you take DC Jack Lowerson so much as a metre off these premises, there'll be hell to pay. Understood?"

They nodded vigorously, and Ryan stalked back around the van and down to the custody entrance to find his opposite number from Durham CID. He didn't have to search for too long; he found Tebbutt filling out the paperwork for Lowerson's transfer on a desk inside one of the smaller conference rooms at the end of the hall.

"I want a word with you, please," Ryan said, closing the door behind him.

If she'd been a younger woman, or a more impressionable one, Joan Tebbutt might have been impressed by the sight of Maxwell Finlay-Ryan spitting with anger. As it was...

Oh, to hell with it. She was still impressed, but she'd have sooner cut off her own arm than admit to any such thing.

"Can I help you?" she said, placidly. "It's late and I'm hoping to finish here before nine."

Her tone was enough to tip him over the edge and he pointed an angry finger towards the door he'd just walked through.

"You've got a detective constable of good standing in there and you're planning to move him into general custody, with half the riff-raff he's helped to put away? Are you trying to get him beaten up, or worse? Why not shaft him in the back now, and be done with it?" he practically roared. "Where's your sense of loyalty, or fair play?"

Tebbutt stood up and put both hands on the table, facing him down.

"At this point, Lowerson is just like any other person facing a murder charge—"

"You better be joking," Ryan snarled.

"No, I'm not. I'm playing by the rules. You should try it sometime," she said.

"Those rules don't apply to a man who is a target for half the people already incarcerated," Ryan said, more softly now. "Joan, where's your pity?"

She looked away as his words niggled beneath her skin, then lifted her chin.

"Lowerson is—"

"A danger to himself," Ryan interjected. "He's at risk, not only from others but from himself. You saw how traumatised he was."

She blew out a frustrated breath.

"That's because you *still* think he didn't kill Lucas," she said. "What if you're wrong?"

"What if you are?"

An awkward silence fell.

"Please, Joan. I'm asking as a favour. Keep him here for another night—just one more night, where we can watch out for him and by the time tomorrow night rolls around you may know even more."

Tebbutt knew she would be kicking herself in the morning, but he'd made her think twice about the whole thing.

Damn the man.

"Fine. He gets one more day."

Ryan let out the air he'd been holding in his chest.

"Thank you," he said simply.

* * *

When he was informed that he'd be spending another night at Police Headquarters rather than in custody elsewhere, Lowerson sank back down on the bed in his cell and stared at the ceiling tiles. It hadn't taken long for damp brown patches to develop there and it reminded him of their last office space; the walls might be different but little else changed.

He couldn't remember a time when he hadn't dreamed of being a policeman. Even as a child, his mother had kept photographs of him dressed up in a miniature polyester uniform and a plastic hat. He'd pretended to search for clues to find hidden treasures around his bedroom, using the magnifying glass he'd found inside a Christmas cracker.

He remembered the day he'd first joined the force from the academy, and the first time he'd met Ryan. As a rookie police constable, he'd been posted as a sentry on the door of a crime scene which, at first, appeared to be a case of death by accidental overdose. It had been springtime and he'd stood there wondering whether he'd made the right career choices, wondering whether he'd be standing on the other side of the door forever. But slowly, by watching and learning, he'd started to move up. Soon after, he was no longer a sentry but a reader-receiver; then, after that, Ryan had helped him to join the training pathway towards becoming a detective.

He probably still had that little plastic magnifying glass, somewhere.

He smiled at the memory, then his vision clouded as tears sprang to his eyes. Perhaps he'd look back on those days as a fond and distant memory from the past, as something he could think of through the long years he'd be spending in prison. He had no doubt that was how things would pan out; his DNA was all over Jennifer's house and probably all over her body.

She'd kissed him on the morning she died—in anger, but a kiss, nonetheless—and their bodies had touched. His hair, her hair. His saliva and hers. His fingerprints everywhere, in every room.

It was a foregone conclusion.

His solicitor said his story fitted the bill for self-defence and that he'd been pushed to his absolute limits. She talked about getting an expert in to support a clear case of coercive control and he had gone along with it, so that he didn't need to keep going over and over his story.

The truth was, he didn't care what happened to him.

The Jack that he used to be was gone; gone far away, disappearing into the sands of time like the little boy who'd enjoyed playing dressy-up.

CHAPTER 33

Ryan's task force reconvened the next morning, on the dot of seven. It was a full hour before most of their shifts were due to start but there had been no complaints, only a willingness to do whatever was necessary to get the job done, and it made him proud. For all the wind-bagging he heard from senior officials, politicians and pundits about police incompetency, Ryan was yet to meet a more dedicated and able workforce than the men and women he was privileged to lead.

A little well-timed injection of sugar certainly helped, mind you, and a tray of freshly-baked croissants was being handed around the room to set them all up for the day. Everyone was in attendance other than Tom Faulkner, who was at his lab, and Captain Nobel, who they assumed had been held up owing to the ongoing transport difficulties.

"We'll make a start," Ryan decided. "First order of business is to look at the CCTV around the Millennium Bridge. Frank? Tell me some good news."

Phillips hastily swallowed a mouthful of pain au chocolat.

"We've got something," he said, coming straight to the point. "One of the cameras positioned on the corner overlooking the traffic lights, beside the courthouse, has a partial view of the north side of the Millennium Bridge. It captured somebody entering at three-oh-nine on Monday morning. It's dark and it's grainy, but it looks like they were wearing a backpack. When they doubled back a couple of minutes later, it looks like they're not carrying anything."

"That must be our guy," Ryan agreed, trying not to get too excited. "Can we enhance the footage? Who are we looking for?"

One of the support staff handed him a printed version of the blown-up image from the CCTV footage and his heart sank again. Given the angle of the frame, all he could see was the side of their suspect's jaw.

"Whoever this is knew what they were doing," he said. "They're wearing dark clothing, nothing too tight to give away build or even gender, and dark shoes to blend in. That looks like a dark woollen hat, too."

"Somebody five-eight or above, maybe," MacKenzie said, scrutinizing the copy she held. "How did they get on to the bridge if it was manned all night?"

"You took the words right out of my mouth," Ryan said. "Who was stationed on the north side?"

Phillips consulted his notebook.

"Couple of locals from Tyne and Wear Command. I've asked to speak to them as soon as they get in, so we can get to the bottom of it but, according to their sergeant, the shift was due to change at three."

Ryan looked up at that.

"Really? Now, that's very interesting, don't you think?"

Phillips gave him a quizzical look.

"Why?"

Ryan opened his mouth to explain, then thought better of it.

"Never mind. Have the phone records come through?"

MacKenzie had taken charge of that side of things and had spent most of the night cross-checking the numbers listed as the victims' most recent calls or texts against their internal database of people and addresses.

"They're still coming in," she said. "We had three of the victims' mobile phones because they were found on their person, which makes life a bit easier. It was a case of marrying up 'unknown' callers and I've included these in a separate list."

Ryan nodded, and held up the list she'd produced that very morning. It was good, efficient work but then he expected no less.

"Thanks. What about the fourth victim—Kayleigh-Ann?"

He watched their eyes flick somewhere over his head to look at her picture, which was still tacked to the wall behind him.

"Only came through this morning, so I haven't had a chance to check all the numbers yet. However, there was one that stood out."

Ryan's eyes grew sharp.

"Oh?"

MacKenzie nodded.

"I've highlighted it several times," she said. "The victim has been receiving calls from that number—although not *making* very many—and texting regularly."

"For a couple of months?" Ryan guessed.

"You've got it."

"That's our man," he said to Phillips, then turned back to the room to explain. "Last night, we spoke to Kayleigh-Ann's mother, who said she believed her daughter had been conducting an affair with a married man. Taking but not making calls? That seems consistent. What times of day?"

MacKenzie gave a half-smile.

"Only during the day," she said. "When our Lothario is out of the marital home and at work, I'd imagine."

"You're such a cynical woman," Phillips said, with admiration. "Don't ever change."

She flashed him a toothy smile, then got back to the business at hand.

"I haven't had a chance to look at any of the victims' social media or e-mail accounts yet," she continued. "I thought the priority was to find out the owner of that mobile number."

"Could just call it," Wilson suggested, taking a bite out of his croissant. "Pretend it's a wrong number."

"That's not really how it works," Ryan said, as he took a marker pen and wrote the number on the board, beneath the image of Kayleigh-

Ann. "If we do that, we put the owner of that number on notice that they're under scrutiny. We lose the element of surprise."

"You don't need to," Phillips said, in a serious tone. "I think I recognise it."

* * *

The room recovered itself quickly.

"Whose is it?" Ryan asked.

"I recognise the last three digits," Phillips explained. "You don't often see '999' at the end of a phone number, do you?"

They waited while he hurriedly took out his phone and began scrolling through his contacts but, in the end, he didn't need to.

"I recognise it too," Wilson said, turning to his colleague with a worried expression. "That's Gary's number."

"That can't be right," Bannerman whispered, and checked her messages until she found Nobel's number. "There, you, see…"

Her eyes flicked between the large numbers written on the board and the number saved on her phone, then her face fell into slack lines of dismay.

"It's the same," she said quietly.

"Aye, it's the same number I've got too," Wilson muttered, and looked up with a worried expression. "Honestly, I had no idea Gaz knew the victim. He never said—"

"He never breathed a word to me, either," Bannerman confirmed, then added hastily, "Look, I'm sure there's some explanation. Gary can be…he can be a bit full of himself, at times, but he's not a killer. I'm sure he couldn't have done this."

"Aye, there's got to be some reason why he never said he knew the lass," Wilson was quick to add. "He's a decent bloke, when you get down to it."

Ryan's face was hard. The stakes were too high to make allowances for professional acquaintances.

"Where is he now?"

"Otterburn," Wilson said, unhappily. "He's at the barracks for a meeting."

Ryan turned to Phillips, who was already getting up from his chair.

"Frank? With me. The rest of you, report to DI MacKenzie."

They left the room at a run.

CHAPTER 34

Otterburn Training Camp and Barracks was located in the countryside to the north-west of the city of Newcastle, in the heart of the Northumberland National Park and a stone's throw from Ryan's home in Elsdon. It covered more than ninety square miles and was used to train thirty thousand soldiers per year. Being the UK's largest firing range for weaponry including AS-90 Artillery and M270 Multiple Launch Rocket Systems, that made it simultaneously one of the most beautiful and most dangerous parts of the county.

It took twenty minutes for Ryan and Phillips to negotiate the city's road diversions, but as soon as they hit the motorway Ryan put the pedal to the floor.

"If I die before my time, I'm tellin' Denise it's all your fault," Phillips said, clutching a hand on the door. "Ever heard of the Highway Code?"

"You worry too much," Ryan said, as they flew past a BMW.

"There! That just proves my point," Phillips said, as it became a speck in the rear-view mirror. "You know you've lost the plot when you're overtaking BMW and Audi drivers because everybody knows they're the most obnoxious."

"What about the blokes who drive a Volvo and stick so rigidly to the speed limit that people think they're drunk?"

"I just like to get from A to B with all my major organs intact," Phillips grumbled.

"If you're scared, close your eyes and I'll tell you when we get there."

Phillips pulled a face but, as he watched his friend manoeuvre, had to admit that an advanced police driving course had given him skills at the wheel he'd never quite had the nerve to try.

"What do you make of Nobel and this lass, Kayleigh?" he asked, changing the subject. "Can't make out why he wouldn't tell us about it."

"Maybe he was ashamed?"

Phillips looked across at him and smiled at such naivety. He might have been fifteen years his junior, but Ryan was an old-fashioned kind of man. When he loved, he loved for life, and he couldn't understand why some men strayed.

As it happened, he agreed with him, but he knew plenty who didn't.

"Not everybody takes the same view on fidelity," he said. "Gary could have been worried about his wife finding out, or many a thing."

"I understand that," Ryan said, guiding the car over dips and peaks as the road wound over the hills and they left the city far behind them. "Or, at least, I try to understand it."

"Let's hear him out," Phillips said. "It looks bad but there could be an explanation."

"I'm all ears," Ryan said, and slowed as they came to the turning that would lead them to the south entrance of the training camp.

They followed a straight road across open fields lined with high, barbed-wire fencing until they came to a series of manned security gates. Ryan slowed the car and wound his window down to speak into the intercom, which was patchy, but eventually he was buzzed through to the next set of gates, where an armed soldier awaited their arrival.

"Bloody hell, it's like Area 51," Phillips muttered. "Wonder if they're hiding UFOs somewhere around here."

Ryan chuckled and wound his window down to greet the soldier who approached them with the kind of natural caution that came from having seen two tours of active service.

"Help you, lads?"

Ryan's eyes were drawn briefly to the sight of a mermaid tattoo curling its way around the man's neck.

"We're here to see Captain Nobel," he said, and reeled off the regiment.

"Got any ID?"

"Sure," Ryan said, and both men produced their warrant cards, which were fully checked.

"Just wait there, please."

He turned away to speak into his radio and then walked back across to stick his head through the driver's window.

"Sorry, Chief Inspector, Captain Nobel isn't currently on site. He was due to be in Newcastle, with you."

Ryan frowned, while Phillips checked with MacKenzie to be sure that they hadn't passed Nobel on the way.

"Nothing from CID," Phillips confirmed. "There's no word from him and he's not answering his phone."

Ryan looked back at the soldier.

"Does Nobel live at the barracks or does he have a place off-site?"

"Captain Nobel spends weekdays at the barracks but weekends at the house his family own," he said, helpfully.

"D'you happen to know where it is?"

"Sure, it's just in Otterburn Village, not far from the castle. Sorry, I don't know the number or anything. Hey," he thought belatedly. "The Cap's not in trouble, is he?"

Ryan smiled thinly.

"Thanks for all your help."

With that, he executed a swift U-turn and headed in the direction of the village.

* * *

They drove around for ten minutes looking for Gary Nobel's Land Rover until they spotted it parked on one of the village side streets. It was sitting haphazardly outside a smart stone house with climbing wisteria around the front door that would be beautiful in bloom.

"There," Phillips said.

"I see it," Ryan replied, and pulled up beside Nobel's car to block him in.

"Nice move," Phillips said.

"This ain't my first rodeo," Ryan muttered, and walked up to the front door.

"Hasn't he got kids?" Phillips asked, just as Ryan had raised his hand to press the bell.

"Bugger," he replied. "That makes things harder. How old?"

Phillips racked his brain but, on reflection, couldn't recall Nobel ever waxing lyrical about his home and family.

"Not sure."

"Alright, let's play this by ear," Ryan decided. "Is there a back door to this place?"

Phillips nodded, pointing towards a side alley that led to a back courtyard.

"I'll make sure he doesn't make a run for it," he said, and Ryan nodded.

The door didn't open at first but after a series of persistent knocks and ringing of the bell, it was finally flung open to reveal a blonde woman in her mid-thirties with a face that was obviously ravaged by tears.

"Look, just go away! We're not interested in whatever you're trying to sell. Stop ringing the bell!"

Ryan put a foot in the door, when she would have slammed it in his face.

"I'm here to see Gary," he said, quickly. "I'm DCI Ryan. He's been working with us on the bombings in Newcastle."

To his surprise, she started to cackle; a hysterical sound that soon dissolved into fresh tears.

"I'll bet he has," she said. "He's been working *such* long hours, lately, I wondered who to blame. Turns out, it wasn't you at all."

She knows, Ryan deduced, but it hardly took Sherlock Holmes to work that one out.

"Is he at home?"

"Oh yes. Come in and see our happy home," she said, in a brittle voice.

Ryan stepped inside and looked around the room, his eye falling on a little boy of three or four sitting cross-legged on the floor in front of the television, holding his hands to his ears.

She followed the direction of his gaze and Maddy Nobel held her head in her hands, hating herself and the man who had caused them nothing but heartbreak.

"Nobel?"

Ryan didn't bother to wait but stepped quickly through the rooms of the house until he came to the kitchen.

And found Gary halfway out of the back door.

"Wait!"

Ryan dashed after him as he ran through the back garden, making for the wooden gate at the end. In his peripheral vision, Ryan spotted a Wendy house and a small climbing frame with a single swing.

"Gary!"

Ryan slowed down as he reached the back gate, already anticipating what was to come. When Nobel wrenched the gate open, he found there was nowhere to run, except directly into Phillips' barrel of a chest.

"Going somewhere, son?"

Phillips held him easily and Ryan caught up with them both, eyeing the man with intense dislike.

"You lied by omission," he said, without any kind of preamble. "You tried to run because you knew we would find out, didn't you, Gary?"

Nobel looked wretched.

"I wanted to be the first to tell Maddy. I didn't want her finding out from someone else."

"How touching," Ryan said.

"Aye, spoken like a true gent," Phillips remarked.

Nobel swallowed, looking over at the kitchen doorway where his wife of ten years stood with his son in one hand and their baby girl in the other.

"Time to go, Gary. You're coming in for questioning. You can either do it voluntarily or under arrest; it's up to you."

"I'll come in," the man replied, wearily.

"Sounds like that's the first good decision you've made lately."

CHAPTER 35

The air inside Interview Room C was both stuffy and cold, a feat that was achieved by a re-circulating air conditioning vent which pumped stale air in a constant, germ-laden whirlwind around the four people seated at a table in the middle.

Ryan had taken MacKenzie in to conduct the interview with Nobel on the basis that, at the very least, it should teach the man a lesson in humility. They were joined by his solicitor, a heavy-set man they recognised from several other investigations as being long on fees and short on legal knowledge.

And that was just fine.

"Mr Nobel, I'd like to start by asking you why you chose to withhold information during an active police investigation," MacKenzie began, diving straight into it. "Why did you choose not to tell us that you had intimate knowledge of one of the Millennium Bridge Attack victims, Kayleigh-Ann Dobson?"

"I didn't think it was relevant," he muttered. "It was a private matter."

MacKenzie leaned forward, linking her fingers atop the metal table.

"Y' see, that's where you're wrong, Gary," she said. "Kayleigh-Ann was a victim of one of the worst crimes ever committed in this city. As a member of the team investigating her death, you had both a moral and a legal responsibility to tell us of your association with her. Why didn't you?"

"As my client has already told you, he mistakenly believed that his private relationship with the deceased had no bearing on the case."

MacKenzie ignored the solicitor completely and continued to stare at Gary with disarming green eyes.

"I don't think that's true, is it, Gary? Which is unfortunate because, as you know, we police have a nasty habit of drawing adverse inferences when people omit to tell us the full truth."

"Is that a threat?" his solicitor boomed, for dramatic effect.

MacKenzie turned to look at him and in the long silence that followed, she watched a flush slowly develop from the folds of skin at the man's neck all the way up his face.

"It's a fact," she said. "Made worse by your client's inability to provide a reasonable explanation for his failure to inform us of key information while having privileged access to our investigation."

"Yeah, convenient, wasn't it, Gary?" Ryan picked up the cue and rolled with it. "You must have thought Christmas had come early when the call came through from Control. Did you laugh, while you pressed the detonator, Gary?"

Nobel's face went hot and then cold.

"I—if you think that I was the one, you must be bloody crazy."

"Now, now," MacKenzie said. "Language."

"I disarm bombs, I don't make them!" Nobel almost shouted, making to get up from his chair. "I don't have to answer any more questions from you."

"Alright," Ryan said, and turned to MacKenzie. "Do you want to do the honours?"

She opened her mouth as if to make a formal arrest, but Nobel held out a hand.

"Wait—wait. Just hold on a minute. I need to think."

"Thinking time's over, Gary," Ryan threw back. "Where were you this morning, between the hours of two and four a.m.?"

Gary lifted a hand in mute appeal, then let it drop again.

"I was with her. With Kayleigh. I told Maddy—my wife—that I was still needed in the city to oversee checks of the bridges. I was at Kayleigh's flat until the morning. I'd only just left when the call came through about...about what had happened."

"And you must have known she'd be on that bridge, all along. You never showed even a hint of surprise, or remorse," Ryan said, with contempt.

"Mighty convenient that your alibi can't be verified, either," MacKenzie hit back. "Kayleigh isn't here to confirm that, is she?"

"It's the truth!" Nobel shouted, and his solicitor placed a hand on his arm.

"You've got a short temper, haven't you, Gary?" MacKenzie whispered, and leaned even further forward, getting into his space. "You don't much like women, either, do you?"

His solicitor blustered.

"That has nothing to do with the matters in hand," he said.

"Maybe it does," she argued, holding eye contact with her quarry. "You love and hate us, don't you Gary? You love conquering us and you love it when we tell you how *big* and *strong* you are but, the fact is, you resent it when we bite back. You don't like any woman telling you what to do, isn't that right, Gary?"

His lip curled, and he shook his head.

"You don't know what you're talking about."

"Oh, I think I do. You like to have a woman at home, somebody you know will always be there to look after your needs, your wants, your children—"

He pointed a finger at her face and Ryan tensed in his chair, ready to step in if needed.

"You *don't* bring my children into this," Nobel shouted.

"You brought them into it the moment you took the decision to kill Kayleigh-Ann and expose your family to an investigation," MacKenzie said. "Why, Gary? Was she threatening you? Was she pressuring you to get a divorce?"

"No! Yes. I mean, she wanted me to divorce Maddy but...I wouldn't kill her for that! What the hell do you take me for?"

"Did she tell you about the baby, Gary? Was that it?"

Ryan watched him closely for a reaction.

"What?" Nobel repeated, sounding confused. "Kayleigh wasn't pregnant."

"You expect us to believe you didn't know?" MacKenzie said, though she was starting to suspect that he hadn't. "It would have ruined your marriage, if Kayleigh told your wife. Isn't that true?"

Nobel rubbed both hands over his face and then into his hair, which stood at all angles in contrast to his usual immaculate grooming.

"I didn't know she was pregnant. I swear, I didn't know," he said, in a very low voice. "Poor kid."

They realised he was thinking of Kayleigh-Ann and Ryan put a finger on the table, a silent signal to MacKenzie that they should hold off and let him speak.

"I would never leave Maddy," Nobel continued, quietly. "She's my everything. It's just that, lately, since we had the baby, it hasn't been the same. She's always tired. And then… I'd seen Kayleigh around when I was in court giving evidence this one time. I don't know…it seemed like fate, that's all."

MacKenzie looked at Nobel with unconcealed repugnance. Here was a man who epitomised the very reason why she'd avoided any long-term relationships for so long, until she'd met Frank. How different they were, she thought. Years earlier, when they'd only been friends and work colleagues, she'd seen how Frank had nursed and cared for his first wife as she'd succumbed to terminal cancer. She'd seen him grieve, seen him forego drinks at work or nights out with his friends, so he could be with her when it mattered. Watching such devotion had probably been the reason why she'd started to fall in love with him in the first place.

There, she thought, was a man worth having.

"Much as my heart is bleeding for you, Gary, it still leaves us with a problem," Ryan said. "As far as I can see, you have a motive, the means to set this whole thing up and, what's more, you had the opportunity."

"I told you, I was with Kayleigh."

"Unless there happens to be footage of you entering and leaving Kayleigh's apartment building, we have no way of verifying that."

Ryan exchanged a glance with MacKenzie, who nodded. He had given them no choice but to hold him, pending further investigation.

"Gary Nobel, I am arresting you on suspicion of the murders of John Walsh, Pritesh Joshi, Anouk Paradis and Kayleigh-Ann Dobson. You do not have to say anything. But it may harm your defence if you do not mention when questioned something which you later rely on in court. Anything you do say may be given in evidence."

"I don't believe this!" he shouted, thrusting up from his chair. "Cheating on my wife doesn't make me a murderer!"

"Yeah, but it makes you a liar," Ryan observed. "And a man who can lie as readily as you is capable of lying about plenty of other things."

CHAPTER 36

DCI Tebbutt pulled up outside a neat house with a well-tended garden and a brand-new car sitting on the driveway. It looked just like any other house in the area; built sometime in the nineties and just starting to weather around the edges. Some of them had solar panels but the Lowersons hadn't opted for that, just yet.

She told her sergeant to remain in the car for now, having already made a judgment call about the best way to approach the task that lay ahead.

And it was no easy task.

She drew in a deep breath and made her way up the short pathway to the front door, which swung open even before she'd had a chance to ring the bell.

"Good afternoon, Mr Lowerson. I was hoping for a word, if I may?"

"Aye, all right. Come in," he said. "Is there any news?"

She took her time wiping her feet and chose not to answer.

"Is your wife at home, too? It would be easier to discuss these things together."

"Yes, I'll just go and get her—she's having a lie down upstairs. If you just have a seat in the living room, I'll not be a minute."

She wandered through to the lounge and took an idle glance around the room, noting the numerous framed photographs of children and grandchildren before coming to stand in front of one in particular which showed Jack and his older brother, Paul, dressed in their school uniform and posing for a photograph sometime in the early nineties. The room itself was like any other of its type; the chimney breast had been painted in a bold shade of green while the rest of the room was papered in a floral mix that seemed to be all the rage. A large, flat-screen television was fixed to the chimney breast and there was a vague smell of furniture polish. Somewhere, the radio was playing 'Sounds of the Seventies' and the strains of *The Eagles* singing about a hotel in California drifted through the house.

A moment later, she heard their footsteps coming downstairs.

"DCI Tebbutt? Sorry to keep you waiting. I was feeling a bit under the weather, so I was lying down."

"Sorry to disturb you, Mrs Lowerson," she said, politely. "Shall we sit down, here?"

"Oh, yes, of course. Would you like some tea?"

"It's very kind of you but, no, I had some before I came."

They each took a seat and Tebbutt watched Wendy reach across to take her husband's hand, preparing herself for whatever news would come.

She cleared her throat.

"I have some bad news," she said. "It concerns your son."

They looked at each other and she watched their eyes fill with tears, no doubt imagining the worst.

"What do you mean?" Wendy whispered, clutching her other hand to her chest. "What's happened to Jack?"

Tebbutt paused for effect.

"Well, it's looking very much like he made false statements to the police and that, in doing so, he has perverted the course of justice."

There was only a momentary relief for the woman who had borne him.

"He's—nothing's happened to him, though? He's alright?"

"That rather depends what you mean by, 'alright', doesn't it, Wendy?" Tebbutt replied. "His professional standing is badly damaged, and he may never work for the police again."

"But wait a minute—he made a confession," Dave spoke up. "Are you saying that confession was false? That you think he didn't kill that woman, after all?"

There had been doubt in his mind, Tebbutt realised. His own father had begun to doubt him, and she suddenly felt a deep sympathy for the young man who was on a twenty-four-hour suicide watch back at Police Headquarters.

"I don't just think it, Mr Lowerson, I *know* he didn't kill Jennifer Lucas," Tebbutt said, and watched the changing expressions on both of their faces.

If there had been any doubt, now she knew for sure.

"How? Have you found the person who really did it?" Wendy asked.

"Oh, yes, most definitely."

"Then, who?" Dave asked.

Tebbutt only smiled.

"Let me start by explaining a little bit about DNA, in very simple terms. Now, I don't know how much you both know about the way we do things but, once we've taken samples at a crime scene, we test it to isolate the unique DNA. In this case, we found a lot of hair and tiny, tiny trace samples from a person's fingers and skin particles. A person who, by rights, shouldn't have touched Lucas's body in the way they did."

They were both silent, listening intently as the postman pushed some letters through the letterbox in the front door with a loud clatter. Nobody noticed.

"Jack gave us a sample of his blood as well as a buccal swab for DNA when he first came in; you remember, when he was protesting his innocence. When he had no reason not to give a sample."

They both nodded.

"We compared his sample with the DNA we were able to recover from Jennifer Lucas's body and those results came back this morning. There was a match."

"A match to Jack's?" his father said. "Well, there's bound to be, he lived there a lot of the time. His hair will be all over the place—"

As he rushed to defend his son, Tebbutt thought that, when all was said and done, it would be something for Jack to hold on to.

"But it wasn't his hair, Mr Lowerson. The match was only a *partial* match. The only circumstances in which we find that kind of match is when there's a familial link. Then, it's just a case of isolating which one."

Wendy and David looked at each other with dazed, uncomprehending eyes.

"You're—you're saying it's one of Jack's family?"

Tebbutt nodded.

"It's amazing how things have progressed in recent years," she said, conversationally, then looked Wendy Lowerson directly in the eye. "We knew it was you, Wendy, because the DNA we found is female. To be a positive, fifty percent match to Jack's own DNA, it could only belong to his mother."

There was a heavy silence in the room as they struggled to accept what she had told them.

"This is a bloody outrage," David ground out. "First, you try and pin this on my boy and now you've got the nerve to come into my house and try to blame my *wife*?"

He looked over at Wendy, wondering why she didn't defend herself, why she continued to say nothing.

Say something, Wendy, he thought. *Please, God, say something.*

"I wanted to come here, to your home, to give you the opportunity to do the right thing," Tebbutt said quietly. "I'm going to ask you once, informally, and it will be the last courtesy I give you. Did either your husband or your son know that you were responsible?"

David began to shake with emotion as he looked at his wife, at the woman he'd loved for over thirty years. The mother to his children.

She turned to him and tears began to spill over.

"Wendy?"

"I-I'm so sorry," she whispered.

Tebbutt watched his face crumble, watched a grown man of sixty-five break down as his life shattered into pieces around him. She had her

239

answer: David Lowerson had not known what his wife had done, nor what she was capable of.

Wendy watched the light die in her husband's eyes, that light she loved so much, and knew then that nothing mattered any more. She had ruined everything, through one single act of madness.

"Jack rang me," she whispered, and they strained to hear her. "He told me about the cat. That silly cat he loved so much. For the first time, he poured it all out, everything. He didn't know where to turn, Dave," she said. "So, he came to his mother."

They remained silent, letting her purge herself of the awful truth.

"He said he was going for a walk, to clear his head," she said, in a colourless voice. "So, I took my chance. He said she would be at home later in the afternoon and that he planned to speak to her that evening. I decided to get there first."

"You didn't go shopping."

Wendy raised her hand as if to touch her husband's face, but he flinched away from her and she let out a sob.

"No, love," she said. "I didn't go shopping."

"What happened when you got there?"

"I only wanted to talk to her," she said. "She answered the door and, do you know what? She acted so nice, at first. 'Hello, Mrs Lowerson,' she said. 'What a lovely surprise.' "

Wendy let out an ugly laugh.

"It was the first and only time I'd ever been invited inside. I think she was curious; she wanted to know how much he'd told me and, who knows? Maybe she wanted to torture me a little, too."

"You talked?" Tebbutt prompted her, when Wendy fell silent.

She looked up.

"Yes, yes we talked. She had a cup of coffee in her hand and offered me some. I told her I wasn't planning on staying long, I only wanted to tell her she should leave my son alone. 'He's too good for you,' I told her. 'He deserves better.' She said…she called me terrible names, said I was just like every other molly-coddling mother on the face of the Earth and that I should try letting Jack make his own decisions. I-I don't know, I just lost my temper," she said, and dashed tears from her eyes. "She was standing very close to me, as close as you are now," she told her husband, who was still seated beside her. "She was taunting me, telling me all the things…well, all the things they'd done together. She was doing it to upset me, I know she was. I shoved her away from me. 'Get away,' I think I said. 'Get away from me.'"

Wendy closed her eyes as she thought back to the awful sound of Lucas's head cracking against the side of the radiator.

"I didn't think I'd pushed her hard—just enough to give us some space," Wendy said. "But—but then, she was falling. She dropped her cup on the floor and I think something else shattered, and then there was this awful sound, a terrible sound…"

"Wendy," her husband whispered, and held his head in his hands.

"Don't cry, Dave, please don't cry," she crooned. "I did it for Jack. I did it to protect him."

He simply shook his head.

"What happened after she fell?" Tebbutt asked.

"She was lying there, and the blood just started pouring from her head," Wendy whispered. "She'd done something to her leg—her ankle maybe. She was trying to say something, maybe asking for help, but then her eyes sort of rolled back and she stopped moving. I just stood there; I panicked, and I started to call for an ambulance. But then, I thought, they'll send me to jail. I've spent my life trying to be a decent person, a decent friend, wife and mother. She was evil, she brought nothing but pain. Why should I be punished? It didn't seem fair."

"That wasn't for you to decide," Dave said, and took the words right out of Tebbutt's mouth. It had not been her decision to make.

"Yes, it was," Wendy argued, twisting her hands together in her lap. "It was like seeing a fallen horse, or an animal writhing in pain. I decided to put her out of her misery, to be sure."

"What did you do?"

241

Wendy looked down at her hands and could remember the terrible power she'd felt, the intense satisfaction as she'd taken Lucas' head and rammed it back onto the edge of the radiator.

Once, then twice.

"I took a fistful of her hair and hit her head against the radiator a couple of times, to make sure she was dead."

David had the look of a man who might faint, or vomit, and Tebbutt spoke briefly into her radio to ask her sergeant to join them.

"All the while Jack was accused, you knew," David said, bitterly. "All the while he sat inside a cell, lonely and confused, you knew. He guessed—I don't know how he must have guessed—and tried to take the blame on his own shoulders because he loves you so much. And you let him, you let your own flesh and blood risk life imprisonment for what you did."

Wendy burst into a flood of fresh tears.

"Please, Dave, it wasn't like that. Please listen."

But he stood up and walked away from her to stand at the window with his back to the room.

"How did he guess, Wendy? Do you know?" Tebbutt tried one final question.

"I had some blood on the bottom of my jeans," she explained. "I'd put them in the laundry basket and planned to wash them. Usually, I'm the one to do the washing around here. But when I came home the other day, I found he'd done a big wash-load for me. He must have seen them. It's the only thing I can think of."

"What will happen to Jack now?" his father asked.

"Well, I'll need to speak to the Crown Prosecution Service and see about that."

"My son is a good man," he said. "Please...I know we don't have the right to ask for anything but..." his voice broke and he was unable to continue.

Tebbutt rose to her feet.

"Wendy Lowerson, I am arresting you on suspicion of the murder of Jennifer Lucas on Saturday 10th February. You do not have to say anything. But it may harm your defence if you do not mention when questioned something which you later rely on in court. Anything you do say may be given in evidence."

David didn't turn around, even as Wendy was led from the room.

CHAPTER 37

When Ryan and MacKenzie returned to the Incident Room, the sun was beginning to set. It filled the room with mellow light and, just for a moment, it lifted their spirits. The city was still locked down with no access across the bridges. Petty crime sprees continued, creating pressure within the police ranks that came to bear on those who were tasked with bringing the madness to an end. They had already been intercepted by the Chief Constable, who had heard of Nobel's arrest and was ever-optimistic that they had turned the corner. She had been less than impressed when Ryan told her he had reservations about them having found the right culprit and had handed him a stern lecture about having been spoilt by too many high-speed, high-octane murder hunts.

"Sometimes, Ryan, it's just the most obvious suspect," she'd said. *"Nobel ticks all the boxes. What the hell do you want? A sign on his forehead saying, 'I DID IT'?"*

No, he didn't need a confession or a helpful sign from God. He just needed the facts to match up with the killer's psychology, and it seemed he wasn't the only one who had his doubts.

"Heard you arrested the Cap," Wilson said, when they re-entered the room.

Ryan swore the walls in Police Headquarters had eyes.

"Yeah," he said. "Seems that bad news travels fast in this place."

Kevin took a slurp of coke and scratched the heel of his hand against his forehead, looking as though he had the weight of the world on his shoulders.

"Look, I've gotta be straight with you," he said. "When I found out Gaz knew that girl, Kayleigh, I thought he was an idiot not to mention it. I mean, I get that he didn't want his wife to know because that'd break up his family, but not telling you about it crossed the line."

"I'm glad we agree on that," Ryan said, with an edge to his voice. "I hope you're not building up to telling us you know one of the *other* victims?"

Kevin gave a short laugh.

"No, don't worry. I was just going to say that, if you'd asked me, 'Hey, Kev, is Gary the type of bloke to cheat on his wife?' then, yeah, I'll be honest and say he probably was. He was always a Ladies Man." He gave another short laugh and toasted his can of coke. "Just ask Sue."

MacKenzie frowned.

"Not Sue Bannerman?"

"The very same," he said. "They were on tour together in Afghanistan eight years ago and they kept each other warm at night, or so he says. After they both got posted into EOD up here, they had a casual thing going on during the week. Like I said, Gary's got a way with the ladies."

"With *some* ladies," MacKenzie corrected him.

"Right. But, I mean, to kill like that? I'll be honest with you guys, I don't think he has it in him."

"He killed as part of his service in the army, didn't he?" Ryan said.

Wilson merely shook his head.

"It's different, man. Over there, you're fighting for Queen and Country. You're defending people, you're following orders. It's all in the line of duty. It's not the same as planning something as cold-blooded as that."

"People can surprise you," MacKenzie said.

Wilson gave a small shrug.

"I guess you're right. Look, I just wanted to get that off my chest, anyhow."

"We'll bear it in mind," Ryan assured him, and when Wilson moved off again he turned back to MacKenzie with a frown.

"What's your take on it, Mac? I have to say, I agree with him. Gary Nobel is a smarmy, opinionated git with a chauvinist view of women and he probably wouldn't make my Christmas card list. He's also got a short fuse, which is precisely why I can't see him planning the kind of execution-style murder that happened this morning. I also can't see him delaying gratification and plotting two other bombings, purely to set up the third."

MacKenzie thought of the psychology of the killer they hunted and nodded slowly.

"You're right," she said. "And most damningly, he's just not smart enough to plan and successfully execute the kind of large-scale chaos we've seen over the past few days. It doesn't feel right. But, if not Nobel, then it's back to the drawing board, isn't it? We need to look again at those victims and see which one was the link. It could take months."

Ryan ran a tired hand over the back of his neck.

"For now, let's look out the CCTV footage of Kayleigh-Ann Dobson's apartment building. If Nobel was where he said he was…" He sighed heavily. "Let's cross that bridge when we come to it. No pun intended," he added, with the flash of a smile.

"Speaking of CCTV, Frank's been supervising the review of all the fresh footage that's been coming in," MacKenzie said. "Something may turn up."

"That's about as likely as Frank giving up bacon butties," he said, to make her laugh, before strolling across the room to see his sergeant.

* * *

Phillips was staring fixedly at the screen of his laptop computer and his desk space bore the evidence of several hours' worth of drinking fizzy pop and chewing nicotine gum, judging by the small mountain of foil wrappers lying discarded beside him. It was getting easier now to handle the old pangs but, every so often, the cravings came back in times of stress.

And it had been a particularly stressful few days.

He ticked off another piece of footage and moved on to the next, which happened to be a batch of recordings from the bus company which operated all the major routes through the city centre of Newcastle and across the bridges into Gateshead.

"Any luck, Frank?"

He looked up when Ryan approached.

"Nothing yet, lad. I keep hoping to see some bloke tiptoeing onto the bridges with a black bag saying 'TNT' on the side, like in the old Bugs Bunny cartoons, but no such luck."

The first piece of footage from the bus company started to run automatically on Frank's computer. Neither man noticed, at first.

"Kev thinks the devices must have been planted well in advance, otherwise it would have been captured on CCTV footage at any number of sites within the past two weeks. As it is…" Phillips paused to yawn widely before continuing. "As it is, most places only keep their footage for up to two weeks and half the cameras belonging to the Council don't work. Same old story."

"What about on the railway lines?"

"They only have cameras within fifty metres of the covered part of the platforms," Phillips told him. On the main sections of the line, it's only at irregular intervals depending on where they've assessed there are weak access points, where kids tend to get in and all that."

"Wait," Ryan said, suddenly, leaning over his shoulder.

"What? What is it?" Phillips said, spinning around in his desk chair.

"I can hardly believe it," Ryan muttered. "Is that a tub of *quinoa salad* sitting on your desk?"

Phillips folded his arms defensively.

"Well, I've got my wedding suit to think of—can't be sitting on my arse scoffing bacon butties all day, can I?"

Ryan gave a funny half-laugh, thinking of the conversation he'd just had with Frank's future wife, when he spotted something that was worthy of genuine alarm.

"Wait," he said again.

"Oh, aye. Don't tell me," Phillips said. "You've spotted the vegetable smoothie I had at lunchtime."

"What?" Ryan looked at him in genuine disgust, then shook it off. "No, I think I caught something on that last video, Frank. Can we take it back to the beginning?"

Phillips turned back to his computer screen.

"It must have started automatically. Let me see now…" He made a funny little humming sound while his fingers flew over the keys with surprising dexterity. "This is the stuff the bus company sent through from their routes going over the High Level Bridge."

He peered at the image, clicked to zoom in a bit closer and then nodded.

"This is from the driver's windscreen camera. They all have those now, so they can cover themselves in case there's ever an accident," Phillips said. "This is the view of the lower level of the bridge just before that minor charge went off, on Sunday morning. This bus was just entering the bridge and ended up crossing over just as the bomb exploded. It was too small to cause any damage to the bus, so it crossed over without any trouble. Do you want me to skip ahead? Where was the bit you saw?"

Ryan simply leaned down and tapped the button, so it moved forward in extreme slow motion.

"There," he said, and paused the footage. "Did you see it?"

Phillips had seen it, but he didn't believe it.

"Rewind that one more time," he muttered. "That can't be right."

They watched the footage again with mounting anger, until Phillips sat back in his chair and put a hand to his face.

"Unbelievable," he growled.

" '*Once you eliminate the impossible, whatever remains, no matter how improbable, must be the truth.*' Arthur Conan-Doyle," Ryan muttered, and flicked his eyes up to the clock on the wall. "We need to hurry."

"I'll make the calls."

CHAPTER 38

Sergeant Sue Bannerman swung a new canvas beach bag on her arm as she waited in the queue to pass through security and on to her departure gate. It had been a long time since she'd had a holiday, and even longer since she'd travelled somewhere exotic without being on active duty. She could hardly wait to sip caipirinhas on Ipanema Beach in a matter of a few short hours. Sun, sea, surf and, most importantly, awkward extradition arrangements with the UK. She'd wait a few days and then draw down all the bitcoins she could. There wasn't anywhere near two million, more's the pity, but she could still live like a queen in Brazil on a few hundred grand.

Her eyes remained alert and watchful, passing over the security personnel as they hurried people along and checked their over-stuffed cabin luggage through the scanning machines.

Nobody was looking at *her*.

Hardly anyone did, she thought with a self-deprecating smile. *Good old Sue*, she thought. Not too pretty, not too ugly, just presentable enough to fill a hole in a man's life until somebody better came along.

Somebody younger, with bigger tits and a fake smile.

Stay calm, she told herself. *Just stay calm, a little while longer.*

She shuffled along the queue with her head slightly bent, trying not to draw attention to herself. She carried just the one canvas bag containing the essentials—and her phone, which was her prized possession. They could take anything else, but not her phone.

"Boots off! Jackets off! Any laptops, Kindles or iPads?"

She smiled pleasantly and bent down to take off her desert boots. Cheesy, maybe, but they were bloody comfortable. She might try out a whole new look, once she was in South America. Maybe she'd dye her hair a different colour and give herself a new, more exciting name, and wear sexier heels.

Her smile dipped.

Maybe if she'd tried those things sooner, Gary would have…

No, she thought. That bastard would always have a roving eye. It didn't matter what she wore, or how she looked. He was the type who was never content with one woman, or even two.

She thought briefly of his wife, Madeleine. She'd met her dozens of times and could almost have written a book on her, considering how much Gary had told her in and out of the bedroom. Maddy Nobel was a sweet, trusting woman who'd married young and hoped for a faithful husband. She'd fallen for Gary's specious charms just as they all had and, until recently, had been blissfully unaware of the kind of man she had married. She lived in a kind of willing ignorance, one where the world was all sunlight and moonbeams and her husband was a demi-god.

But she'd never seen Gary cry like a baby, never seen him struggle with the grief of having killed a man in combat. She'd never held him and rocked him, then soothed him with her body. Maddy could never know the depths of love that she had experienced with Gary because her house was built on nothing but sand.

Sand and lies.

"Miss?"

Sue jerked out of her reverie and realised she was holding up the rest of the queue.

"Sorry," she said, and quickly shoved her jacket into one of the plastic tubs.

"Mobile phone? Tablet?"

She hesitated for a second, then retrieved it from the side pocket of her bag and placed it in the tub. It was standard procedure, after all. Nothing to worry about, and it would look strange if she didn't.

"Go on through," the security guard told her, with a nod.

She glanced around the security hall again and, seeing nothing unusual, stepped beneath the arched security barrier.

Bleep.

Sue let out a short sigh. Nothing to worry about; it happened all the time. Sometimes, they did random checks and it was all part of the procedure.

"Any jewellery, love? Any metal?"

She shook her head.

"Alright, can you step through again, please?"

Sue focused on taking deep breaths in and out.

"No problem," she said, and barely recognised her own voice.

She stepped beneath the archway again.

Bleep.

She could have howled with frustration but, by now, the other security guard had come over and their faces were no longer smiling and approachable. They were suspicious.

"Come and step into this cubicle, please," one of them said, pointing towards a plastic tube which detected dangerous chemicals and tiny metal devices. She should know; she'd been fully trained in their use. "Just put your hands above your head."

She had seen one or two passengers being subjected to the same thing, earlier in the queue, so she tried not to panic. There was nothing to find, anyway. She had already checked her body with a hand-held sensor they kept back at Otterburn and there had been no chemical traces.

"Higher, please," the security guard said, and she raised her arms as the scanners whirred.

The lights began to flash red and there came a series of *bleeps.*

"This is ridiculous," she told them. "I haven't got anything dangerous on me. I have a plane to catch."

"I'm sure you'll still make your plane, Miss, but not before we've done our checks. You can't be too careful, these days."

She almost laughed at the irony of it all; a bunch of glorified monkeys in suits were lecturing *her* about enhanced security.

"Just let me grab my phone," she said, casually. "I don't want somebody stealing it out of the tub."

"Matty? Look after this lady's phone, will you?" the guard called out. "I'm just going to do a quick fingertip search in one of the private rooms and then we can all be on our way, alright love?"

Sue looked into the guileless eyes of the security guard and reminded herself that she was feeling overly paranoid. The place was awash with passengers hoping to catch long-haul evening flights, so it was little wonder they had extra security in place. She would have commended them for it, in her old life.

"No problem," she said, and gave her best impression of a smile.

"Just through here," the guard said, and led her to a small room with an unmarked door. Inside, there was a table and four chairs, a film camera and recording device, and two men waiting for her with stony faces.

"Hi, Sue. Long time, no see."

She spun around to leave but found the exit barred, and her only insurance was lying at the bottom of a plastic tub beside a conveyor belt.

CHAPTER 39

Sue Bannerman started to laugh, and it was a sound close to mania. "What's all this about, Ryan? Thinking of coming on holiday with me?"

Ryan spoke very carefully, keeping his anger in check.

"The only holiday you'll be taking is a bus trip at Her Majesty's Pleasure."

"I've already given most of my life to Her Majesty," she said. "The rest belongs to me."

"And what about the lives you took, Sue?" Phillips asked, softly. "What about them?"

Her throat worked, and she swallowed sudden tears, which rose every time she thought of the others who had died.

She hadn't meant…

She wouldn't think about that.

"In war, there is always collateral damage," she said, in a shaky voice. "I was taught to cope with that, unlike the rest of you, who swan around pretending to save the world. Why don't you leave it to the Big Boys, eh, Frank? You two are just small fish in a much bigger pond."

"Small fish or not, we appear to be reeling you in," Ryan shot back. "Any last words, before we arrest you on suspicion of murder?"

"Here's a word for you, Ryan: BOMB."

A muscle twitched in the corner of his mouth, but his demeanour never altered.

"The question you need to ask yourselves is: where have I planted the next bomb? You didn't think I wouldn't be prepared for this very eventuality, did you?" she said, affecting an air of supreme confidence. "I admit that I never thought you'd look further than Gary—the man has 'guilt' written all over him, in more ways than one—but that doesn't matter now. I have my insurance."

Phillips scratched the side of his face with a rasp of fingernails against stubble and let out a long, gusty breath.

"Ah, but do you, though? D'you know what I think? It's all bluff."

"Why do you think we waited until you'd passed through security?" Ryan asked. "We know you're not carrying anything, Sue, because you've just been scanned and your phone is currently sitting in a secure lock-box awaiting its disposal."

"We like to be prepared too," Phillips said, cheerfully.

She looked between them and smiled again, shaking her head as though they were a pair of minor nuisances.

"How on earth did you guess it was me?" she asked, as if she was settling down for a cosy, fireside chat.

"How do you think, Sue?"

She thought of all the steps she had taken, all the careful planning, and drew a frustrating blank.

"I planned the perfect murder," she said.

"There's no such thing," Ryan replied. "You were caught on camera, Sue. Nobody flinches before a bomb actually explodes, unless they know what's about to happen."

She followed the dots and closed her eyes in silent acceptance.

"The bus. The bloody bus on the bridge," she said.

"Why'd you do it, Sue? Simple revenge?" Phillips asked.

She didn't have to tell them her reasons and, in that moment, Sue was sorely tempted to remain silent. She could take her reasons to the grave and they'd carry on with their lives, make their own conclusions and live to fight another day.

Whereas she…

Sue reached out to grasp the back of the chair and she drew it closer, so she could sit. Her body felt exhausted, more tired than she could ever remember being in her whole life.

"You have to admit, I had you all going for a while," she said, with a girlish smile they found vaguely nauseating. "I thought that, if I was on the bridge while an explosion went off, you'd never suspect me. What bomber would put themselves in danger like that?"

She laughed, a bit too brightly.

"Only a mad one," she finished for them. "But you don't need to know 'how', because you've already worked it all out, haven't you? You've slotted it all together in your minds."

When they remained silent, she glared at them.

"I did it for every woman who ever felt cheated. For every woman who was told, 'I love you' by some lying scumbag and believed it," she said. "I gave that bastard eight years. *Eight years* of my life and then I find he's been shagging some little receptionist on the side?"

"How do you think his wife feels?" Ryan put in, ever so smoothly.

"She's different," Sue muttered. "You don't understand."

"Try me."

"Maddy was like a mother to him. She was his wife in name only. *I* was his wife. *Me*, not her."

As Ryan listened to her ravings, he began to feel an emotion he had not anticipated.

It was pity.

"We all make mistakes, Sue. We recover from them and move on," he said, thinking of his own history. "We don't kill people."

"No, you make excuses for them instead. Nowadays, it's a sex addiction, right? It's just a made-up label, so that people like Gary can be the victim and his wife can forgive him because she can tell herself it isn't his fault."

"Medical professionals would disagree with you," Phillips pointed out.

"Quacks," she told him. "Listen to me, Frank. I know you don't want to hear this and I know the world will say I was just another crazy ex; some fragile little woman who was out for revenge. It might have started that way," she admitted. "But it became more than that. So much more. It was about righting the balance in the world."

"By killing?" Ryan said, just to be clear.

"Think of it like this," she said, as if she was explaining the basics of trigonometry and not discussing mass slaughter. "By removing Kayleigh-Ann Dobson, I've removed one of the people responsible for causing heartbreak and for breaking up happy homes. If she did it once, she'd have done it again, make no mistake. Think of her as a lieutenant in a terrorist organisation, if it makes it easier for you."

"And Nobel is—what? The leader of your fictional organisation?" Ryan asked.

"Yes," she said. "But if he were killed, he'd be glorified. His name would be martyred in the ranks of the army, as if he'd been a poster boy for all that was good and right instead of all that was mendacious and *wrong*."

Her hands started to tremble, so she held them together on her lap.

"So, I decided he could be tried in a court and found guilty."

"Seems a bit one-sided," Phillips said.

"Sometimes, the fairest outcome isn't the one that conforms to the laws of man," she snapped.

Ryan and Phillips exchanged a look. They had almost heard enough.

"And all those others who died, the child who almost died, the four other people who were seriously injured in your holy cause…where do they figure in all this?"

"They're necessary losses. Sometimes, we must make sacrifices to serve the greater good. You wouldn't understand."

"Oh, I don't know," Ryan mused. "For example, I've been forced to listen to your navel-gazing attempts to justify premeditated murder for, gosh, ten minutes now. But, as you say, it's all in the service of the greater good." He turned to Phillips. "Frank? Book her."

"With pleasure," his sergeant replied.

CHAPTER 40

Around the same time that Ryan and Phillips were securing hand-cuffs on the woman who had fashioned herself as '*The Alchemist*' but who would come to be known as the infamous '*Bridge Killer*', DCI Tebbutt opened the door to Jack Lowerson's cell.

The expression in his eyes was one of such infinite sadness and she understood, now, what had caused it.

"We know the truth, Jack," she said. There was no point in sugar-coating it; they both knew who had dealt the lethal blow.

He let out a deep sigh and leaned back against the wall.

"How did you find out?"

"DNA. How else?"

"I didn't think—I just wanted to protect her. She's in her late sixties and she's my mum."

Tebbutt nodded. She needed no other explanation for why he had tried to shield his mother. He felt responsible, as if it were his fault that the woman had taken it upon herself to teach Lucas a lesson and warn her off.

Besides, he loved his mother.

He thought she loved him but, in the end, she'd loved herself even more. That particular truth would be harder to accept, in the fullness of time.

"Your dad is waiting for you upstairs," she said.

"How did he take it?"

Tebbutt thought of the man's devastation and shook her head.

"That's for the two of you to discuss," she said.

He nodded, then asked the burning question.

"Are you going to charge me?" he asked. "I accept what I did."

She looked at him for a long moment for, like his friend Ryan, she had her own moral compass to follow and the decision she had made did not sit easily on her shoulders.

But she had made it, all the same.

"I have not recommended that the matter be pursued by the CPS," she said. "It is not in the public interest, especially as we have found the person responsible. Your mother is co-operating fully."

Lowerson's chin wobbled but he bore down and nodded his thanks.

"What about…" He stopped himself, having already come to his own decision. "I'll tender my resignation first thing tomorrow morning."

"Why on Earth would you want to do that?"

They both looked up in shock at the sound of a new voice in the room, and Ryan stepped into the doorway. They'd deposited Sue Bannerman down the corridor and he'd look forward to questioning her later but, for now, there was Jack.

"I-I can't come back," Lowerson said. "Not after everything that's happened."

Ryan stuck his hands in his pockets and considered what was the best thing to do with him.

"You need some time to heal," he said, frankly. "You've been through all kinds of hell and you need to take time to process all that. Take whatever time you need and then come back, fighting."

"I don't know if I *can* come back," Jack said. "Or if Morrison would take me back, after the decisions I've made."

"Leave that to me," Ryan said, and caught Tebbutt's eye-roll. "As Joan says, it's not in the public interest to have you out there doing God knows what. You'd probably end up working as a waiter in one of those hideous hipster bars in town. I'd see you twiddling an enormous oiled moustache while you sipped a fruity cocktail from a mason jar, or something equally ridiculous."

Lowerson felt laughter bubble up, when he had thought he would never laugh again.

"There'll always be a place for you on the team, Jack. It'll be waiting for you, whenever you're ready."

Jack couldn't find his voice, so he just nodded.

"My dad will need help to get through it," he said. *And so will I,* he added silently.

"You have friends," Ryan said. "Let us help you, if we can, and in the meantime find somewhere quiet and peaceful, where you can get to know yourself again."

"I hear Holy Island is a lovely place for rest and relaxation," Tebbutt suggested, forgetting the reports she'd read of their experiences on the island a couple of years previously.

Ryan and Lowerson exchanged a grin.

"Just watch out for the tides," Ryan said, gravely. "They can be deadly."

EPILOGUE

Ryan was standing on top of a ladder when the familiar tinkle of the *Indiana Jones* theme tune filled the hallway.

"Want me to get it for you?" Anna asked, from her position at the foot of the ladder she'd been holding steady so that Ryan could hang a large painting on the wall.

"I'll come down."

Ryan caught it on the last ring and frowned at the unusual country code.

"Hello?"

"Am I speaking with Detective Chief Inspector Ryan?" the caller asked, in heavily-accented Italian.

"Yes. And you are?"

"I am Jacopo Romano, Direttore Generale della Polizia Criminale," the other replied, in his native tongue. "I hope you don't mind the intrusion. However, I have already spoken with your forensic expert, Faulkner. He tells me to call you."

"Oh?"

"It was I who rang him," he explained. "He is the only other to have searched the European database for a specific DNA sample, aside from our department. We are searching for a missing person in our country, *signore,* and it would appear that their DNA has found its way to you. We do not know how, or what the connection may be."

Ryan thought of the postcard that had arrived in the midst of all the bridge bombings. There had been no time to turn his attention to Nathan Armstrong then, not while danger lurked on their very doorstep. But things were different now.

And here was a fresh lead, where none had existed before.

"Who does the DNA belong to?"

"I cannot discuss it over the telephone," Romano said, lowering his voice. "The person is *known,* Chief Inspector. A person of note, in our country, and I must be careful."

After a lengthy conversation, Ryan ended the call and stared at the new picture he'd just hung on the wall in their hallway.

"Well?" Anna burst out. "What was all that about?"

Ryan turned to her with a serious expression marring his handsome face.

"I need to go to Italy," he said. "We talked once before about the risks involved if you were to come with me, so I won't repeat myself, but I want to be sure that you understand. I can't protect you in the same way, if I needed to, Anna. It won't be my turf and we'll be guests of the *Polizia di Stato.*"

She thought of the university classes she had to teach, of the work she had to do, and then tried to imagine doing it all while she worried for her husband, thousands of miles away.

"I'm coming," she told him. "The university will have to handle it."

She hoped.

"What about CID? What will Morrison say?"

Ryan had already thought of that.

"She knows that, by rights, Nathan Armstrong should be incarcerated by now. Instead, he's roaming the four corners of the world hurting countless more people. It's time to bring it to an end and she knows that. The man has our home address," he added, softly. "We'll never sleep soundly until he's brought to justice."

"When do we go?" she asked.

"We'll leave for Rome in three days," he said. "Armstrong is due to be in Florence the week after that, which gives us time to stay ahead of him."

"I've never been to Florence," she said, with some excitement, and Ryan moved across to cup her face in his hands.

"Anna, this isn't a holiday," he said, urgently. "We need to be careful, always, and remember to be vigilant. There'll be other times we can go, when the circumstances are different."

"Don't worry," she told him. "I understand what this means."

He lowered his head to kiss her deeply.

"Ryan? Why does he send the postcards? Why leave a trail, at all?"

"It's an invitation," Ryan said, grimly. "One which I accept."

DCI Ryan will return…

If you would like to be kept up to date with new releases from LJ Ross, please complete an e-mail contact form on her Facebook page or website, www.ljrossauthor.com

AUTHOR'S NOTE

Seven Bridges of course refers to the seven bridges connecting the cities of Gateshead and Newcastle for the stretch of a mile across the River Tyne. There are many more lovely bridges as the river meanders its way out into the countryside but for the purposes of the story I have written, I decided to concentrate on the most iconic section. Each bridge is noteworthy, but most people who are not local to the area might recognise the Tyne Bridge as it bears a striking resemblance to the Sydney Harbour Bridge, in Australia. They share the same architect, Mott, Hay and Anderson, and both derived their inspiration from the Hell Gate Bridge in New York City.

I have a particular childhood memory of walking along the Quayside to see the Tall Ships sailing in to drop anchor and of thousands of people flocking to see them, in all their old-world beauty. Bunting lined the riverbank and stalls were set up selling all kinds of food and floppy velvet hats which were, of course, a staple fashion item during the early nineties! I still feel that old magic, whenever I take a stroll along the river to the Baltic Art Gallery, where there's an unrivalled view of all seven bridges. If there's fog on the Tyne, even better!

I hope I've managed to capture a flavour of the urban scenery around that part of Newcastle and into Gateshead but, inevitably, I have not been able to mention every landmark or place of note for to do so would affect the pacing of the story. However, there will be many more stories to tell in the future and I hope to be able to showcase so much more of the beautiful scenery I'm proud to call home.

LJ ROSS

May 2018

ABOUT THE AUTHOR

Born in Newcastle upon Tyne, LJ Ross moved to London where she graduated from King's College London with undergraduate and postgraduate degrees in Law. After working in the City as a regulatory lawyer for a number of years, she realised it was high time for a change. The catalyst was the birth of her son, which forced her to take a break from the legal world and find time for some of the detective stories that had been percolating for a while and finally demanded to be written.

She lives with her husband and young son in her beautiful home county of Northumberland.

If you enjoyed *Seven Bridges*, please consider leaving a review online.

If you would like to be kept up to date with new releases from LJ Ross, please complete an e-mail contact form on her Facebook page or website, www.ljrossauthor.com

ACKNOWLEDGMENTS

Seven Bridges is the eighth novel in the DCI Ryan mystery series and is also the fourth book to have made it to the coveted Number One spot on the Kindle bestsellers chart in the UK, even before it was properly released! I am delighted and humbled to know there are so many kind and supportive readers who, like me, enjoy finding out what lies in store for Ryan and his team on their next adventure. Thanks to all of you.

I have been fortunate to enlist the help of a good many kind and knowledgeable people during the writing of this book. I would like to thank Kirsty "Train Queen" Maule, for her invaluable advice around train operating procedures, policies and all manner of interesting titbits from her experience as an engineer—unfortunately, not all of it could be included in the book but I shall save it for another time! I'd also like to thank all the kind bloggers and beta readers who have taken the time to read *Seven Bridges,* your wonderful encouragement has been a cornerstone for the past three years.

I am so grateful to all my family and friends who have enabled me to continue doing the job I love because, without them, it would not be possible. Enormous thanks to my husband, James, and to my son, Ethan. Everything I do, I do for these two blue-eyed boys who, between them, make me smile, laugh and strive to be a better person every day. All my love, always.

Finally, I am grateful to Joan Tebbutt and Jennifer Lucas, two incredibly kind women who donated generously to charity in exchange for a character in one of my books. I hope the fictional alter-egos I have created will bring a few smiles!

Made in the USA
Columbia, SC
20 September 2020

21250974R00164